DEATH TRAP

"They know we're here," said Father Christmas. "Look at her, dressed in gold and glitter and leaning out over the edge of the balcony. They're using her as bait."

"For me?" asked Nighthawk.

"Who else?"

"And they think I'm going to burst into the building and shoot my way up to the third floor because she's standing there?"

"Yeah," said the older man. "Pretty damned foolish, aren't they? So what do we do now? Go back to the hotel?"

"You can go if you want."

"What about you?"

"Me?" repeated Nighthawk. "I'm going to burst into the building and shoot my way up to the third floor."

"I thought I just explained: That's exactly what they're expecting."

"They're expecting a man," replied Nighthawk, checking his pistol and thrusting it back into a pocket. "What they're getting is the Widowmaker."

The Widowmaker

MIKE RESNICK

BANTAM BOOKS
New York Toronto London Sydney Auckland

THE WIDOWMAKER

A Bantam Spectra Book/August 1996

SPECTRA *and the portrayal of a boxed "s" are trademarks of Bantam Books, a division of Bantam Doubleday Dell Publishing Group, Inc.*

ISBN 0-553-57160-5

Published simultaneously in the United States and Canada

Bantam Books are published by Bantam Books, a division of Bantam Doubleday Dell Publishing Group, Inc. Its trademark, consisting of the words "Bantam Books" and the portrayal of a rooster, is Registered in U.S. Patent and Trademark Office and in other countries. Marca Registrada. Bantam Books, 1540 Broadway, New York, New York 10036.

PRINTED IN THE UNITED STATES OF AMERICA

OPM 0 9 8 7 6 5 4 3 2 1

Prologue

◆ ◆ ◆ ◆ ◆ ◆ ◆

A mile beneath the glittering surface of Deluros VIII, the capital of mankind's sprawling Oligarchy, two men rode a slidewalk down a long, dimly lit corridor, their voices echoing in the vast emptiness. One wore gray, one white. They passed a door, then four more.

"I wonder what he'll be like?" mused the man in gray.

The man in white shrugged. "Old and sick."

"I know," agreed the man in gray. "But I've seen so many holos of him when he was . . . well, you know."

"When he was the most famous killer in the galaxy?" asked his companion sardonically.

"He did most of his killing on the side of the law."

"So the legend goes."

"You sound like you think otherwise," said the man in gray.

"No. But I know how legends get made."

The slidewalk brought them to a security checkpoint, then stopped until their ID badges and retinas had been scanned. It began moving again, only to stop once more at a second checkpoint fifty yards farther on.

"Is this really necessary?" asked the man in gray.

"The richest men and women in the Oligarchy lie helpless down here," came the answer. "They are totally defenseless—and believe me, *nobody* gets that rich without making enemies."

"I know," said the man in gray. He gestured ahead to two more checkpoints. "I was just wondering if we're going to have to pass through one of these stations every forty or fifty yards."

"Absolutely."

"I was afraid of that."

"Add it to your bill," said the man in white.

After another two hundred yards the corridor branched off, and they chose the slidewalk that veered to the right. The doors came more frequently now, as did the checkpoints, but finally they came to a halt in front of a door that appeared no different from any of the others.

"We're here," said the man in white, allowing the scanner above the door to verify his retina and palm print.

"I feel nervous," said the man in gray, as the door slid into the wall long enough for them to pass through.

"It's a simple enough procedure."

"But he doesn't know who we are."

"So?"

"What if he's happy the way he is? What if we annoy him? What if he kills people for bothering him?"

"If he was in any condition to kill people, he wouldn't be here," said the man in white. "Lights!"

The room was instantly bathed in a dim blue glow.

"Can't you make it any brighter than this?" asked the man in gray.

"He hasn't opened his eyes in more than a century," replied his companion. "The room will wait until it knows his pupils are adjusting before it gets any brighter." He walked past a number of drawers built into the wall, checking their numbers, then came to a stop. "Drawer 10547."

A drawer slowly emerged from the wall, stretching to its full eight-foot length. The two men could barely make out the shape of a human body beneath the translucent covering.

"Jefferson Nighthawk," mused the man in gray. "*The* Jefferson Nighthawk." He paused. "It's not what I expected."

"Oh?"

"I thought there'd be all kinds of wires and tubes attached to him."

"Barbaric," snorted the man in white. "There are three monitoring devices implanted in his body. That's all he needs."

"How does he breathe?"

"He's breathing right now."

The man in gray stared, trying to detect the tiniest sign of movement.

"I don't see anything."

"He's doing it so slowly that only the computer can tell. DeepSleep slows the metabolism down to a crawl; it doesn't *stop* it, or we'd be down here with thirty thousand corpses."

"So what do you do now?"

"I'm doing it," said the man in white. He walked over to the drawer where the body lay, laid his hand over a scanner until it identified his fingerprints, then tapped in a code on a keyboard that suddenly extended from the scanner.

"How long will this take?"

"For you or me, probably a minute. For the people we've got down here, maybe four or five minutes."

"Why so long?"

"If they weren't dying, they wouldn't be here in the first place. In their weakened conditions, they take longer to respond to external stimuli." The man in white looked up from the body. "More than one has died from the shock of being awakened."

"Will he?"

"Not likely. His heart reads pretty close to normal, considering."

"Good."

"But if I were you, I'd brace myself for when he finally wakes up."

"Why? You've already told me he won't die, and that he's too sick to pose a threat even if he wanted to. So what's the problem?"

"Have you ever seen a man in the advanced stages of eplasia?"

"No," admitted the man in gray.

"They're not pretty. And that's an understatement."

They both fell silent as the body in front of them gradually began acquiring color. After two more minutes the translucent top slid into the wall, revealing an emaciated man whose flesh was hideously disfigured by the ravages of a virulent skin disease. Patches of shining white cheekbone protruded through the flesh of the face, knuckles pierced the skin of the hands, and even where the skin remained intact it looked like there was some malignancy crawling across it and discoloring it.

The man in gray turned away in disgust, then forced himself to look back. He half expected the air to smell of rotting flesh, but it remained pure and filtered.

Finally the eyelids flickered, once, twice, and then, slowly, they opened, revealing light blue, almost colorless eyes. The diseased man remained motionless for a full minute, then frowned.

"Where did Acosta go?" he croaked at last.

"Who is Acosta?" asked the man in gray.

"My doctor. He was here just a minute ago."

"Ah," said the man in white, smiling. "Dr. Acosta has been dead for more than eighty years. You yourself have been here for one hundred and seven years, Mr. Nighthawk."

Nighthawk looked confused. "One hundred and . . . ?"

"And seven years. I am Dr. Gilbert Egan."

"What year is it?"

"5101 G.E.," said Egan. "May I help you sit up?"

"Yes."

Egan lifted the frail, skeletal figure until it was sitting erect. The moment he stopped supporting it, it collapsed onto its side.

"We'll try again when you're feeling a little stronger," said Egan, adjusting Nighthawk so that no ravaged limbs flopped over the side. "You've been asleep a long time. How do you feel?"

"I'm starving," said Nighthawk.

"Of course you are," said Egan with a smile. "You've gone more than a century without a meal. Even with your metabolism slowed down a hundred-fold, your stomach has probably been empty for a decade or more." Egan attached a tube to Nighthawk's left arm. "Unfortunately, you're in no condition to eat, but this will supply your body with the nourishment it needs."

"I might as well get used to eating," rasped Nighthawk, "now that I'm cured." He paused. "A hundred and seven years. It sure as hell took you long enough."

Egan looked at the frail, diseased man with some compassion. "I am afraid that a cure for eplasia has not yet been developed."

Nighthawk turned and stared at the doctor. It was the kind of stare that made Egan happy his patient was not armed and healthy.

"I left explicit instructions that I wasn't to be awakened until I was cured."

"Conditions have changed, Mr. Nighthawk," said the man in gray, stepping forward.

"Who the hell are *you*?" demanded Nighthawk.

"My name is Marcus Dinnisen. I am your solicitor."

Nighthawk frowned. "My lawyer?"

Dinnisen nodded. "I am a senior partner in the firm of Hubbs, Wilkinson, Raith and Jiminez."

"Raith," said Nighthawk, nodding vaguely. "He's my lawyer."

"Morris Raith joined the firm of Hubbs and Wilkinson three years before his death, in the year 5012. His great-grandson worked for us until his retirement last year."

"All right," said Nighthawk. "You're my lawyer. Why did you feel I had to be awakened?"

"This is somewhat awkward to explain, Mr. Nighthawk," began Dinnisen uneasily.

"Spit it out."

"At the time you elected to undergo DeepSleep, you turned your entire portfolio over to my firm."

"It wasn't a portfolio," said Nighthawk. "It was six and a half million credits."

"Exactly so," said Dinnisen. "We were instructed to invest it and to keep up the payments for this facility in perpetuity, or until a cure for your disease was developed."

"So it took you one hundred and seven years to lose all my money?"

"Absolutely not!" said Dinnisen heatedly. "Your money remains intact, and has been earning an average of 9.32% per annum for more than a century. I can supply you with all the figures if you wish to review them."

Nighthawk blinked, a puzzled expression on his grotesque face. "Then if I'm not broke and I'm not cured, what the hell is going on?"

"Your account has been earning slightly more than six hundred thousand credits a year," explained Dinnisen. "Unfortunately, due to an inflationary spiral in the Deluros economy, this facility now charges a million credits a year. This makes for a shortfall of almost four hundred thousand credits per annum. We cannot make the payments with your dividends, and if we dip into capital, you will be destitute in a decade. Nor is there any guarantee that a cure for eplasia will be found by then."

"So you're telling me that I'm being thrown out of here?" asked Nighthawk.

"No."

"Well, then?"

"I require a decision from you," responded Dinnisen, staring at the hideous countenance in fascination. "If anyone else could make it, I would never have awakened you until . . ."

"Until I was broke," Nighthawk concluded wryly. "All right, go on."

"We—that is to say, your solicitors—have received a most unusual communication, one that may solve your financial problems and allow you to remain here until the cure for your disease has finally been found."

"I'm listening."

"Have you ever heard of Solio II?"

"It's a planet on the Inner Frontier. Why?"

"The governor of Solio II was assassinated six days ago."

"What's that got to do with me?"

"Simply this," said Dinnisen. "Knowledge that the notorious Widowmaker was still alive has somehow reached the Frontier, and the planetary government of Solio II has offered you a bounty of seven million credits to hunt down the killer—half now, half when you succeed."

"Is this some kind of joke?" demanded Nighthawk. "I can't even sit up!"

Dinnisen turned to Egan. "Doctor, would you explain, please?"

Egan nodded. "While we have not yet effected a cure for your disease, Mr. Nighthawk, we *have* made progress on other fronts, especially in the field of bioengineering. When the offer was tendered to Mr. Dinnisen, he came up with a proposal that is acceptable to the government of Solio II if it is acceptable to you."

"Bioengineering?" repeated Nighthawk. "You're going to clone me?"

"With your permission."

"When I went into DeepSleep, I was told that I had no more than a month to live," said Nighthawk. "How do you expect me to wait until the clone has grown to manhood? Or, if you're going to put me away and awaken me in another twenty or thirty years, what makes you think Solio will be willing to wait?"

"You don't understand, Mr. Nighthawk," said Egan. "We no longer have to raise a clone from infancy to maturity. During the past quarter century, we have devised a method whereby we can create a clone of you at any age: sixty minutes or sixty years. We propose to create a twenty-three-year-old Jefferson Nighthawk, a young version of yourself at the peak of your physical abilities."

"Will he have the disease?"

"If we took the cells from you today, the answer would be yes. But there is a museum on Binder X that has on display a knife with which you were stabbed when you were a young man. Do you recall the incident?"

"I've been stabbed more than once," replied Nighthawk.

"Well, yes, I suppose you have," continued Egan uneasily. "At any rate, we have been in contact with them, and they say that they can supply some of your blood cells from the blade. In all likelihood they'll be contaminated, but we have ways of purifying them."

"You still haven't answered my question: if you make my clone from these blood cells, will he have the disease?"

"Almost certainly not, since *you* didn't have it at that age. However, he will be susceptible to eplasia, and will very likely contract it as he grows older—just as you did."

Nighthawk frowned. "This disease rots my flesh off my bones. I look like a child's nightmare. I wouldn't wish it on my worst enemy; how can I give it to someone who's even closer to me than a son?"

"He's just a shadow, a copy of the original," said Dinnisen. "His sole purpose, the only reason he will be brought into existence, is so that *you* can remain alive until a cure is found."

"Consider it this way," added Egan. "If you give your permission to create a clone, you may both survive long enough for us to develop a cure. If not, one of you will surely die and the other will never be born."

"It's an easy choice when you put it that way," admitted Nighthawk. He sighed deeply. "God, I'm tired. You'd think I'd have a little more energy after a hundred-year nap."

"I anticipated that," said Dinnisen, producing a pocket computer. "I've got a copy of the Solio II agreement here, as well as permission for us to create the clone. Your thumbprint is all that we need to make them legal and binding." He paused and smiled. "Then we'll put you back into DeepSleep."

"How soon will the clone be ready?" asked Nighthawk, struggling helplessly to lift his hand. Finally Egan helped him place his shriveled thumb on the surface of the lawyer's computer.

"If we accelerate the process, perhaps a month."

"That fast?"

"I told you: we've made enormous progress in the field of bioengineering."

Nighthawk nodded, then looked up at the medic.
"I need some food."

"No, you don't," said Egan. "Now that you've satisfied the legalities, there's no need for you to remain
awake."

"And find me a bed," continued Nighthawk.

"I don't think you are listening to me . . ." began
Egan.

"In a month you're going to have a perfect,
twenty-three-year-old, disease-free replica of me,
right?" asked Nighthawk.

"Yes."

"Are *you* going to teach him how to kill?"

"No," said Egan, surprised.

"How about you?" said Nighthawk, turning to
Dinnisen.

"Of course not," replied Dinnisen.

"Then it's up to me."

"I'm afraid not," said Egan. "You probably can't
live for a month, and I can't put you back into
DeepSleep until the clone is ready and then awaken
you—the process of starting and stopping your metabolism would be harder on you than just keeping you
awake."

"You can't send him out there without any training!" snapped Nighthawk.

"We have no choice," said Egan. "You are in no
condition to train him."

"He won't last a week," mumbled Nighthawk, his
eyelids drooping, his speech slurring. "You've killed us
both."

Suddenly he lost consciousness, and Egan
straightened the bedding beneath him.

"Well, that's your client," he said. "What do you
think of him?"

"I don't think I'd have liked meeting him when he was young and healthy."

"That's too bad," said Egan, touching a button that caused the translucent cover to lock into place. "Because that's precisely what you're going to do in about a month."

"I'll be meeting the duplicate, not the original," replied Dinnisen. "He won't be carrying any of Nighthawk's grudges, just his skills."

"His *potential* skills," noted Egan. "Nighthawk was right about that."

"They'll be enough," said Dinnisen. "Why do you think Solio wanted *him*, when there are so many other killers and bounty hunters to be had?" He looked down at the diseased body. "When Jefferson Nighthawk was twenty-three years old, he had already killed more than *thirty* men. Gun, knife, freehand, there wasn't a man alive who could touch him. The instincts will be there, all right."

"Instincts aren't skills," said Egan. "What if you're wrong?"

"We've fulfilled our end of the contract. We'd rather have all seven million, but half is better than nothing."

Egan studied Nighthawk's face for a long moment. "Have you considered what might happen if you're right?"

"I beg your pardon?"

"What if the clone's every bit as efficient a killer as the original was?"

Dinnisen looked puzzled. "That's what we're hoping for."

"How will you control him then?"

"The original Widowmaker repressed all his emotions. This one won't have any reason to—and loyalty has an emotional basis."

"Have you considered the fact that you'll only have a few weeks to give him a moral and ethical code of behavior at the same time you're teaching him a hundred ways to kill?"

"*I'm* not teaching him anything," answered Dinnisen defensively. "I'm a solicitor. I'll be hiring specialists—not just specialists in killing, but in behavior as well. How difficult can it be?"

"I'll bet Pandora said those very words just before she opened the box," replied Egan as the drawer containing Jefferson Nighthawk slid silently back into place.

Chapter 1

⬧ ⬧ ⬧ ⬧ ⬧ ⬧

◈

The jungle planet of Karamojo was the jewel of the Quinellus Cluster. A fierce, primitive world, it was a hunter's paradise, overflowing with enormous horned grass eaters and deadly carnivores.

The Oligarchy, having seen what happened to such overexploited worlds as Peponi and Karimon, had declared Karamojo off-limits for colonization. Instead, it became an exclusive planet for sportsmen, and hunting licenses were strictly limited. It took an awful lot of money, or clout, or both, just to land on Karamojo, and even more to be allowed to hunt there.

Aficionados said that the fishing was better on Hemingway, out in the Spiral Arm, but everyone agreed there was no better hunting to be found anywhere. It made the men who visited the planet willing to put up with its hardships: swarms of deadly insects, an atmosphere so thin that a hunter's blood had to be medically oxygenated every fifth day, a temperature that rarely dipped below 30 degrees Celsius even at night, and a landscape that made adrenaline pills all but mandatory.

Only nineteen hunters in the planet's history had been granted permanent licenses. One was the fabled Fuentes, considered by most experts to be the best hunter who had ever lived. Another was Nicobar Lane, whose trophies filled museums across the galaxy.

And yet another was Jefferson Nighthawk, known as the Widowmaker.

It had taken almost a day for Nighthawk and his companion, a small, balding man named Ito Kinoshita, to clear Customs. His fingerprints checked out. So did his retinagram and his voiceprint. Preliminary DNA tests seemed also to confirm his identity—but he was more than a hundred and fifty years old, and the man who bore his name was clearly under twenty-five, and hence a clone.

Finally the authorities decided that a clone had the right to use the original's license, and he and Kinoshita disappeared into the endless alien bush for four days. When they emerged, it was with the carcasses of two enormous Demoncats, the seven-hundred-pound carnivores that preyed on the huge herds.

Kinoshita drove their safari vehicle toward Pondoro Outpost, a luxurious fortress in the middle of the bush where tired, wealthy hunters could relax in comfort. The outpost contained a restaurant, a tavern, an infirmary, a weapons and ammunition shop, a map shop, a taxidermist, and one hundred chalets, which could hold up to four hundred Men. There were only three such outposts on the planet—Pondoro, Corbett, and Selous—and at no time were more than fifteen hundred humans hunting or relaxing on a planet that possessed almost twice Earth's surface area.

Upon reaching the outpost, they unloaded their Demoncats at the taxidermy shop, retired to their chalet to bathe, shave, and change into fresh clothes, and then met at the restaurant for dinner. The menu consisted of imported game meats, as there was something about the indigenous Karamojo animals that humans couldn't metabolize.

Then they headed over to Six-Finger Blue's, the tavern run by a huge human mutant whose skin was tinted a striking shade of blue. His left hand ended in a shapeless mass of bone, while his right possessed six long, multi-jointed, snakelike fingers. He had been a fixture on Karamojo for the better part of thirty years; if he had ever left the planet during that time, no one could remember it.

Blue himself was no hunter, but he believed in creating an ambience that would appeal to his clients, and so the heads of Demoncats, Fire Lizards, Battle-tanks, Silverskins, and half a dozen other local species were stuffed and mounted on the walls, making the tavern look far more like a rustic hunting lodge than a bar from the 52nd Century of the Galactic Era.

Blue kept a colorful blue-red-and-gold Screech-owl in a large cage over the bar. Customers were encouraged to feed it, and a small supply of live lizards was always handy. Just beyond the cage was a computer readout, constantly being updated, of the current exchange rates in credits, Maria Theresa dollars, Far London pounds, and half a dozen other currencies.

One wall was lined with a discreet set of holographic screens, as remote cameras stationed all over the area flashed scenes of animals and where they could be found. A few short-timers, men and women in for one-day safaris, watched the screens intently. Whenever the animal they were looking for came up, they went out after it. There was no such thing as a white hunter or a guide, not in an age when the safari vehicle could read spoor and track game on its own.

Upon reaching the table, Kinoshita moved the chairs, then sat down and gestured for his young companion to do the same.

"You're through rearranging the table?" asked Nighthawk, staring at him curiously.

"Never sit with your back to a door or a window."

"I don't have any enemies yet," replied Nighthawk.

"You don't have any friends either, and where you're going, that's more important."

Nighthawk shrugged and took a seat.

An alien servant, humanoid in form and speaking Terran with a harsh accent, approached them and asked for their drink orders.

"A pair of Dust Whores," said Kinoshita.

The alien nodded and walked away.

"Dust Whores?" repeated Nighthawk.

"You'll like them," Kinoshita assured him.

Nighthawk shrugged and looked around the room. "Interesting place. Feels exactly like a hunting lodge should."

Kinoshita nodded in agreement. "There's a place just like this on Last Chance."

Nighthawk shook his head. "No, it's on Binder X."

Kinoshita smiled. "You're right, of course. My mistake."

Well, your memory—or whoever's memory you've got—is functioning perfectly, you poor bastard.

The alien waiter returned with the drinks. Nighthawk stared at his dubiously.

"They're good," Kinoshita assured him.

"They're green," he replied.

"Trust me, Jeff," said Kinoshita. "You'll love it."

Nighthawk reached out for a glass, brought it slowly to his lips, and took a sip.

"Cinnamon," he said at last. "And Borillian rum. And something else I can't quite put my finger on."

"It's a fruit they grow on New Kenya. It's not quite an orange or a tangerine, but it's in the citrus family—as much as an alien fruit *can* be, anyway. They wait until it ferments, then process and bottle it."

"Good," said Nighthawk, taking another sip. "I like it."

Of course you like it. The real Widowmaker was practically addicted to these things.

Nighthawk downed his drink, then looked across the table at his companion.

"Are we going out again tomorrow?" he asked.

"No, I don't think so. We wanted to see how good you were with your weapons after a month of training. We saw."

"Too bad," said Nighthawk. "It was fun."

"You think being charged by a Demoncat is fun?"

"Well, it's certainly not dangerous," came the answer. "Not when I've got a rifle in my hands."

"The taxidermist would probably agree with you," remarked Kinoshita.

"I beg your pardon?"

"When I brought the carcasses in, he said that you didn't just shoot them in the *eye* to avoid damaging the heads, you shot them in the *pupil*."

"Like you told me when we started, it's just like pointing your finger."

"I lied," said Kinoshita. "But you seem to have turned it into the truth."

A disarmingly boyish smile crossed Nighthawk's face. "I did, didn't I?"

Kinoshita nodded. "You did."

"Damn!" said the young man happily. "That calls for another drink!" He signaled to the alien waiter. "Two more Dust Whores." Then he turned back to Kinoshita. "So what do we do next?"

"Nothing," said Kinoshita. "Today is your graduation."

"Wasn't much of an exam," said Nighthawk.

It hasn't started yet. Aloud, he said, "You'd be surprised how many men have been killed by Demoncats. You had less than half a second to aim and fire, you know."

"*You* were the one who wanted to go into heavy cover after them," noted Nighthawk.

"I wanted to test your reactions under the harshest field conditions," said Kinoshita.

"Do you do this a lot?"

"Go into thick bush after Demoncats? No, thank God!"

"I meant train men to fight."

"You're the first."

"What *do* you do, then?"

"A little of this, a little of that," replied Kinoshita noncommittally.

"Have you ever been a lawman or a bounty hunter?" persisted Nighthawk.

"Both."

"And a soldier?"

"A long time ago."

"What about an outlaw?" asked Nighthawk.

"I give up," said Kinoshita. "What *about* an outlaw?"

"Have you ever been one?"

"Depends on who you ask," said Kinoshita. "No court ever convicted me of anything."

"How did you wind up working for Marcus Dinnisen?"

"He's got a lot of money to spend. I need a lot of money. It's only natural that we got together."

"When is your job over?"

Kinoshita stared at the head of a Fire Lizard, which stared blindly back at him. "Soon."

The young man frowned unhappily. "How soon?"

Kinoshita sighed. "Oh, I might come out to the Frontier with you for a week or two, until you're settled, but after that I'd just be in the way. It's not very likely that the man you're after will simply announce himself. You've got a lot of work to do, and the sooner you start, the better." Kinoshita sipped his own drink. "The Frontier's as empty as the Oligarchy is crowded. It's almost impossible to sneak up on anyone out there. They see you coming from too far away."

"They won't see me at all," said Nighthawk. "I'll be in a ship until I land."

"I was speaking metaphorically." Nighthawk looked unconvinced. "Look," continued Kinoshita, "I was right about the drinks. Trust me, I'm right about this too. I'd be a hindrance."

"If I'm the guy who has to do the dirty work, I should be able to make some of the decisions."

"Once you're out there on your own, you'll be making *all* the decisions," Kinoshita assured him.

"Then I should decide whether I go alone or not."

"I don't want to argue with you," said Kinoshita.

"We had a nice, satisfying hunt and a nice, satisfying meal. We'll talk about it later." *If I can figure out a graceful way to explain to you that you're expendable but I'm not.*

Nighthawk shrugged and nodded his agreement. "All right. Later."

The young man was considering ordering yet another round of drinks when suddenly Six-Finger Blue walked over to the table.

"Hello, Ito!" he said in his deep bass voice. "I *thought* I spotted you when you came in. Where the hell have you been keeping yourself?"

"Oh, here and there," said Kinoshita.

"Last I heard, you were shooting bad guys out on the Rim."

"Gave it up," answered Kinoshita. "Decided I liked the thought of living to an old age."

"Yeah, making it past forty has got a lot to recommend it," agreed Six-Finger Blue. He turned and stared at Nighthawk. "Who's your friend? His face is familiar, but I can't quite place it."

"His name's Jeff," said Kinoshita.

Nighthawk extended his hand, and Blue wrapped his six fingers around it. "Howdy, Jeff. You been out here to the Frontier before?"

"No," answered Nighthawk.

"Well, if you're half the man your pal is, you'll make out just fine," said Six-Finger Blue. He stared again. "Damn! I could swear I've seen your face somewhere!"

He wandered off to greet other patrons, and Kinoshita turned to Nighthawk. "An old holograph, probably," he suggested as a possible explanation. "I could almost guess when and where, because by the time you were twenty-three you were wearing a huge handlebar mustache. It didn't look like much, but it added ten years to your appearance."

"It wasn't a holo of *me*," answered Nighthawk. "You're confusing me with *him*."

"You *are* him, in a way," said Kinoshita. "Now that I've worked with you, in a *lot* of ways."

Nighthawk shook his head. "He's an old man, dying of some horrible disease. I'm a young man with my whole life ahead of me. Once I take care of this business on Solio II, I've got a lot of places to see and things to do."

"What kind of things?" asked Kinoshita.

Nighthawk tapped his head with a forefinger. "As real as these things seem to me, I know they can't be my memories. I'm going to replace them with *real* ones. There's a whole galaxy out there to see and experience."

"It sounds like you've been giving it some serious thought."

"Well, I've been working all my life—all forty-eight days of it." Nighthawk smiled awkwardly at his rudimentary attempt at humor. "I'm looking forward to my first vacation." He paused thoughtfully. "Though for the time being, I'll settle for just one night of sleep when I'm not plugged in to an Educator Disk."

"It was necessary," replied Kinoshita. "You've been force-fed the equivalent of twenty years of living in little more than a month. We couldn't send you out there with no knowledge and no social skills Hell, you wouldn't even be able to speak yet if it hadn't been for the Disks."

"I know, and I'm grateful," said Nighthawk. "But I still have *my* life to live, once I'm through saving *his* life." He looked around the room, over the mounted heads on the wall, then back to Kinoshita. "I want to see him before I leave."

Kinoshita shook his head. "He might not survive being awakened again—at least, not until we have a cure for him."

"I don't have to talk to him," persisted Nighthawk. "I just want to *see* him."

"They say he looks pretty awful."

"I don't care. He's the only family I've got."

"They won't allow it, Jeff. Why not plan on seeing him after you've done your job and science has found a way to cure him?"

"Science hasn't made any progress in a century. Why should I expect them to find a cure now?"

"I'm told they're getting close. Just be patient."

Nighthawk shook his head. "I don't have a father or a mother. All I've got is him."

"But there's more to it than that, isn't there?" said Kinoshita.

"Why should you think so?"

"Because I've already told you what an unpleasant experience it will be to see him. Now, what's the real reason?"

"I want to see what's in store for me if they *don't* come up with that cure."

"You've got enough things to think about, Jeff. You don't need to carry around an image of what this disease can do to you."

"*Will* do."

"*Can* do. You might not contract it."

"Come off it, Ito. I'm not his son; I'm his *clone*. If *he* got it, *I'll* get it."

"They could have a vaccine in two years, or ten, or twenty. You're physically twenty-three years old. He didn't contract it until he was in his late forties."

"That's not so far off," said Nighthawk.

"It's far enough."

"You won't let me see him?"

"It's not up to me," said Kinoshita.

Nighthawk sighed. "All right." He paused. "I'll have another Dust Whore. They kind of grow on you."

You gave in too easily, Jeff. The real Nighthawk would have demanded what he wanted, and then if I hadn't helped him, he'd have taken it himself. If he wanted to see a frozen body, God help anyone who stood in his way. That's what made him the Widowmaker. We had to tone you down, make your controllable, but now I wonder if you're tough enough to do what must be done.

Two more drinks arrived, and Kinoshita looked around the tavern. His gaze fell on two burly men standing at one end of the bar.

They're here, just as we'd been tipped they would be. He glanced surreptitiously at Nighthawk. *It's time for your final exam, Jeff. I hope you're up to it.*

"You see those two guys at the bar?" asked the small man.

Nighthawk nodded. "You know them?"

"In a manner of speaking," answered Kinoshita. "I know *of* them." He paused and studied the two men. "The one with the beard is Undertaker McNair, an assassin from out on the Rim. The other one's his bodyguard."

"What does an assassin need with a bodyguard?"

"Everyone needs someone to watch his back— especially a man with *his* reputation and enemies."

Nighthawk frowned. "If you know who he is, so must Customs. Why would they allow a hired killer to hunt here?"

"Because he can afford it."

"That's the only reason?"

"This is an exclusive place. People are expected to pay for that."

"How much has this cost *us* so far?"

"Don't worry about it," said Kinoshita. "You're about to earn more than enough to cover the cost."

"You're being optimistic. It could be months before I finish my work on Solio II."

"No. You're going to earn it right now."

Nighthawk looked puzzled.

"There's paper on Undertaker McNair—half a million credits, dead or alive." Kinoshita paused. "Dead is easier."

"I don't even know him," said Nighthawk uncomfortably.

"You won't know the man you're after on Solio, either."

"That's different. Besides, I'm not armed."

"I've taught you forty-three ways to kill with your hands and feet," said Kinoshita. "This is as good a time as any to see how much you've learned."

"But he's not bothering anyone," said Nighthawk. "I can't just walk up to him and kill him."

"I agree. Kill the bodyguard first."

Nighthawk looked at the two men, then back at his tutor. "Don't make me do this, Ito."

"I can't make you do anything," said Kinoshita.

"What'll happen if I say no?"

The small man shrugged. "We'll pack our bags and go back to Deluros."

"And then?"

Kinoshita paused a moment and stared into Nighthawk's eyes. "And then they'll destroy you quickly and painlessly, and we'll make the next clone a little more aggressive."

"You'd let them do that to me?" demanded Nighthawk.

"I couldn't stop them," said Kinoshita. "They're playing for huge stakes, and their first duty is to the old man who pays their bills."

Nighthawk looked at the two men, then back to Kinoshita. "What do I say to them?"

"Anything you want, or nothing at all."

"What if they're armed?"

"They're not supposed to be, not in here."

"But *if* they are?"

"Then you'll have to think fast, won't you?" said Kinoshita.

"That's *it*?" said Nighthawk. "That's all the advice you're going to give me?"

"I won't be around to give you advice when you go up against the man you were created to kill. You might as well get used to it."

Nighthawk stared at Kinoshita silently.

All of a sudden you'd rather kill me than them. What the hell did I say that got you so pissed off? Suddenly a sense of outrage possessed him, outrage that his sole purpose for existing was to kill. Yet he couldn't change it, so he tried to focus it on his targets.

"Wait here," said Nighthawk.

The young man got to his feet and walked over to the bar, where Undertaker McNair and his bodyguard were standing. He strolled casually past them, then suddenly whirled and brought his hand down heavily on the back of the bodyguard's neck. There was a loud cracking sound, and the man dropped like a stone.

McNair was startled, but his instincts were good, which is all that saved him from Nighthawk's first blow: a haymaker that was aimed at his head but struck his shoulder as he turned and tried to protect himself.

"What the hell is going on?" muttered McNair, backing away and striking a defensive posture.

Nighthawk said nothing, but launched a spinning kick that would have beheaded McNair if it had landed. McNair blocked it, reached inside his tunic, and suddenly was holding a long, wicked-looking knife in his hand.

"Who *are* you?" demanded McNair, feinting twice with the knife, then thrusting toward Nighthawk's neck. Nighthawk blocked the thrust, grabbed the assassin's wrist, ducked and twisted—and McNair flew through the air and landed next to his bodyguard with a resounding *thud*!

The young man, not even breathing hard from his exertions, kicked the knife out of McNair's hand and across the room, then gestured for him to get to his feet.

"What do you want?" rasped McNair. "Is it money? We can deal!"

Nighthawk feinted for McNair's groin, then took the heel of his hand and landed a powerful blow to McNair's nose, driving into his brain and killing him instantly.

Nighthawk heard a humming noise behind him, and turned to find himself facing a fully charged laser pistol.

"Hold it right there, son," said Blue, holding the pistol in his good hand.

"There was paper on them," said Kinoshita, who hadn't left his table.

"Not my concern," said Blue. "You don't kill people in my establishment."

Nighthawk shot a quick glance at Kinoshita. It seemed to ask: *Do I kill him too?*

Kinoshita shook his head, and the young man relaxed.

"We'll be happy to leave as soon as you put your pistol away."

"I haven't said that I'm going to put it away," replied Blue.

"And we'll make restitution," continued Kinoshita.

"Yeah?" The interest was in Blue's voice; his face was without emotion, his unblinking eyes trained on Nighthawk.

"There's six hundred thousand credits due on those two," said Kinoshita. "Half a million on McNair, the rest on his friend. We can't have racked up *that* big a bill in just three days. I'll instruct the authorities to turn the reward over to you. Pay our tab with it, and keep the rest."

"And the Demoncats?"

"What about them?"

"Always a market for good trophies."

"They're yours."

Blue stared at Nighthawk for another moment, then put his pistol back behind the bar. "You got yourself a deal," he announced. "Have one more Dust Whore—on the house."

"That's very generous of you, Blue," said Kinoshita, gesturing Nighthawk to leave the bar and rejoin him at the table. "We accept."

Nighthawk plunked a coin down on the bar. "I can afford to pay for *my* drink," he said with a hint of childish pride.

"You did well, Jeff," said Kinoshita. "Those were

tough, hard men you killed. You pulled it off with a minimum of effort, and with no damage to yourself."

"So what?"

Kinoshita smiled. "*That* was your graduation ceremony. We will each drink a Dust Whore. Then we'll go back to the chalet, and in the morning you'll take off for Solio II." The small man paused. "When we entered this establishment, you were a clone, all potential, all promise." He raised his glass in a salute. "Now you are as good as any man, and better than most."

"I always was."

"I know, but—"

"You don't know anything," said Nighthawk angrily. "You think I was created in a laboratory just to kill someone on Solio II."

"You were, Jeff," said Kinoshita. "We've never hid that from you."

"*I'll* decide what I was created for," said Nighthawk in low tones. "I'm a man, just like you." He stared unblinking into Kinoshita's eyes. It was not a pleasant stare. "*Don't you ever forget it.*"

Well, now I know what got you so riled.

"You saw what I did to those two," continued Nighthawk, gesturing toward the corpses and downing his drink with a single swallow. "I could get to where I *like* killing things."

He got to his feet and stalked out of Six-Finger Blue's, heading toward his chalet.

Kinoshita watched him go.

Yeah, no question about it; you're the Widowmaker, all right. You just needed to get your blood up. Kinoshita smiled a strangely satisfied smile. *I guess maybe we made you tough enough after all.*

Chapter 2

Solio II wasn't much of a world, not for a young man who had been born two months earlier on Deluros VIII and whose head was full of memories of glittering worlds he had never been to. There were less than a million inhabitants: about eight hundred thousand were human, the rest aliens of various species.

The planet's primary business was trade. It served as one of the handful of transitional worlds, officially part of the Frontier but in reality acting as an economic conduit between the mining and farming worlds of the Inner Frontier and the conspicuous consumers of the Oligarchy. It was said that Solio II was the Breadbasket to a Thousand Worlds, though it was a supplier rather than a breadbasket, and it traded with closer to three hundred worlds than a thousand, which was still not exactly a trifling number.

The Solio system had been ruled by dictators for the past half century. The most recent, Winslow Trelaine, had been in office for almost eight years before his assassination. He was the fourth governor in the past half century to die violently; governors of Solio II had a habit of not surviving long enough to retire.

Colonel James Hernandez, the government's chief of security, had made the initial contact with Nighthawk's legal representatives, and it was to his office that the young man reported when he finally touched down on Solio II.

Hernandez was a tall, lean man with thick black hair, an aquiline nose, a narrow jaw, and dark brown eyes. His chest was covered by row upon row of medals, despite the fact that the Solio system had never gone to war with anyone. A stack of orders was piled neatly on one corner of his desk, awaiting his signature—although his computer, which hovered above the left side of the desk, was quite capable of duplicating his signature thousands of times per minute.

The rest of the office was spotless, as if he'd just completed inspection. Every cabinet top was pristine, every painting was hung at the perfect angle to the floor, the various holoscreens were arranged by size. Nighthawk imagined that a speck of dust would be treated as an enemy invasion.

Hernandez got to his feet, his eyes appraising the young man who had entered his office. "Welcome to Solio, Mr. Nighthawk. May I offer you something to drink?"

"Later, perhaps."

"A cigar? Imported all the way from Aldebaran XII."

Nighthawk shook his head. "No, thanks."

"I must tell you I can hardly believe I'm here speaking with the Widowmaker himself!" said Hernandez enthusiastically. "You were one of my heroes when I was a boy. I think I read everything ever written about you. In fact," he added with a smile, "you might say that *you* are the reason I became what I am."

"I'm sure the Widowmaker would be flattered to know that," said Nighthawk in carefully measured tones as he sat down opposite Hernandez on a straight-backed chrome chair. "But I am not him."

Hernandez frowned. "I beg your pardon?"

"The Widowmaker is currently on Deluros VIII, awaiting a cure for the disease that afflicts him. My name is Jefferson Nighthawk, and I'm just someone who's here to do a job."

"Nonsense," said Hernandez, genuinely amused. "Do you think we haven't heard of your exploits on Karamojo? You killed Undertaker McNair with your bare hands." He paused, staring at Nighthawk. "You're the Widowmaker, all right."

Nighthawk shrugged. "Call me what you want. It's just a name." He leaned forward intently. "But remember that you're dealing with *me*, not *him*."

"Certainly," said Hernandez, studying him carefully for a moment. Finally he turned and lit a thin cigar. "Mr. Nighthawk, do you mind if I ask you a couple of questions that are not related to your mission here?"

"What kind of questions?"

"You're the first clone I've ever met," continued Hernandez, taking a puff of his cigar, "and I'm naturally curious about you. For example, I know that you didn't exist two months ago. How did you learn to speak the language so rapidly?"

"You make me sound like a freak," said Nighthawk, openly annoyed. "I'm a flesh-and-blood man, just like you."

"No offense intended," said Hernandez smoothly. "It's just that I will almost certainly never have the opportunity to speak to another clone. It is said that there are less than five hundred of you in the galaxy. Your creation is outlawed on almost every world in the Oligarchy. We had to cash a lot of political IOUs to get you made." He paused. "So it's only natural that I take advantage of the opportunity while you're here."

Nighthawk stared coldly at him for a long moment, then forced himself to relax. "I was given intensive sleep therapy," he replied at last.

"I know we've made great strides in sleep therapy," said Hernandez. "But I can't imagine anyone could master colloquial Terran that quickly. Did they perhaps start teaching it before you were . . . ah . . . fully formed?"

"I don't know," said Nighthawk.

"Fascinating! Did they use the same means to teach you to use the physical attributes you so obviously possess?" A tiny bit of ash fell on the desk; Hernandez meticulously ran a miniaturized vac over it.

"I suppose so. I also worked out with Ito Kinoshita."

"Kinoshita," repeated Hernandez. "I've heard of him. A formidable man."

"A friend," said Nighthawk.

"Far preferable to having him for an enemy," agreed Hernandez.

"Now let me ask you a question."

"Certainly," replied Hernandez. He noticed that his cigar had gone out and lit it again.

"Why me?" demanded Nighthawk. "You could

have hired Kinoshita, or someone like him. Why did you spend all those IOUs and all that money for *me*?"

"I think the answer's obvious," said Hernandez. "You are the greatest manhunter in the history of the Inner Frontier. Greater than Peacemaker MacDougal, greater than Sebastian Cain, greater than any of the legendary lawmen and bounty hunters." He paused. "Winslow Trelaine was a good leader and a dear friend; he deserves to be avenged by the best."

"I've done my homework, Colonel Hernandez," said Nighthawk. "Winslow Trelaine was a dictator who grew fat at the public trough."

Hernandez chuckled. "You sound as if you were contradicting me."

"Wasn't I?"

"Not at all," said Hernandez. "Do you think only democratically elected leaders can attain greatness? Let me suggest that how one reaches power has nothing to do with how one exercises it."

"I think it does."

"And well you should," replied Hernandez. "You speak with the innocence and idealism of youth, and I can appreciate that."

"I'm not *that* young."

An amused smile crossed Hernandez's face. "We'll discuss it again when you're a year old."

"Are you *trying* to insult me?" asked Nighthawk, an ominous note in his voice.

"Not at all," Hernandez assured him. "*I'm* the reason you exist. Of all the men that I could have had, I chose to create you. Why would I insult you?"

"*You* didn't create me."

"Oh, I didn't take the skin scrapings and fill the test tubes and prepare the nutrient solutions or whatever it is they do, but you exist for one reason and one reason only: because *I* threatened some politicians, bribed others, and paid an inordinate amount of money to your legal representatives for the sole purpose of creating a young, healthy Jefferson Nighthawk to hunt down the assassin of Winslow Trelaine." Hernandez stared at him. "Don't tell me they also gave you the Book of Genesis during your sleep therapy."

Nighthawk stared at him but said nothing.

Finally Hernandez shook his head. "We've obviously gotten off on the wrong foot. Perhaps we should talk about what you plan to do now that you're here."

Nighthawk waited for the tension to flow out of his body. "I'll have that drink now," he said at last.

Hernandez crossed the office to an ornate cabinet and pulled out an oddly shaped bottle and two large crystal glasses. "Cygnian cognac," he announced. "The best there is."

"I've never had any."

"Well, you're starting at the top," said Hernandez. "From this day forward, every cognac you drink will be a disappointment, for the memory of this will never leave you."

Nighthawk took a sip, resisted the urge to ask for a Dust Whore, and forced a smile to his face. "Very good," he said.

Hernandez took a small sip from his own glass. "Wait for the aftertaste," he said.

Nighthawk waited what seemed an appropriate amount of time, then nodded his head in agreement.

"And now," continued Hernandez, "I think it's time to get down to business."

"That's what I'm here for."

"As you know, Winslow Trelaine was assassinated nine weeks ago." Hernandez grimaced. "He was killed with a solid beam of light from the muzzle of a laser rifle, fired at a distance of approximately two hundred meters."

"Where did it happen?" asked Nighthawk.

"Ironically, as he was getting out of the car to attend the opera."

"Ironically?" repeated Nighthawk.

"Winslow *hated* the opera," said Hernandez with a smile. "He was there to make peace between two feuding factions among his supporters."

"Could one of them have done it?"

"Not a chance," replied Hernandez with absolute certainty. "We had all of them under surveillance."

"Could one of them have commissioned it?" persisted Nighthawk.

"One of them *did*," answered Hernandez. "They knew he'd be attending the opera that night, though his loathing for it was well documented. They even knew which government vehicle he'd be arriving in." He paused. "That information could only have come from an insider."

"Was this the first attempt on his life?"

"The third."

"Tell me about the first two," said Nighthawk.

Hernandez sighed. "I would love to tell you that my quick-witted security staff anticipated and thwarted them, but the fact of the matter is that both attempts were thoroughly botched or else they might well have succeeded."

"I assume you captured the perpetrators?"

"The *would-be* perpetrators," Hernandez corrected him. "Yes, we caught them both."

"And I assume they had no connection to the assassin who succeeded?"

"Not as far as we can tell," agreed Hernandez. "Both were members of the lunatic fringe. Well, *differ-*

ent lunatic fringes. One wanted to help the sales of his book, which was a dismal critical and commercial failure. The other thought Trelaine and his entire administration were puppets of some alien race and were preparing to enslave the planet for his dark masters."

"Is either one alive?" asked Nighthawk.

Hernandez shook his head. "Both were executed. Besides, as I said, they acted alone—and they were crazy. *This* was a meticulously planned political assassination."

"And there are no leads at all?"

"None."

"Well," said Nighthawk thoughtfully, "there's no sense questioning Trelaine's cabinet or his personal friends, at least not yet. They'll all deny everything, whether they're telling the truth or not, and I don't suppose I have the authority to . . . ah . . . *extract* the information I need?"

"No, I'm afraid not."

"Pity." Nighthawk followed Hernandez's gaze, saw that it had come to rest on his almost-untouched glass of cognac, and forced himself to take another sip. "Well, Trelaine was obviously killed by a hired gun. Who's the likeliest?"

The smile returned to Hernandez's face.

"Did I say something funny?" asked Nighthawk.

"Not at all. I am just pleased to see that you are reasoning like the Widowmaker."

Nighthawk sighed and placed the glass down on the edge of the desk. "All right. Who am I looking for?"

"I will give you his name in a moment," said Hernandez. "But first, I want it made clear that I am not accusing him of murder. I am not saying that he pulled the trigger." He paused. "But out here killers and bandits tend to be territorial. If this man didn't take the commission himself, he undoubtedly approved whoever *did* take it."

"Fine," said Nighthawk. "Who is he?"

"Have you ever heard of the Marquis of Queensbury?"

Nighthawk shook his head. "No."

"He is the most lethal man within hundreds—perhaps thousands—of light-years," said Hernandez, not without a tiny note of admiration. "Present company excepted, I hope. Anyway, armed or unarmed, you couldn't ask for a more formidable opponent. Further, having built a criminal empire, he has demonstrated remarkable skill at running it."

"Have you any idea where he might be?" asked Nighthawk.

"I know precisely where he is."

Nighthawk frowned. "Then why haven't you—?"

"It's not that simple," interrupted Hernandez. "Not only do most of the Frontier worlds make their laws in a haphazard fashion, when they have any laws at all—but almost all of them lack extradition treaties with each other. That's why bounty hunters flourish out here."

"So he's on a world that won't extradite him?"

"He's on a world that hasn't seen a lawman or a law since the first Man set foot on it eight centuries ago."

"If they don't have any laws, it should be easy enough to just go there and hunt him down," suggested Nighthawk.

"Ah, the exuberance and confidence of youth!" replied Hernandez with a smile. "How I wish I still shared it with you!"

"Okay," said Nighthawk. "What am I missing *this* time?"

"Seven light-years from here—three star systems away—are the nearest habitable planets. And I use the word 'habitable' *very* generously. They are sister planets, mining worlds named Yukon and Tundra. Each is an almost unbroken sheet of ice. The average daytime temperature lingers around minus-twenty degrees Celsius—and each possesses literally hundreds of outlaws who are totally loyal to the Marquis."

"Which one is he on?"

Hernandez shrugged. "I've no idea. He divides his time between them."

"They sound . . . unappealing," remarked Nighthawk.

"They're unappealing on good days," said Hernandez. "On bad days they're a lot worse—but they're his headquarters."

"Why not just drop a bomb?"

"Because you would be killing thousands of innocent men and women," answered Hernandez.

Nighthawk shrugged. "Oh, well—it was an idea."

"Not a practical one."

"I assume there's no way to sneak up on him?" continued Nighthawk. "I mean, if he controls the planets, he knows who comes and goes."

"I'll give you credentials as a miner," said Hernandez. "That should get you through the door, anyway."

"An interesting situation," commented Nighthawk dryly.

"It is an outrageous situation," said Hernandez. "That is why we have come up with an outrageous solution and are paying an outrageous price." He lit another cigar. "Remember this: The Marquis is as

◆ ◆ ◆   39

dangerous as you are. If I were you, I'd shoot him on sight."

"I don't know what he looks like."

Hernandez reached into his desk drawer and withdrew a small, multicolored cube. He studied it for a moment, then tossed it to Nighthawk.

"Run that through your ship's computer. It's got all the data we possess on the Marquis, including a current holograph."

"Thanks," said Nighthawk, putting the cube into a pocket. He stared across the desk at Hernandez. "If I shoot him on sight, how will he be able to identify his employer for us?"

"If you can get it out of him, so much the better," said Hernandez. "But frankly, my office is under enormous pressure to produce the killer. My own preference, of course, is for finding the man who hired him, and we'll continue to work on it, but there are certain political realities that I must face if I wish to keep my job."

"Give 'em someone to hang or they'll hang you instead?" suggested Nighthawk with a smile.

"Something like that."

"Is there anything else I should know?" asked Nighthawk.

"Probably," said Hernandez. "If I think of it, and it's not on the cube, I'll transmit it to your ship."

Nighthawk got to his feet, and Hernandez rose as well. "I'll spend tonight in orbit about Solio, just in case you remember anything else you want to tell me." He paused. "I assume the coordinates and star maps are on the cube?"

Hernandez nodded.

"Thank you for your time," said Nighthawk. "I'll report to you whenever it's practical."

"Good luck," said Hernandez as Nighthawk left his office.

The officer sat down and took a final sip of his drink. "Did you hear that?" he said at last.

A small, olive-skinned man wearing a major's uniform entered the office through a hidden door. "Every word of it," he said.

"Have somebody follow him," said Hernandez. "If he goes anywhere except straight to his ship, I want to know about it."

"Do you really think he can take the Marquis, sir?" asked the major.

"I hope so. He's the best there's ever been—or at least, he *was*." Hernandez paused, lost in thought for a moment. "Yes, I think he's got a chance."

"Can he also come out of there alive?"

"Well, that's a different proposition. He might be good enough to get in there and kill the Marquis, but there's no way that he's going to be able to fight his way back out. And that, of course, will save us the completion fee for the job." He contemplated his cigar thoughtfully for a long moment. "Poor, ignorant clone. The real Widowmaker would doubtless have spotted my purpose halfway through our interview; this one is too young and too innocent to even know what he's dying for."

Chapter 3

•   •   •   •   •   •   •

Tundra was everything Hernandez had said, and more. Almost as large as Earth, it was completely shrouded in snow and ice. Mountains, valleys, plateaus, buttes, all shone such a brilliant white in the midday sun that a man without polarized lenses would go snow-blind in a matter of minutes.

The planet had once provided the Oligarchy with a bounty of gold and diamonds and fissionable materials. For almost two centuries it had been ripped open and plundered until, at long last, its vast riches were only a memory. Ghost towns littered the face of the planet. Smelting and refining plants stood empty, encrusted in ice or buried under hundred-foot snowdrifts. Here and there small communities of Men still existed, extracting the last bits of treasure from centuries-old mines, but most of the miners had long since moved on to younger, riper worlds.

There were still goods to be assayed and shipped, miners to be fed and medicated and entertained, remnants of businesses to be tended. Most of the people remaining on Tundra gathered in Klondike, a once-prosperous city.

Nighthawk set his ship down at the Klondike spaceport, checked the outside temperature, found that it was 46 degrees below zero Celsius, and decided to travel the half mile to the city in his spacesuit rather than in the protective outer garments that Hernandez had supplied.

As he passed among the spaceships that stood like frozen needles in the sun, he noted that two of them were transport vessels from Solio II, delivering foodstuffs and liquor to the isolated dome-dwellers. Almost all of the others, some four hundred in number, were private ships and bore insignia from all across the Inner Frontier.

He had cleared the spaceport and was riding a rented powersled toward the city when he saw a sudden movement off to his left. He stopped, turned, and tried to pinpoint it against the glare of the snow. Then he saw it again—a brief, feeble, jerking motion. Curious, he altered course and a moment later came to a small, underweight man twitching in the snow, his thick coat, fur gloves, and fur boots obviously not adequate against the cold.

Nighthawk crouched down and helped the man to a sitting position. His eyes focused briefly and he said something, but Nighthawk, wearing his space helmet, could not hear, nor did he have any intention of removing the faceplate in this temperature.

By gestures he tried to ask if the man could

stand. The man shook his head, and Nighthawk set him onto his feet, pointed toward the city, and prepared to load him onto the powersled. The man resisted weakly, then passed out, and a moment later the sled was taking them both toward Klondike.

When he reached the city, Nighthawk tried to figure out what to do with his burden. The deserted streets and sidewalks were being plowed continuously by robotic machines, but he couldn't spot any people. There were some imposing buildings—an opera house, a theater, a museum—but all were deserted and coated with ice, as if they belonged to some more prosperous era in the planet's history.

Nighthawk slowly surveyed the city, left to right. Offices, stores, bars, a sports arena, a small colosseum—all frozen, all deserted. Finally he felt a hand poke him weakly. It was the small man he had rescued, and he pointed to a building off to the right.

Nighthawk immediately directed the sled toward it, and as he got closer he saw the glow of artificial light coming from a small window. When he reached the front door it dilated long enough for him to enter with the small man slung over his shoulder, then quickly contracted back into place.

He passed through an airlock and found himself in a small tavern. Two orange-skinned aliens in the corner glanced briefly at him, then went back to conversing in low hisses. A man sanding at the bar stared at him in open curiosity, but made no motion to join or help him. The bartender—tall, broad-shouldered, potbellied, and golden-eyed—nodded to him, smiled briefly, and then went back to whatever he had been doing.

Nighthawk carried the small man to a table, lowered him gently into a chair, then quickly clambered out of his spacesuit and walked over to the bar.

"Dust Whore for me, something hot for my friend," he said. "Bring them over when they're ready."

He returned and sat down next to his new companion, who seemed to be recovering his senses. Now, in the light, Nighthawk could see that the man's skin was leathery, giving the impression of row upon row of hard scales.

"How do you feel?" asked Nighthawk.

"Awful." Pause. "Where are we?"

"We're in Klondike."

The man moaned. "Now I feel even worse. I was trying to tell you to take me to your ship."

"I have business here," responded Nighthawk.

"Well, I have business anywhere else," said his companion, coughing feebly. "I was trying to get *away* from Klondike when you interfered."

"You'd have been dead in another ten minutes," replied Nighthawk.

"I might have made it to my ship."

"Not even if you had wings."

"Well, at least it would have been painless," muttered the little man. "Freezing to death's not a bad way to go."

"Compared to what?" asked Nighthawk.

"Compared to what's gonna happen to me if I don't get off this iceball of a world right away."

"You're in no condition to go anywhere."

The small man sighed. "You've got a point," he admitted. "By the way"—he extended his hand weakly—"I haven't thanked you for saving my life." Nighthawk stared at the scaled fingers without moving. "It's okay, friend. They wouldn't have let me on the planet if I had anything contagious." Nighthawk considered the statement, then reached out and shook his hand. "The name's Malloy—Lizard Malloy."

"Jefferson Nighthawk."

"I've heard that name—or something like it," said Malloy. "A long time ago. So it couldn't have been you, could it?"

"No," said Nighthawk. "And I've never met anyone called Lizard Malloy before."

"Used to be simple John Jacob Malloy," answered the little man. "Asteroid miner. Made a goldstrike over in the Prego system, just before the star went nova. They warned us it was going to blow, but I thought I had another day's time to get my stuff out. Turned out I was wrong. Sun exploded into a zillion glowing dustballs. Stuff went right through my spacesuit. When I got out of it, I found my skin looked like *this*." He held out his arm for inspection. "You should have seen what I did to Geiger counters for the next three years! Drove my doctors crazy. And of course, I had to dump my gold for a tenth of its value; it's got to sit in a vault somewhere for a couple of centuries before anyone can touch it."

"But you're not hot anymore?"

"Nope. I can walk through a spaceport today and not set off a single machine. One day I woke up and all the radiation was gone. Drove my doctors crazy a second time!" Malloy chuckled in amusement. "Whenever I need to raise a grubstake, I go back to the hospital and let them try to figure out what happened."

"I assume they haven't come up with an answer yet?"

Malloy shook his head. "Nope. I'm one of nature's mysteries." He paused. "You'll find a lot of us on the Frontier, one way or another." He gestured to the approaching bartender. "Even Gold Eyes here is one of us. Only he was born that way."

The bartender set their drinks on the table and grinned down at Malloy. "Word is out that he's looking for you," he said.

"Now tell me something I *don't* know."

The bartender chuckled and walked back to the bar.

Malloy rose to his feet. "I gotta get out of here." But he was overcome by dizziness, tried to steady himself, and collapsed back onto his chair.

"The only place you should be going is a hospital," said Nighthawk.

The small man shook his head vigorously. "I'll be okay in another minute."

"Sure you will," said Nighthawk sardonically.

"They don't call me Lizard just for the scales," countered Malloy. "The damned nova gave me a lizard's metabolism, too. I get too cold, I go comatose. You warm me up, I'm fine." Suddenly he grinned—a reptilian grin. "Put me in a sauna, I have so much energy I can't sit still." He paused. "Anyway, I'll be fine soon, and then I'm gone before *he* knows I was here."

"Who are you talking about?"

"Who else? The Marquis."

"The Marquis of Queensbury?" asked Nighthawk.

Malloy grimaced. "You know any other Marquises?"

"What does he have against you?"

"Well, that's kind of a long and involved story," said Malloy. "I'm sure it wouldn't interest someone like you."

"Everything about the Marquis interests me," said Nighthawk.

Malloy stared at him long and hard. "Look,

Jefferson Nighthawk," he said, "you saved my life, so let me return the favor. You're a nice young man. If you want to live to be a nice old man, go home."

"Explain yourself."

"There are only two reasons for a man on Tundra to be interested in the Marquis. You either want to join him or kill him—and somehow you don't strike me as the joining type." He paused. "You're just a kid. He's the Marquis. You haven't got a chance."

Nighthawk downed his Dust Whore. "I haven't got a choice."

"He'll kill you."

"I doubt it," said Nighthawk seriously. "I'm pretty good."

"Every graveyard on the Frontier is filled with kids who were pretty good," said Malloy. "Go home."

"I can't. But there's something I *can* do. From this moment on, you're under my protection."

"What are you talking about?" demanded Malloy.

"Just what I said," replied Nighthawk. "Anyone wants you, they have to go through me to get you."

"Fuck it!" said Malloy, jumping to his feet. "I've got better things to do than play bait for the Marquis. He'll kill us both." He turned toward the door. "I'm out of here!"

Nighthawk shoved the small man back onto his chair, and an instant later Malloy was staring down the barrel of a wicked-looking gun.

"You don't have any choice in the matter," said Nighthawk, his conversational tone belying the meaning of his words. "I saved you. Your life is mine. I'll spend it any way I choose."

Malloy looked long and hard into Nighthawk's eyes before moving, or even breathing deeply.

"You'd really do it, wouldn't you?" he said at last. "You'd really kill me!"

"I'd prefer not to."

"Yeah, but you'd do it."

"Without hesitation," said Nighthawk, holstering his gun and sitting back down.

Malloy was silent for a moment. "I could make a break for it," he said at last. "The door's not that far away."

"You could," agreed Nighthawk.

"Just how good a shot are you?"

"Pretty good."

"Pretty good," repeated Malloy sardonically. "I'll bet you could hit a speck of dirt at four hundred feet."

"Maybe even five hundred," said Nighthawk easily. "Now, have a drink and relax. I'm buying."

Malloy frowned. "I don't understand you at all. First you save me, then you threaten to kill me, and now you're buying my drinks."

"It's easy enough. As long as you are under my protection, I pay your way."

"And how long is *that*?" asked Malloy suspiciously.

"You'll know when it's over." Nighthawk signaled the bartender to bring two more drinks.

"No more for me," said Malloy. "I want to be sober enough to duck if I have to."

"Just relax. Nothing's going to happen to you."

"What makes you any better than every other kid who's gone after the Marquis? They were all good, and now they're all dead. Are your hands any faster? Are your eyes any better? Why should you succeed when so many have failed?"

"Because I'm the best there is."

"You're just a kid, maybe twenty-two, twenty-three years old," said Malloy derisively. "Who'd you ever kill? What makes you the best?"

"Take my word for it," said Nighthawk.

"If we were just two guys talking in a bar on some other world I would—but we're on *this* world and you're using me as bait, so no, I don't take your word for anything. Who have you killed?"

"Cherokee Mason," said Nighthawk. "Zanzibar Brooks. Billy the Knife."

"Wait a minute!" said Malloy. "What kind of idiot do you take me for? Those guys are all out of the history books!"

Nighthawk shrugged. "So am I."

Malloy stared at him and frowned. "Jefferson Nighthawk, Jefferson Nighthawk," he repeated. "It's familiar, but I don't place it. And you're not out of any book more than a year or two old."

"Maybe you know me by another name," said Nighthawk.

"Maybe I do," replied Malloy dubiously. "What is it?"

"The Widowmaker."

"Bullshit! He died a century ago."

"No he didn't."

"Well, if he's alive, he's a hell of a lot older than *you.*"

"He's in DeepSleep in a cryonics chamber on Deluros VIII," said Nighthawk.

"What are you trying to tell me?" demanded Malloy.

"I'm his clone."

"I don't believe it!"

The two orange-skinned aliens looked up briefly

at Malloy's exclamation, then went back to conversing in their low, hissing voices.

Nighthawk shrugged again. "Believe what you want."

Malloy stared at him, puzzled. "Why would they clone him? You even *think* of cloning a human, you're looking at thirty to life on a prison planet." Suddenly his eyes narrowed. "Are you telling me they cloned you just to kill the Marquis?"

"That's right."

"What happens to you after you're done? Do they send you back to the factory?"

"I don't think they've thought that far ahead," said Nighthawk. He paused. "But *I* have."

"And you're really the Widowmaker?"

"Yes."

Suddenly Malloy grinned. "I'll have that drink now." He turned to the bartender. "Hey, Gold Eyes. Another round here!" As the bartender prepared the drinks, he turned back to Nighthawk, speaking in low tones. "You know, there may be a way for everyone to profit from this."

"How?"

"Watch."

The bartender approached them and delivered their drinks.

"Hey, Gold Eyes, what's the odds on the kid here living till tomorrow?"

The bartender shrugged. "Beats me."

"What are the odds if he goes up against the Marquis tonight?"

Gold Eyes stopped and scrutinized Nighthawk for a long moment. "Three hundred to one, against."

"I'll take twenty credits' worth of that," said Malloy.

"Where's your money?"

"Hey, Jefferson," said the small man, "loan me twenty credits, will you?"

"I buy your drinks," said Nighthawk. "I don't pay for your bets."

Gold Eyes kept staring at Nighthawk. "Are you here to kill the Marquis?"

"I never said that," replied Nighthawk.

"Then you're not?"

"I didn't say *that*, either."

"Want a piece of advice?" said Gold Eyes.

"How much are you asking for it?"

"It's gratis."

"Then keep it," said Nighthawk. "It's probably worth about what you're charging for it."

Gold Eyes chuckled. "I like you, kid. Take my advice and get the hell out while the getting's good. He already knows you're here."

"Where is he?"

"Who knows?" said Gold Eyes. "But this is his world. Nothing goes on here that he doesn't know about." He picked up the empties and headed back to the bar.

"What happened to your money?" asked Nighthawk, turning to Malloy. "When you said the Marquis was after you, I figured you'd swindled him somehow."

"I did," said Malloy unhappily.

"How?"

"I had the most perfect set of cards you ever saw," said Malloy. "They were beautiful. I mean, *nobody* could spot them. Even if you knew they were marked, you couldn't read them until I showed you how." He paused. "I took the Marquis for two hundred and seventy-five thousand credits last night."

"And he spotted them?"

"No. I told you no one could spot them. Hell, if he had, I'd have been dead before morning."

"What happened, then?"

"Since I was planning to leave, I sold the deck to one of the locals for a couple of thousand credits." Malloy smiled ruefully. "Wouldn't you know we'd have the first blizzard in a month? No ships could take off, so I came back here for a little warmth and companionship—and found out that the son of a bitch I'd sold the deck to had cashed in by fingering me to the Marquis! I hid out until morning, and then tried to make it to the spaceport."

"So?"

"So what?"

"So where's the money?"

"Taped behind one of the chemical toilets in the men's room in his casino," answered Malloy.

"All right," said Nighthawk, slapping some money on the table. "Let's go get it."

"I beg your pardon?"

"Your money," said Nighthawk. "I assume you want it?"

Malloy blinked furiously, like a lizard suddenly exposed to the sun. "You don't propose to just walk into the Marquis' casino, take the money, and walk right back out with it?" he demanded.

"Oh, we might stop for a drink or two, just to make sure we're spotted."

Malloy studied him for a long moment. "You're *sure* you're the Widowmaker?"

Nighthawk didn't answer but started putting on his spacesuit, and Malloy finally climbed into his coat and boots.

"How far?" asked Nighthawk.

"Halfway down the next block," answered Malloy.

"Can you make it?"

"I have two hundred and seventy-five thousand credits waiting for me there," said Malloy. "What do *you* think?"

The door dilated as they passed through to the frigid street.

"God, I *hate* this iceball!" said Malloy, already starting to shiver. But Nighthawk, as before, refused to remove his faceplate, and so could not hear his companion. They walked rapidly to the casino and wasted no time entering it. Nighthawk left his spacesuit and helmet in an Anti-Thief Field just inside the airlock, and Malloy—who couldn't afford the protective device—simply hung his coat on a wall.

If Gold Eyes' tavern had been empty, the Marquis' casino was overcrowded. The walls changed color to match the mood of the live music, and the place was brilliantly illuminated although no light source was visible. Built to comfortably accommodate perhaps one hundred and fifty Men, it currently held upward of two hundred, plus another forty aliens. Floating three feet above the floor were tables for roulette, baccarat, ten variations of craps (with six-sided, eight-sided, and twelve-sided dice), and even two tables of *jabob*, an alien game that had become incredibly popular all across the Inner Frontier. A sleek chrome bar, stocked with intoxicants from a hundred worlds, lined one wall, and hovering a few feet above it was a tiny stage that featured a sultry half-clad girl whose undulations passed for dancing. Holographs of beautiful females—both human and alien, mostly nude—lined the walls, glowing gently as they spun slowly in the air.

"He does pretty well for himself," remarked Nighthawk.

"Ninety percent of these guys work for him," answered Malloy, his features becoming more animated as he became warmer. "They're just playing with money he gives 'em." He looked around nervously. "I don't want to ask any embarrassing questions or anything—but have you thought of how you're gonna get out of here if you *do* kill him? There's a couple hundred guns in here. Even the Widowmaker wasn't *that* good."

Nighthawk made no answer, but scanned the crowd, checked all the exits, and measured the distances involved while his brain computed the odds.

"You know, if *I* could figure out what you're here for, it ain't gonna be too long before someone else does, too," whispered Malloy. "Let's get the hell out of here. I can get my money some other time."

He started walking toward the door, but Nighthawk reached out and grabbed his arm. "We're staying."

Malloy seemed about to jerk his arm free, then thought better of it. "Well?" he insisted as they turned back in to the casino. "Are you taking them *all* on?"

"Not unless I have to," said Nighthawk.

"Then what *are* you gonna do?"

"I'm working on it."

"What if one of *them* works faster?"

"He'll wish he hadn't."

"Look," said Malloy in low tones, "maybe you Frontier legends don't feel any fear, but us real people, we get scared shitless at the thought of facing a couple of gunmen, let alone a couple of hundred. Tell me something comforting about why I shouldn't worry."

"Shut up and think about your money."

"Right now all I can think is that it'll pay for one hell of a fancy funeral," complained Malloy. "I mean, you *seem* sane, but you don't look even a little bit afraid, and that makes you either stupid or crazy." He paused. "*Are* you crazy? Did you maybe just imagine all this about the Widowmaker and everything?"

Nighthawk turned away from Malloy, an expression of distaste on his face. As he did so, his gaze fell upon a new dancer atop the floating platform. Her appearance was striking: her hair was auburn, her eyes almost colorless, her figure lean and lithe. But it was her skin that captured Nighthawk's attention: it was light blue.

The music began again, an alien melody with an insistent rhythm, and the blue-skinned girl started dancing atop the platform. Tiny chimes attached to her fingers and ankles augmented the primal rhythm as she spun and whirled in the confined quarters with an almost inhuman grace.

"Who is she?" asked Nighthawk.

"Her?" replied Malloy. "I don't know her real name. They call her the Pearl of Maracaibo. Comes from somewhere in the Quinellus Cluster."

"A mutant?"

Malloy grinned a reptilian grin. "Unless you know anyone else with blue skin."

Nighthawk continued staring at her. "Just that mutant bartender." Pause. "She's very beautiful, isn't she?"

"A lot of people think so. The smart ones keep it to themselves."

"Oh?"

"She belongs to the Marquis."

"You mean she works for him?" said Nighthawk.

"I meant what I said."

"Didn't they fight eight or nine wars to abolish slave labor?"

"For all the good it did."

Nighthawk smiled. "I stand corrected." He paused. "Interesting man, the Marquis."

"Does that matter?"

"Maybe so, maybe not," said Nighthawk without taking his eyes off the Pearl of Maracaibo. "You never know."

Chapter 4

◆ ◆ ◆ ◆ ◆ ◆

*The music stopped and the blue-skinned girl vanished be-*hind the floating platform.

"Go tell her that I'd like to buy her a drink," said Nighthawk.

"I don't know where she is," said Malloy with obvious relief.

"Then tell the bartender to send her one with my compliments."

"Doesn't it bother you that you're completely surrounded by all these cold-blooded killers whose only loyalty is to the Marquis?"

"The only thing that bothers me is that you're talking to me instead of walking over to the bartender."

Malloy got up and stared long and hard at Nighthawk. "You ain't *him*," he said at last.

"I beg your pardon?"

"I know *he* lived to see forty. No way you're going to." And turning on his heel, Malloy approached the bar. He forced his way between two shaggy Lodinites, signaled to the bartender, said something to him, pointed to Nighthawk, then returned to the table.

"You know any prayers?" asked Malloy, taking his seat.

"Nope. Why?"

"Probably just as well. I don't think you're gonna have time for one."

"What's it like to spend your whole life being afraid?" asked Nighthawk, genuinely interested.

"Healthy," said Malloy. "And if you're *not* afraid, you've got a gene missing or a screw loose or something. These guys don't know you're a legend come back to life. They think you're a just a kid—and any moment now, when the bartender shoots his mouth off, they'll think you're a kid who listens to his gonads instead of his better judgment."

"I can't help what they think."

"Yes, you *can* help it," said Malloy bitterly. "Or at least you could have until you sent me over to buy a drink for some goddamned mutant who probably can't metabolize it anyway."

"You worry too much. It's going to make you old before your time."

"Yeah? Well, you're going to make me dead before my time!"

"I saved you, remember?"

"To use as bait!"

"Only if I have to." Nighthawk looked over Malloy's shoulder. "And it's starting to look like I won't."

Malloy spun around on his chair and saw two

men and a hulking, gray-skinned alien from Pellenorath VI approaching the table.

"I don't have a weapon!" whispered Malloy urgently.

"You won't need one."

"You don't know who they are! The one on the left is Bloody Ben Masters. He's killed maybe twenty men all by himself—and I've seen the Pellenor rip men to pieces!"

"Shut up and keep out of the line of fire," said Nighthawk calmly. He looked up as the three killers reached his table. "Is there something I can do for you, friends?"

"Yeah," said Masters. "You can be very careful who you buy drinks for when you're in Klondike."

"You mean my friend Lizard?" he asked innocently, gesturing toward the leather-skinned Malloy. "He looked thirsty."

"You know exactly who I mean," said Masters.

"Ah! You're speaking about the lovely young dancing lady."

"You got it."

"But she looked thirsty, too. Besides, it hardly seems fair that the Marquis of Queensbury should have a whole world and her, too."

"You are pushing your luck," said the Pellenor in heavily accented Terran.

"Just consider this a friendly warning," continued Masters.

"Well, I thank you for your concern," said Nighthawk. "And I'll certainly be careful about who I buy drinks for."

"Good."

"Oh, I'll still buy them for the young lady," said Nighthawk, getting to his feet as the three were turning to leave. "But I'll make sure I never offer any to scum like you or your ugly gray pet here."

Bloody Ben Masters had his pistol out before he had fully turned back to the table, but Nighthawk was even faster. There was a brief hum of power, and Masters and the other human collapsed to the floor, their flesh charred and smoking from Nighthawk's laser gun.

The bulky Pellenor emitted a roar and lunged for Nighthawk, but the young man was too quick, sidestepping him and bringing the barrel of his gun down with killing force on the back of the alien's head. The skin broke open, shooting out jets of purple blood, and the alien collapsed to the floor.

"You all saw it," said Nighthawk without raising his voice.

"A clear-cut case of self-defense," added Malloy, amazed to find himself still alive. "Bloody Ben went for his gun first. I'll testify to it!"

Nobody said a word for almost a full minute, while Nighthawk kept his laser pistol in his hand, hanging down past his hip but ready to use again if he had to. Finally someone spoke up: "So whose deal is it?" and a few seconds later everyone went back about their business.

"Have you got any law officers here?" asked Nighthawk, holstering his weapon and sitting back down.

"Not much point to it," answered Malloy. "We ain't got no laws on Tundra, except those the Marquis makes up."

"So who's going to take care of the bodies?" continued Nighthawk, staring at the three corpses that lay where they had fallen.

"There are some maintenance mechs somewhere,"

said Malloy. "When they see the mess, they'll come on over and cart the bodies away."

"And they're just going to lie here until then?" asked Nighthawk, surprised.

"I suppose so."

Nighthawk looked around the casino. No one paid any attention to the bodies; they could have been invisible. "It's like it never happened. I thought maybe you were kidding when you said they didn't have any laws here."

Two small robots suddenly approached with an airsled. They placed both human corpses on it, then piled the alien atop the humans. There was a whirring of overtaxed motors, and the sled gently sank to the floor. The robots studied the situation for a moment, then rolled the alien off the sled and left with the two men.

"You're awfully good," said Malloy admiringly. "I half think you might have a chance against the Marquis after all. In a fair fight."

"Thanks."

"Doesn't make much difference, though," added Malloy. "The Marquis doesn't believe in fighting fair."

"I assume he's on his way here?"

"If he's on Tundra."

"And if he's not?"

"Don't worry—*someone* will be laying for you," answered Malloy. "You killed three of his people. He can't let you get away with that. It's bad for business."

Nighthawk studied the room again, wondering where the next attack might come from. Finally he turned to Malloy.

"I want you go up to the bartender again," he said.

"You're not buying her another drink?" said the little man incredulously.

Nighthawk shook his head. "I want you to go and tell the bartender that if the next person to come after me isn't the Marquis, I'm going to consider it a direct attack by *him* and this place will need a new bartender two seconds later."

"Are you sure?" asked Malloy. "I mean, hell, *he* can't help who tries to kill you."

"Who do you think passed the word to those three?" responded Nighthawk irritably. "I'm through with underlings. If the Marquis is around, he'll know how to contact him."

The two robots came back with an empty airsled to collect the Pellenor. Malloy watched them load the body and leave, then looked up. Suddenly his leathery face registered total fear.

"Uh, that ain't gonna be necessary," he said, his voice shaking.

Nighthawk turned in the direction Malloy was looking. A tall man was staring at him. He had wild red hair, bright blue eyes, and as square a jaw as Nighthawk had ever seen. He was tall—close to six feet eight or nine inches—his shoulders were broad, his waist solid without being fat, and he possessed an animal grace that was rarely seen in men a foot shorter. There was a deep scar on his left cheek, from just below the corner of his eye down to his jaw, but rather than looking bizarre or ugly it only seemed to add to his charisma.

And charisma he had: he seemed to fill the room just by being in it. Everything about him was just a bit bigger than life. He wore no visible weapons. He carried a bottle of alien liquor in one hand and an empty glass in the other.

Nobody had to tell Nighthawk that this was the Marquis of Queensbury. The crowd parted as if by prior signal as the huge redheaded man approached his table.

"You're dead," he said to Malloy, then ignored him as if he were some insignificant insect and turned his attention to Nighthawk. "Your name's Jefferson Nighthawk."

Nighthawk simply stared at him.

"You killed three of my men."

Nighthawk made no reply.

"You don't talk much, do you?" asked the Marquis of Queensbury.

"I haven't heard any questions," replied Nighthawk.

The Marquis nodded his approval. "A good answer." He sat down at the table, commandeered an empty glass, and poured himself a drink from the bottle he was carrying. "You want a question? I'll ask one." The blue eyes bored into Nighthawk's own. "Who gave you permission to kill three of my men in my casino?"

"They went for their weapons first," answered Nighthawk.

"Makes no difference," said the Marquis. "They belonged to me, and you killed them." He paused ominously. "How are you going to make that up to me?"

"Well, I suppose I could go out and recruit three more fools," said Nighthawk.

"Are you calling my men fools?"

"Yes."

The Marquis stared at him for a long moment, then laughed aloud. "I *like* you, Jefferson Nighthawk!" He shook his head with mock sadness. "It grieves me to have to make an example of you."

"Then don't," said Nighthawk.

"It can't be helped," said the Marquis. "How long could I stay in business if I let everyone make advances to my woman and kill my men?"

"Longer than you can stay alive if you don't walk away," said Nighthawk. He placed the muzzle of his laser pistol against the Marquis' belly beneath the table, where no one else could see it.

The Marquis looked nonplussed. "You're going to kill me in front of two hundred witnesses?"

"I'd rather not."

The Marquis chuckled. "I'll just bet you'd rather not."

"On the other hand, I don't plan to let you kill *me* in front of two hundred witnesses, either," said Nighthawk.

"Put the pistol away," said the Marquis. "I'm not armed."

"I'm told you're a man of your word," said Nighthawk. "Promise not to kill me and I'll let you walk away."

"I can't promise that," said the Marquis. "Who knows what the future holds?" He paused. "But I'll promise not to kill you today. Good enough?"

Nighthawk nodded.

The Marquis got up, turned his back, and began walking away—but just as Nighthawk thought the situation had been diffused, or at least postponed, he felt his arms being grabbed and twisted behind his back. He was yanked painfully to his feet and held motionless by half a dozen men.

"It's nice to have friends," said the Marquis as he turned back to Nighthawk. "Of course, you wouldn't know about that, would you?"

Nighthawk grimaced, and for a moment his gaze

fell on Malloy, who hadn't moved since the Marquis had entered the room.

"Him?" said the Marquis with a contemptuous laugh. "That's not a friend, that's a parasite."

"Let me go, and you'll be surprised how few friends I need," Nighthawk countered.

"Ah, the bravado of youth!" said the Marquis, amused. "Half adrenaline, half testosterone, and totally foolish."

He nodded to two of his men, who quickly removed Nighthawk's visible weapons, frisked him for hidden ones, and came away with two knives and a small sonic pistol.

"You have an impressive number of toys," observed the Marquis. "Now that we've removed them, perhaps you'll tell me why you were looking for me."

Nighthawk glanced around, found himself surrounded by a hostile crowd of men and aliens, and then looked back at the Marquis.

Think fast. What would he have done?

"I have a business proposition for you," he said at last.

"Well, it's fortunate I came by when I did, isn't it?" said the Marquis. "Before you had totally decimated my customers, that is."

"I thought it might get your attention," admitted Nighthawk.

"Oh, it did that, young Jefferson," said the Marquis. "You offer whiskey to my woman, and instead of announcing your presence like a normal visitor, you kill three of my men. It certainly does attract my attention." He paused and stared at Nighthawk. "Just what is it that you want?"

"Hire me."

"I beg your pardon?"

"I'm better than any twenty men you've got," said Nighthawk. "And I'll only charge what you pay ten of 'em."

The Marquis stared at him with an amused expression. "I can't decide whether you're very young or very foolish."

"I'm very good."

"Do you know how many very good men I've killed?"

"I haven't the slightest idea."

"Sixty-four."

"And how many of them were being held motionless before you?" asked Nighthawk.

Another grin, half amused, half satisfied, appeared on the Marquis' face. "Let him go."

Suddenly Nighthawk's arms were hanging loose at his sides.

"All right," said the Marquis, folding his hands into a massive pair of fists, "let's see what you can do. And in the meantime, I'm going to show you what happens to brash young men who kill *my* men on *my* world."

His hand shot out. Nighthawk saw it coming, but even his youthful reflexes weren't good enough, and an instant later he felt the cartilage in his nose give way.

"You okay?" asked the Marquis with false solicitation. "You look terrible."

"I'll live," answered Nighthawk, spinning and delivering a kick that would have knocked the Marquis halfway across the room if it had landed, but the Marquis sidestepped it.

"Oh, one more thing," said the Marquis, feinting with a left, then barely missing with a thunderous right.

"What's that?" asked Nighthawk, connecting two quick jabs to the Marquis' chin, then attempting a chop to the bridge of the nose, only to have it blocked.

The Marquis picked up a glass filled with Cygnian cognac and hurled the contents into Nighthawk's eyes. "We fight by the Marquis of Queensbury rules."

"What the hell are they?" said Nighthawk, backing away quickly and blinking his eyes furiously.

The Marquis grinned. "I thought you'd never ask," he said, lifting a chair over his head and hurling it at him. "They're whatever I say they are."

He followed up with a flying kick, but Nighthawk ducked, reaching an arm beneath the Marquis' legs, and lifted upward. His equilibrium upset, the Marquis landed on his back with a loud thud.

Nighthawk kicked him twice, and was about to deliver a third when the Marquis recovered, grabbed his foot, and twisted. Nighthawk went sprawling, but was up in an instant.

"You know, you're not half bad," said the Marquis as he slipped a punch, stepped in close, and delivered a flurry to Nighthawk's belly.

Nighthawk doubled over to protect himself. Then, as the Marquis moved even closer, he brought his head up quickly, splitting the Marquis' chin open.

"*Goddamn!*" bellowed the Marquis as blood gushed down over his shirt. "That *hurt!*"

"It was supposed to," rasped Nighthawk, following up with a left that closed the Marquis' right eye.

The Marquis fell to the floor, but even as he did so, he whipped out his legs and tripped Nighthawk.

"You're good, I'll give you that," panted the Marquis as he regained his feet.

"You're not so bad yourself," mumbled Nighthawk through his split lips.

"Tell you what," said the Marquis. "Let me buy you a drink and then we'll have Round Two."

"Sounds good to me," said Nighthawk, following him to the bar. The bartender slid two large beer mugs over to them.

"You're not going to be too proud to let me pay, are you?" demanded the Marquis.

"I like it when other people pay," said Nighthawk.

"Good," said the Marquis. "We're going to get along fine."

"We've made a pretty good start, haven't we?"

The Marquis threw back his head and guffawed. "You've got a fine sense of humor, Jefferson Nighthawk!" Suddenly he hurled the beer mug at Nighthawk's head. It split his forehead open and careened off.

Nighthawk almost dropped to his knees, but managed to hang on to the bar with one hand. He saw a kick coming, and just managed to grab a floating barstool to protect himself. The Marquis bellowed in rage as the stool upset his balance; the huge man's head bounced off the bar, and his knees were suddenly wobbly.

Nighthawk wiped away the blood that was pouring down into his eyes and cautiously closed in for the kill. He landed a left, two rights, and a chop to the shoulder that deadened the Marquis' arm. He was so intent on putting the Marquis away that he didn't see the huge thumb coming for his ear until it was too late. A million bells chimed inside his head, and suddenly he had difficulty keeping his balance.

He sensed that the Marquis was coming toward

him, but all he could do was spin crazily to his left, extend his arms, and hope for the best. He felt the edge of his hand chop across the Marquis' neck, and then he was grabbing the bar again, trying desperately to stay on his feet.

He waited for the Marquis' final charge, wondered what form it would take, wondered if he would even be able to see it coming . . . but for a moment nothing happened.

Then the Marquis laughed again. "By God, Jefferson Nighthawk, I do believe you're as tough as you think you are!"

Suddenly Nighthawk felt a powerful arm supporting him.

"We'll have another drink, and then we'll go to my office and talk business." The Marquis paused and looked out at the crowd. "From this minute forward, this man works for me and speaks for me. An insult to him is an insult to me, and if anyone cheats him in any way, they've cheated me. Is that clear?"

The crowd reaction—total silence, and a number of bitter glances—told him that it may not have been popular, but it *was* clear.

"What about my friend?" asked Nighthawk, indicating Lizard Malloy.

"I'm feeling generous today," answered the Marquis. He turned to Malloy. "Listen to me, you little swindler: You return my money before you leave the casino, and maybe I'll let you live. You take one step outside before I get what's mine, you're dead meat. Do you understand?"

"What's this 'maybe' shit?" demanded Malloy. "If I give you your money, I get to walk."

The Marquis turned to a burly bearded man. "Kill him."

"Wait a minute!" shrilled Malloy. "Wait a minute. It's a deal!"

The man aimed his weapon at Malloy and looked at the Marquis.

"You're sure it's a deal?" asked the Marquis. "I mean, I do admire bravery in a man."

"It's a deal," repeated Malloy, deflated.

The Marquis nodded, and the gunman put his weapon away.

"And now, my friend," said the Marquis, turning to Nighthawk, "let's go enjoy the comfort and privacy of my office."

"If your furniture's any good, maybe we'd better stop bleeding first," suggested Nighthawk.

"Good idea," said the Marquis. He pulled a banknote out of his pocket and slapped it on the bar. "Fifty credits says I stop before you do."

Nighthawk matched the bet. "You're on."

The Marquis grinned again. "Jefferson, my boy, I have a feeling that this is the beginning of a beautiful working relationship."

Chapter 5

♦ ♦ ♦ ♦ ♦ ♦ ♦

❖

The Marquis of Queensbury's office reflected its owner's tastes. The furniture was rugged, built for large, muscular men. The bar was well stocked. There was a glass-enclosed room filled with boxes of cigars from all over the galaxy. Music—*human* music—was piped in. A reinforced window offered a view of Klondike. Paintings and holographs of human and alien nudes, far more provocative than those in the bar, hung on the walls or floated just in front of them. A trio of display cases held jeweled alien artifacts.

As they sat down, the huge man looked intently at Nighthawk for a long moment, trying to see past the blood and the swellings.

"You're a clone, aren't you?" he asked at last.

"Yes."

"I *thought* so!"

"It was the name, right?"

The Marquis shook his head. "No. Out here people change names like they change clothes. There are probably a dozen Jefferson Nighthawks on the Frontier."

"Then . . . ?"

"There are other ways of telling. For one thing, I've seen holos of the Widowmaker." He paused. "I've never seen a clone before. I find *that* more interesting than whose clone you happen to be."

"Oh?"

"Yes. For example, how old are you?"

"Twenty-three."

"Not physically, but actually?"

Nighthawk sighed. "Three months."

The Marquis grinned. "I *thought* so!" He continued to stare at Nighthawk. "What's it like to have no past, no memories?"

"I have them," answered Nighthawk. "They're just not my own."

"Whose are they?"

Nighthawk shrugged. "I've no idea."

"Who trained you? The original?"

"No, he's dying from some disease he picked up more than a century ago. He was in his forties when he contracted it, and he was sixty-two when it finally disabled him."

"Frozen?"

Nighthawk nodded. "On Deluros VIII."

"Let me see if I can put it together," said the Marquis. "Someone had a job for the Widowmaker. Somehow they knew he was alive, but when they tried to find him, they discovered that he was frozen. Probably they knew it up front, since he'd be well over a century old. But old or not, he was supposed to be the best, and they wanted him anyway—so they bribed every well-placed official they needed in exchange for a clone."

"That's about it."

"Oh, no, there's more," continued the Marquis. "Why are you here, at this place, at this time? Well, it could be that you're after one of my men—but the message you sent was for me, not for them. So why are you after me? What crime have I committed that's so important they cloned the Widowmaker?"

"You're doing pretty well so far. What's the answer?"

"Easy. You're obviously here to hunt down Winslow Trelaine's killer."

"That's right."

"Well, I didn't kill him," said the Marquis. "Hell, I *liked* him. He left me alone, I left him alone. We had an understanding."

"An understanding?"

"He and Hernandez let me plunder the planet six ways to Sunday in exchange for a few favors."

"But you know who *did* kill him—and who paid for it?"

"It's possible," said the Marquis easily. "I know a lot of things."

"So why not tell me?"

The Marquis chuckled. "If I told you other people's secrets, you'd never trust me with your own."

"I don't plan to anyway." Nighthawk paused. "So what happens now?"

"What happens?" repeated the Marquis, leaning back on his chair, which floated gently just above the floor. "Back in the casino you offered to come to work for me, remember? We're negotiating your contract right now. I don't give a damn what brought you here.

I need a good lieutenant; there's none better than the Widowmaker."

"I'm not the Widowmaker. I'm *me*."

"Same thing."

"It's not," protested Nighthawk. "He's not even a man anymore. His skin is covered with a hideous disease, and he's more than a hundred years old. He's a *thing* that used to be Jefferson Nighthawk."

"And you're a laboratory creation, three months out of the test tube," said the Marquis. "So what? I prefer to think of you both as men."

Nighthawk grimaced. Thoughts about his own relationship to humanity made him uncomfortable.

The Marquis lit up a thin cigar imported from distant Antares III. An ashtray sensed the smoke and floated over to hover just beside his hand.

"Care for one?" he asked, offering a cigar to Nighthawk.

"I don't know. I can't remember."

"Try one. It's the only way to find out."

Nighthawk agreed, accepted a cigar, and lit up. He decided he would have to try a few more before he knew if he liked them.

"Anyway," continued the Marquis, "what the hell do you owe those people back on Deluros? If they didn't want something, you wouldn't be here. You're not legal anyway; it's a felony to clone a human, so they broke a bunch of laws just to make you. You catch their man for them, they'll probably hire you out again or turn you into a vat of protoplasm; either way you haven't got much of a future to look forward to."

"What kind of future are *you* offering me?" asked Nighthawk.

"The very best," answered the Marquis with a

smile. "Skip being a man altogether. Go right from test tube to kingship! I control eleven worlds already; by the time I'm through, I'll have an empire of twenty-five worlds, maybe thirty. You'll be my majordomo. You want a couple of worlds of your own, just prove your worth to me and they're yours."

"I thought the Oligarchy didn't look too kindly on upstart emperors," remarked Nighthawk wryly. "Even when the total populations of their empires don't equal the population of Solio II."

"We're doing them a favor," answered the Marquis firmly. "No matter how vast the military becomes, the galaxy's always going to be too big for us to gobble up whole. So out here on the Frontier, enterprising men assimilate it piecemeal. In the long run, what difference does it make to history whether the Oligarchs control these planets or *I* do? They're controlled by the race of Man, and that's what really matters."

"That's as eloquent a justification for pillage, plunder, and wholesale slaughter as I've heard," said Nighthawk.

"*I* thought so," agreed the Marquis, still smiling. "You don't like that explanation? Then try this one: You'll have more power than you ever dreamed of."

"I don't know," said Nighthawk. "I have pretty big dreams. I might even want something *you* have."

The smile vanished and the Marquis stared coldly at him. "You try to take anything that's mine and you're the sixty-fifth footnote to my biography, just a slab of dead meat waiting to be carted away." He paused. "On the other hand, do what I tell you to do, and do it well, and you'll find that everything's negotiable."

"Including the Pearl of Maracaibo?"

"*Almost* everything," amended the Marquis. "She's private property, Widowmaker. Don't even think of it."

"I told you: I'm *not* the Widowmaker. And she's free to make her own choice."

"Nonsense. No one's ever free. You belong to your masters on Deluros—and when you leave them, you'll belong to me."

"And who do you belong to?" asked Nighthawk.

"I owe bits and pieces of me all across the Frontier."

"I thought you were in the business of killing and robbing people, not owing them."

"Would you rather I killed and robbed you?" asked the Marquis with an amused laugh. "I can, you know."

"Maybe."

"I thought I just proved it out in the casino."

"You're as good as you're going to get," responded Nighthawk seriously. "I'm still learning."

"A telling point. Let's hope we never have to find out how much you've learned."

Nighthawk got to his feet.

"You leaving?" asked the Marquis.

"Just looking around at the spoils of conquest," replied the younger man, studying the alien artifacts in the display cases.

"I haven't got an eye for art," said the Marquis. "I just pick up what appeals to me. The rest gets sold to collectors on the black market."

"How did you get started?" asked Nighthawk. "Were you a thief? Or a killer?"

"Me?" said the Marquis. "I was a detective."

"You're kidding!"

"Not at all. About fifteen years ago I tracked down a suspect out here on the Frontier. Jewel thief.

M i k e   R e s n i c k

He was sitting on a pair of diamonds as big as your eyes. I tried to take him alive, but he put up a fight and I had to kill him. Well, the more I got to thinking about taking those diamonds back and turning them over to my superiors—who I knew were corrupt enough to pocket the diamonds and kill my report—the more it seemed like an exercise in futility."

"And they were worth a fortune."

"And they were worth a fortune," agreed the Marquis. "So they vanished, and I vanished with 'em. I took a new name, got into some trouble, shot my way out of it, and then I became the Marquis of Queensbury."

"What's a Marquis?" asked Nighthawk.

"Damned if I know, but some guy called the Marquis of Queensbury created the rules for karate, or maybe it was judo. Anyway, on my world I create the rules, so it seemed an appropriate name." He paused. "After a couple of years I realized that a competent motivated man could become a hell of a lot more than a successful thief out here. He could, in fact, become an emperor. I started with Tundra and Yukon—it's not hard to take over a couple of worlds that haven't got two thousand inhabitants total—and then I just started expanding."

"What does owning a world entail?"

"Well, for starters, I'm the tax collector."

"Protection money?"

"That's such a vulgar term," said the Marquis with an expression of distaste. "I prefer to call it a Security Assessment."

"Have you ever had to supply security?"

"Not yet, knock wood," answered the Marquis. "But I've got enough manpower to hold off almost anyone except the Navy."

78

"If those three I killed were an example of it, I'd say you're in big trouble if someone tries to move in."

"Apples and oranges. They were just three men, and you're the Widowmaker. That's different than sending three hundred hardened killers against an expeditionary force controlled by another . . ."

"Warlord?" suggested Nighthawk.

"I was going to say *entrepreneur*," replied the Marquis.

"Yeah, well, I still wouldn't count too heavily on them."

"I don't," replied the Marquis. "I'm counting on *you*."

"My first obligation is to find Trelaine's assassin."

"I'm counting on *that*, too." The Marquis flashed him a grin. "You know he couldn't have killed Trelaine without my approval. You know you can't beat his name out of me, and that if you luck out and kill me, you still won't get it. So the logical course of action is for you to do such a brilliant job that you win my trust and place me under obligation to you—right?"

"Perhaps," agreed Nighthawk. "On the other hand, I may disappoint you and find the assassin without your help."

"I've been disappointed before. I'll survive." *You may not*, was the strong implication, *but I will*.

"Still, until I do find him, I might as well work for you. I'll need a job once my current one is over."

"Even the Widowmaker must genuflect to logic," said the Marquis with a satisfied smile.

"From time to time," agreed Nighthawk. "Where do I start? What do I do?"

"First, you take a few days to recover. I'm just egocentric enough to think I did you some damage. Use the time to learn your way around Klondike, meet

◆ ◆ ◆ 79

some of the men and women who work for me. I keep a suite on the sixth floor of the hotel down the block; it's yours for the time being."

"Where will *you* stay?"

"On the tenth floor," replied the Marquis with a grin. "I like penthouses." He paused. "Anyway, I'll send a medic by to stitch you up and straighten your nose. If there's anything you want, just order it through room service. If you go anywhere in town for food, drink, clothes, anything at all, just tell 'em who you are until they get to the point where they recognize you. I'll pass the word before you leave that you're working for me."

"Does everyone who works for you get this kind of service? I'm surprised the merchants haven't left for better pickings."

"I'm a businessman, not a philanthropist," laughed the Marquis. "How can I tax them if they don't make any money? No, only you and Melisande have carte blanche."

"Melisande?"

"That's the girl you're never going to touch."

"The Pearl of Maracaibo?"

"Her professional name. Like the Marquis of Queensbury, or the Widowmaker."

"Okay, she's Melisande and I'm Jefferson Nighthawk. Who are you, really?"

"My name wouldn't mean a thing to you."

"I'd like to know it anyway."

"I'm sure you would," said the Marquis. "But I've no intention of telling it to you. It's much better if everyone thinks I'm dead."

"As you wish," said Nighthawk with a shrug. "But it hardly seems fair."

"Of course it's not fair," said the Marquis. "I'm

the boss and you're not. What's fair got to do with anything?"

"Not much, I guess."

"You have an interesting expression on your face."

"I do?"

The Marquis nodded. "It says, 'Someday when he least expects it, I'm going to remind the Marquis of what he just said—probably after I take his woman away and shoot his legs out from under him.' " He paused. "Forget it. It's not going to happen."

"It's your fantasy, not mine," said Nighthawk.

"What's yours—and how many women does it involve?"

"None."

"No women at all? What kind of fantasy is that?"

"I'll tell you someday when I know you better," said Nighthawk. "I might even enlist your help."

"How comforting."

"It is?"

"Certainly," said the Marquis with a smile. "It means that it doesn't involve killing me."

"To borrow an old expression," said Nighthawk, "I've got bigger fish to fry."

And perhaps a very old one to kill, before his attorneys and medics decide to kill me.

"Really?" said the Marquis, interested. "So you think the assassin is a bigger fish than I am?"

"You want the truth?"

"Definitely."

"I think you *are* the assassin."

"I told you I wasn't," replied the Marquis.

"I know. But I don't believe you."

"And what do you plan to do about it?"

"I plan to hunt for evidence. As slowly as I can. And hope that you're right."

"I don't think I understand," said the Marquis, frowning. "I thought you explained to me that your first obligation was to bring in the assassin."

"My first obligation is to hunt for him. I'll be just as happy if I don't find him."

"Ah, I was right!" said the Marquis with a smile, finally comprehending. "You fulfill your mission and it's back into the vat with you."

"Not if I can help it."

"Just stay out here and they'll never find you."

"There's one man back there who can find me wherever I go," responded Nighthawk.

"Nonsense! You're the Widowmaker."

"So is *he*—and if they cure him, he'll be after me the next morning."

"What makes you think so?"

"It's what I'd do—and I'm him."

"It's foolish," protested the Marquis. "Why should the Widowmaker want to kill his clone—especially if no one is paying him to do so?"

"You can't have two Jefferson Nighthawks walking around at the same time. I've got something that he spent his whole life acquiring: his identity. He'll want it back."

"I don't know how you can be so sure."

"Because I want to kill him for the same reason," answered Nighthawk. "As long as he lives, I'm just a shadow. I'm not even legally alive. Every credit I make is his, everything I do, both good and bad, accrues to him." He paused, trying to order his thoughts. "Jefferson Nighthawk's just a name. I can answer to it as well as any other. But Widowmaker's a *definition*. I won't be the Widowmaker until *he's* dead."

"But he doesn't have that problem," noted the Marquis. "He *is* the real"—Nighthawk winced—

"forgive me, the original, Widowmaker. His money, his identity, they're his own."

"But who will they hire when they want the Widowmaker—an old man they can't even stand to look at, or me? He can't let me live any more than I can let *him* live. God didn't mean for there to be two of us alive at the same time."

The Marquis stared at the young man for a long minute. "I wouldn't have your dreams for anything," he said at last.

"My dreams are very pleasant," said Nighthawk wryly. "It's just my life I have problems with."

"Well, we'll simplify and improve it, starting tomorrow."

"I hope so," said Nighthawk, getting up to leave. He heard a door dilate behind him and saw the Pearl of Maracaibo's image in a mirror as she emerged from another room, one with a large unmade bed in it.

But somehow I doubt it, he added mentally as he left the office and went back to join Malloy in the casino.

And for just a moment it seemed that a very old, very diseased man was walking beside him with an unseemly vigor.

You think it's going to be this easy? asked the old man. *You think you're going to kill the bad guys and get the girl and spend your life hunting villains on the Inner Frontier?*

I hadn't thought that far ahead, admitted Nighthawk. But it's a pleasant future.

It's a pipe dream. Do you really think I'll let you live once I'm out of that frozen tomb? God made one Widowmaker, not two.

How will you stop me? You're an old man, and I'm in my prime.

♦   ♦   ♦   83

But I'm the real Widowmaker. You're just a shadow that will vanish in the light of my day. Think about it: The better you are, the sooner I can dispose of you.

Then the image vanished . . . but the words stayed with Nighthawk long after he reached the casino.

Chapter 6

• • • • • • •

◆

The Marquis proved to be a man of his word. Whatever Nighthawk asked for he received, and payment was never requested.

Nighthawk spent a couple of days exploring the city of Klondike. He visited each of its four restaurants, all of its many bars and casinos and brothels. The drug dens he avoided; his borrowed memories were increasingly vague as they were replaced with his own experiences, but those that remained told him that nothing good or useful ever came of drugs or their users.

Most of his time, though, was spent in the Marquis' casino, where he was on call for anything the Marquis might want. Lizard Malloy stuck close to him, as if he were the little man's only protection in this hostile environment, and in exchange for offering that protection Nighthawk picked his mind, learning the names and dubious accomplishments of most of the men and women who worked for the Marquis.

There was another reason for spending time in the casino, and Malloy was quick to spot it.

"Don't even think about her," he said as Nighthawk watched the Pearl of Maracaibo undulating atop her floating platform.

"Last time I thought about her, it got me a job with the Marquis," replied Nighthawk.

"All the more reason not to push your luck twice," said Malloy.

"I wonder what she sees in him?"

"You mean, besides the fact that he's ten feet tall and owns forty or fifty worlds?" asked Malloy.

"He's not that tall, and he only owns eleven worlds."

"Well, that makes all the difference in the universe," said Malloy sardonically.

"Where does she come from?"

"I don't know."

"Find out for me, by tomorrow," said Nighthawk, smiling up at the Pearl of Maracaibo as she finished her dance.

"You got yourself a serious death wish, you know that?" said Malloy.

"Just do it."

Malloy shrugged and fell silent. A moment later one of the Marquis' men approached Nighthawk and took him to the office.

"What's up?" asked Nighthawk as he sat down opposite the Marquis.

"We've got a little problem over on Yukon that I want you to clean up."

"Oh?"

The Marquis nodded. "Seems someone has set up

shop there without my permission. I sent an emissary to explain that this was a breach of etiquette, and she killed him on the spot. We can't allow her to get away with that. Too many other people might start flexing their muscles."

" 'She'?" repeated Nighthawk.

"Name's Spanish Lace."

"Sounds intriguing."

"There's nothing intriguing about her. She's operating on my territory without a permit. That's against the law."

"*Your* law?"

"You know of any other?" said the Marquis.

"Not on Yukon and Tundra," admitted Nighthawk.

"Well, then, that's your job."

"I'm not quite clear," said Nighthawk. "Do you want me to sell her a permit to operate, or run her off?"

"I want you to kill her," said the Marquis. "And then I want you to take what's left of her and nail her to a cross or hang her from a tree—anything out in the open—as a warning to anyone else who might be having similar ideas."

"There are only a few thousand people on Yukon," noted Nighthawk. "How many are likely to see her stretched out on a cross or spinning slowly in the wind?"

"It's cold there. She'll keep."

"Why not just charge her a couple of million credits and send her packing?" suggested Nighthawk.

"I'm going to answer you this time," said the Marquis, "because you've just started working for me and you don't know that I have a reason for everything I do. You haven't learned that you *never* question one of my orders; that's the same as arguing with me, and I won't tolerate that in an employee." He paused. "If you ever question another order, you'd better have a nice cemetery plot picked out. I don't care how good you are, I'll kill you on the spot—and if *I* can't, I've got two hundred men who'll see to it that you don't live long enough to leave Klondike."

Nighthawk simply stared at him without saying a word.

"All right," continued the Marquis. "If you fine her and chase her off Yukon, you'll have made a powerful enemy who'll think that I have wrongly humiliated her and appropriated her money, though of course I have every right to whatever money is brought to one of my worlds. If, on the other hand, you kill her, we'll have at least as much of her money, probably even more, and we *won't* have a bitter and successful woman out there"—his vague wave encompassed half the galaxy—"plotting ways to get her money back and punish me for appropriating it."

"So you don't really care whether anyone sees the body?"

"Certainly I do, but that isn't my primary purpose for killing her." The Marquis paused. "Any more questions?"

"What's her line, and how many men has she got?"

"Spanish Lace? It all depends on which world you ask that question. She doesn't believe in specialization. She's a bank robber, an arsonist, an extortionist, an assassin. She usually works alone, but she may have brought a little protection along."

"She's an assassin, you say?"

"Don't look so interested. She had nothing to do with Trelaine."

"How do you know?"

"Nothing goes on in this sector that I *don't* know."

"All right," said Nighthawk. "When do you want me to leave?"

"Immediately. Why else would I be telling you all this?"

"Where will I find her?"

"I've already had the landing coordinates fed into your ship's computer. Take that little snake-skinned bastard Malloy along with you. He's been to Yukon before; maybe he can be of some use to you." The Marquis chuckled. "At least he won't block your vision or get in your line of fire. I don't think I've ever seen a bigger coward."

"That's probably why he'll outlive us both," replied Nighthawk.

"It's possible—but you have to consider the quality of that life."

"*He* considers the quality of his death," said Nighthawk with a smile. "Hasn't found one that lives up to his high standards yet."

"Somebody should explain to him that very few of us fuck ourselves to death," said the Marquis.

"I'll try to remember that."

"Especially when you're around Melisande," added the Marquis meaningfully.

"I'm not going to get myself killed over a blue-skinned mutant," said Nighthawk.

"Nothing personal," replied the Marquis. "I like you, I really do. But you were put together in a lab three months ago. How the hell do *I* know what you will or won't get killed over?"

"I'm as much a man as you are!" snapped Nighthawk heatedly.

"If you weren't, I wouldn't worry about your doing something stupid because of Melisande."

The answer seemed to mollify Nighthawk, and he relaxed visibly.

"Well, now that you've made up your mind not to kill me, get the hell out of here and go kill the person you're being paid to kill," said the Marquis.

Nighthawk nodded and got to his feet.

"Cigar?"

"I still haven't decided if I like them," answered Nighthawk.

"By the same token, you really can't know if you like blue-skinned ladies, can you?" asked the Marquis meaningfully.

"Don't start on me again!" snapped Nighthawk. "There's more to me than just a killing machine!"

"And you'll kill me to prove it?"

Nighthawk glared at him for a moment, then turned and left the office.

He hunted up Malloy, got into a spacesuit, and found one for his companion. Then they made their way across the ice fields to the spaceport. Within an hour they were ensconced in the pilot's cabin of Nighthawk's ship, leaving Tundra behind them and heading for Yukon.

"I *hate* traveling within a solar system!" complained Malloy, looking at a viewscreen. "It takes longer to go from one world to another than from one *star* to another."

"Can't do light speeds within a system," answered Nighthawk. "You know that."

"Yeah, but I don't have to like it."

"Find some way to occupy yourself. Like telling me about Melisande, for instance."

"I found out what you wanted to know," said Malloy. "She comes from Greenveldt."

"That's a Frontier world?"

"Right."

"Are all the colonists on Greenveldt blue-skinned?" asked Nighthawk.

Malloy shook his head. "She didn't evolve, she mutated."

"Explain."

"She's a sport—there's just one of her."

"I like that," said Nighthawk.

"You do? Why?"

"Let's just say I have a certain fondness for people who are one of a kind."

"Then you ought to love Spanish Lace," said Malloy. "There ain't never been anyone like her."

Nighthawk checked his navigational computer and found that he had almost forty minutes before the ship entered Yukon's orbit. "We've got time," he said. "Fill me in."

"Didn't the Marquis tell you?"

"Just that she's moved in on his territory and he wants her off."

"He didn't tell you that she's killed the last three men who had your job?"

"No."

"Or that she's not quite human?"

"Explain," said Nighthawk.

"She *looks* pretty much like a normal human woman," said Malloy. "But I've heard stories about her. She's got powers that no human ever had."

"For instance?"

"I don't know."

"So it could just be bullshit."

"If it was, would the Marquis' last three hired guns be dead?"

"Go on," said Nighthawk. "I need details."

"Nobody knows any. She's robbed some banks back in the Oligarchy, I know that. And they say she killed Jumbo Willoughby with her bare hands. Oh, and there was that affair on Terrazane—"

"What affair?"

"Somebody blew up the whole parliament. Killed about three hundred men and women. Nobody ever proved anything, but they say it was *her* doing, that if she didn't set off the bomb herself she at least arranged for it to go off."

"She sounds interesting."

"What she is is *deadly*," said Malloy devoutly. "Don't worry—you won't have to meet her."

"No way. I'll be at your side."

Nighthawk stared at him. "You don't have to."

"I don't care. I'm coming with you."

"I'd have thought you'd be happier keeping out of the line of fire."

"I'm supposed to wait in the ship or some bar wondering who's going to come to meet me, you or the worst killer on the planet?" demanded Malloy. "No, thanks! First time a door or a hatch opened, I'd be wound so tight I'd probably explode."

"To hell with your reasons," said Nighthawk. "I thank you for your loyalty." He paused. "It's strange, but you're just about the only friend I've got."

"I'm not your friend," said Malloy. Nighthawk started to protest, but Malloy raised his hand for silence. "But let's pretend that I am for a minute, so I can give you a piece of friendly advice." Nighthawk stared silently at him, and he continued. "I know you've never had a mother or a family, and you've probably never even had a woman, let alone lived with one. I know you're probably looking for people to talk to and drink with at the same time you're hunting for victims. Well, let me tell you something, something the first Jefferson Nighthawk must have known to have lived so long: Out here on the Frontier, you must never mistake self-interest for friendship. They're a harder breed out here than back in the Oligarchy. They came out here for a reason, and they *stay* out here for a reason, and friendship isn't it. So be as cordial as you like, Widowmaker, and most people will be cordial right back at you because of who you are and what you can do if you get mad at 'em—but *never* think that a cordial overture out here will lead to friendship. If it leads to another day's survival, that's enough."

Nighthawk considered what Malloy said for a long moment, then shook his head. "I don't buy that. You're too cynical by half."

"You were created solely to kill people, and *I'm* cynical?" said Malloy sarcastically.

"Killing is what I *do*," said Nighthawk. "It's not what I *am*."

"Not yet," agreed Malloy. "But you'll grow into it. Or die."

They fell silent for a few minutes, and then Malloy spoke again.

"What's he paying you to go up against her?"

"Nothing."

"You're facing Spanish Lace for *free*?" demanded Malloy.

"Not exactly," answered Nighthawk. "He's paying me a ton of money to do a job. This is part of the job description. Probably today I'm being underpaid;

yesterday and tomorrow I'll be overpaid. It all evens out in the end."

"That depends on when the end comes," noted Malloy.

"If you can tell me what to prepare for, maybe it won't come too soon," suggested Nighthawk.

"I don't know her powers. I just know that a couple of times they had her dead to rights, but she's still alive and everyone who's ever tried to kill her is dead."

"Maybe she's just good with her weapons," offered Nighthawk.

Malloy shook his head again. "She's faced odds even *you* wouldn't face, Widowmaker."

"But she comes of human stock. Just how many strange talents can she have?"

"Enough," said Malloy unhappily, as the ship entered Yukon's frigid atmosphere.

Chapter 7

◆ ◆ ◆ ◆ ◆ ◆ ◆

◈

The ship touched down in the city-state of New Siberia, which differed from its namesake only in that it was bigger, colder, and a few hundred thousand light-years away. Nighthawk and Malloy were about to exit the ship and take the heated tram to the spaceport tower when a voice rang out through the ship.

"Passports, please."

"When we get to Customs," answered Nighthawk, staring at the young woman's face that had suddenly appeared on all the viewscreens.

"This *is* Customs, sir," she replied. "So few people come and go here that we found it more convenient to clear you before you leave your ship rather than set up a permanent booth in the tower."

The two men held up their titanium passport cards for scanning.

"Welcome to Yukon, Mr. Nighthawk. Welcome back to Yukon, Mr. Malloy. What is the purpose of your visit?"

"Tourism," said Nighthawk.

"We don't have a tourist industry, Mr. Nighthawk."

"That's hardly my fault," he said. "I plan to see such natural wonders as your lovely planet affords."

"I think you are here to gamble, Mr. Nighthawk," continued the woman, oblivious to his answer.

"You make it sound like it's against the law."

"Absolutely not. In fact, it is encouraged. I see that you have recently opened an account on Tundra. We can bill your account for a gambling license if you will give us permission."

"And you don't have tourist licenses, is that it?" asked Nighthawk with a smile.

"Verbal permission will be sufficient," she continued. "A holocopy of this conversation will be kept on file."

"You have my permission."

"I am sure you will enjoy your stay here, Mr. Nighthawk, and I wish you good luck at the gaming tables." Pause. "Your purpose for visiting Yukon, Mr. Malloy?"

"I'm with him."

"I cannot find any account bearing your name and voiceprint in either the Inner Frontier or the Oligarchy, Mr. Malloy," she said. "How will you pay for your gambling license?"

"Bill me," interjected Nighthawk.

"If you wish," she said. "However, the laws of Yukon require me to tell you that the purchaser of a license is responsible for all debts incurred on that license."

"I see," said Nighthawk. He paused for a moment. "Mr. Malloy will purchase his own license with cash when he finally reaches one of your casinos. Is that acceptable?"

"Quite," said the woman. "I should further point out that until he places a certain minimal amount on deposit here, any purchase he makes is payable in cash. In advance."

"He understands."

"I must hear *him* say it."

"I understand, I understand," muttered Malloy.

"Fine. You are each cleared to remain on Yukon for seven days. If you wish to go beyond the borders of New Siberia, you will have to ask and receive permission from whichever country you plan to visit. If you wish to extend your vacations, please check in here again more than one Galactic Standard day before your current visa expires. Are there any further questions?"

"Yes. Where can I find a map of New Siberia?"

"Please wait. . . . A map has just been transferred to your ship's navigational computer."

"And how does one get around on New Siberia?"

"There are powersleds for rent at the tower," was the answer. "They are heated, and come with radar, a radio, and a three-day supply of food for a crew of six men."

"Do I *need* a crew of six?"

"No. That is the maximum number a sled can transport at one time."

"Thank you," said Nighthawk. "You've been most helpful."

The screen deactivated.

"Bring up the map and find Spanish Lace,"

Nighthawk ordered the computer. "We might as well see exactly where the hell we're going."

The computer threw the map on a viewscreen, then cross-indexed it against the planetary census, and suddenly a tiny spot, some forty miles distant, began blinking brightly.

"Nearest city?" demanded Nighthawk.

There was a blinking right next to the spaceport.

"Nearest neighbor?"

Another spot, some fifteen miles away, began blinking.

"Off."

The screen went dark, and Malloy turned to Nighthawk. "She doesn't seem to like crowds."

"An understatement."

"So what do we do now?"

"We rent a powersled and pay her a visit."

"She's got to have defenses," said Malloy. "She'll know you're coming."

"Probably."

"Why not contact her from here? You could talk."

"I'm not being paid to talk."

"You're not being paid to get killed, either," said Malloy.

"I don't plan to die."

"Neither did the three guys who went before you."

"If you're frightened—" began Nighthawk.

"Of course I'm frightened!" snapped Malloy. "Only a crazy man wouldn't be frightened!"

"Then stay here."

"What if she kills you?"

"You've got more chance to get away if you're here than if you're standing next to me."

"Too cowardly," said Malloy.

"But you *are* a coward," replied Nighthawk with a chuckle.

"But I'm not blatant about it."

"In other words you want to stay here, but you want a good reason to—one that will keep your self-respect intact."

"Basically," admitted Malloy.

"All right. You don't know what powers she possesses, right?"

"Right."

"Does anyone?"

"Not to my knowledge."

"Then stay here and keep in radio and visual contact with me, and if she uses those powers to kill me, you can report what she's got to the Marquis. You might even get yourself a nice reward for that kind of information."

"You really think so?"

Nighthawk smiled. "Not a chance. But you *will* be bringing him information he needs."

"Well, that's all fine and well for *you*," said Malloy. "After all, you work for him. But I don't."

"Then don't go back to Tundra. Get as far away as you can and send him a subspace message offering to sell what you know."

"Now, *that* makes sense!" said Malloy.

"And it's more in keeping with your character," added Nighthawk sardonically.

"We can't all be heroes and killers," said Malloy defensively. "Some of us are just normal men." He looked at his scaled hands and arms and smiled ruefully. "Well, maybe not exactly *normal*," he amended.

Nighthawk donned a spacesuit, then began going through the ship's minimal stores.

"What are you looking for?" asked Malloy. "You're already packing three different kinds of weapon."

"Four," corrected Nighthawk. "I'm looking for an eye."

"You leave your eyes lying around in cabinets?" asked Malloy, confused.

"A three-hundred-and-sixty-degree camera," explained Nighthawk. Suddenly he reached out and picked up a small, circular object, less than an inch in diameter. "Got it."

"That must be spy gear," said Malloy. "I never saw anything like it before."

"I'll put it down on a chair or table," said Nighthawk, ignoring his remark. "It'll transmit a visual of the entire room it's in—walls, floor, ceiling, everything. The computer will receive the signal, sort out all the angles and images, and display something that makes sense to you."

"What if she's got a killer pet that eats it?"

"Then you'll see what the inside of its digestive system looks like, and you'll have to sell your information to a exoveterinarian instead of the Marquis." He paused. "I'll keep my communicator activated. If she hasn't got some way to nullify the signal, it should transmit everything we say."

"Are you sure you'd rather go alone?"

"As a matter of fact, I'd much rather have company," said Nighthawk, repressing a smile. "Give her two targets instead of just one."

"Damn it!" exploded Malloy. "You were supposed to say that you wanted to face her alone!"

"I do, really. I just wanted to see your reaction."

"Cold-blooded killers aren't supposed to have a sense of humor," muttered the little man.

"Then I must be a hot-blooded killer."

"Let's just hope you're a long-lived one."

"One of me is."

Nighthawk left the ship, found a waiting tram, and got off at the tower, where he rented a heated powersled. It was a type with which he was unfamiliar, so he had the saleswoman program it for him.

"You're *sure* these are the coordinates you want?" she asked.

"Why not?"

"I'll need a larger deposit," she said apologetically. "Lots of people go out to the Ice Palace. Almost none of them come back."

"What happens to them?"

"Beats me," she said. "I don't know. I don't *want* to know. I just want a bigger deposit."

Nighthawk pressed his thumb against a contract rider that she produced.

"You got any advice for someone going to the Ice Palace?" he asked while waiting for the thumbprint to be cleared and approved.

"Don't believe your eyes."

"I don't think I understand," said Nighthawk, as the computer approved his print.

"She *looks* human, but she's not."

"What is she?"

"If you survive and return the sled, maybe you can tell me," said the woman.

Chapter 8

· · · · · · · ·

◆

Nighthawk could see the Ice Palace from five miles away.
It appeared, truly, to be a structure of snow and ice,
blindingly white in the midday sun. There were huge
turrets, crenellated walls, towers and ramps and balus-
trades, and literally millions of icicles hanging down
from every section and structure. All that was missing
was a moat, and he was sure it was only because it was
too cold for water.

He approached to within a mile, then slowed the
powersled to half speed, alert for any possible danger.
Small white animals scurried to and fro, some even
racing alongside the sled for a moment, but they
veered off as he neared the main gate.

Finally he came to a halt in front of the Ice Palace and stepped off his sled. He looked around for
guards and was mildly surprised not to find any. He

walked up to the gate and tried it. It was locked, and he turned his laser pistol on it, melting both the locking mechanism and the latch itself.

He stepped cautiously inside. The walls and floor still seemed to be made of ice, but his spacesuit told him that the temperature was 23 degrees Celsius. He cautiously removed his helmet, then quickly slipped out of his suit. He touched some icicles that hung down from the ceiling; they were quartz, and quite warm to the touch. Spheres of light—not quite solid, with no discernible power source—floated near the ceiling, illuminating the room.

He walked through a number of chambers, accompanied by about half the spheres, which seemed to sense his presence and anticipate his needs, racing to provide light whenever he turned his head to look in a new direction. The walls and floors glittered like polished diamonds. Some of the chambers were furnished with pieces that matched the magical decor of the palace; others were empty. Nowhere was there any sign of life. No humans, no aliens, no pets, no guard animals, nothing.

Finally he came to an exceptionally large room, perhaps sixty feet on a side. Lilting alien music came from a tiny speaker that hovered near the ceiling at the exact center of the room, and a number of the light spheres floated about it in a stately dance that had no pattern but displayed a form and grace that seemed to match the music perfectly. Lining the walls were exquisite statues of ice, or perhaps quartz that resembled ice; Nighthawk couldn't tell which.

As he crossed the room, a door slid into place behind him. He whirled, gun in hand, as he heard the sound, then quickly moved toward the next doorway.

A glittering white door slid shut before he was halfway there.

A low chuckle told him that he wasn't alone, and he turned to find himself facing a small, lithe woman with wild dark hair and matching eyes. She was dressed in a formfitting black outfit made of a delicate lace.

"How did you get in here?" demanded Nighthawk.

"This is my home," she replied. "I come and go as I please."

"You're Spanish Lace?"

"And you are Jefferson Nighthawk."

"Who told you so?"

"I have my sources," she replied. She stared at him. "Of all the lackeys the Marquis of Queensbury has sent, you are the youngest. You must be very skilled at your trade."

"I'm not a lackey."

"But you *are* a killer?"

"I'm many things," he said. "That's one of the less important ones."

She uttered a mocking laugh. He stared at her for a moment, then began examining the room, walking through it, studying the artifacts, while she stood perfectly still, watching him intently. Finally he stopped and turned back to her.

"What's so special about you?" he asked. "Why does he want you dead?"

"He wants me dead because he fears me," said Spanish Lace.

"He doesn't strike me as a man who is afraid of anything," replied Nighthawk.

"If he doesn't fear me, why did he send you to do his dirty work?"

"Because I'm not afraid of you either—and he's got all the money," answered Nighthawk with a smile.

"Have you thought of how you are going to get back?"

"Same way I got here."

"I don't think so," she replied. "Why not go and check for yourself?"

"After you."

She shrugged and retraced his route through the palace. Doors dilated or slid back as she approached, and in less than a minute she came to the main gate. As it slid into the wall, she stepped aside and Nighthawk saw what remained of his powersled, a crushed, twisted mass of metal.

"What the hell happened to it?" muttered Nighthawk, more to himself than to Spanish Lace.

"Poor Jefferson Nighthawk," she said. "How are you to leave here now?"

Suddenly Nighthawk was aware of the freezing cold, of the wind whipping across his face and body. He turned to Spanish Lace, who stood next to him, totally oblivious to the wind and cold. His first instinct was to stay out there and outlast her, to prove that he could stand anything she could stand, but he quickly realized that it was precisely that kind of machismo which could get him killed, for she seemed truly impervious to the elements.

He turned and walked back into the Ice Palace. Spanish Lace fell into step behind him.

"You asked a question a few moments ago," she said when they had reached the chamber they had left.

"I did?"

"I think your precise words were: 'What the hell happened to it?'" She smiled. "*I* happened to it."

"You were with me."

"I know."

"You did it before you came into this room?"

"I did it *while* I was in this room," she replied.

"How?"

"I promise you will discover that before this day is over, Jefferson Nighthawk." She sat down in a chair that looked like sculpted ice. "Have you decided how you will kill me yet? Will it be death by heat or death by sound? Will I die before a weapon, or beneath your fists? Will my end be swift or slow?"

"I haven't said I would kill you at all," replied Nighthawk. "I only said that I was *sent* to kill you."

"Ah," she said, smiling again. "You await a counteroffer."

"Not necessarily."

She looked puzzled. "Then what?"

"Let's just talk for a while."

"Why?"

"Have you got anything better to do?" asked Nighthawk.

She stared at him for a long moment. "What kind of killer *are* you?"

"A reluctant one. Why does he want you dead?"

"I am a rival, and he is very territorial. What better reason is there?"

"Offhand, I can think of hundreds," said Nighthawk. "Why is life held so cheaply on the Frontier?"

"Probably because it *is* the Frontier. Life is never very expensive on the farthest borders of civilization."

"You people have pasts and futures. Don't you want to hang on to them?"

"*You* have a past and a future too," she pointed out. "Why should anyone else's attitude puzzle you?"

He shook his head. "I have no past, and my future is, at best, uncertain."

"How can you have no past?" she demanded.

He merely stared at her.

Suddenly her dark eyes widened. "Of course! You're a clone!"

He nodded an affirmative.

"Remarkable! I've never seen one before." She got to her feet and approached him. "And that explains why you are so young." She reached out a hand. "May I touch you?"

He shrugged and made no reply as she ran her fingers over his face and neck.

"Remarkable!" she said again. "You feel human."

"I *am* human."

"I mean that there is nothing artificial about you."

"That goes with being human."

She stared at him, obviously fascinated. "And who were you, Jefferson Nighthawk? A mass murderer? A decorated soldier? A celebrated lawman?"

"I am . . . I *was* . . . the Widowmaker."

"Ah. A bounty hunter!"

"And a lawman."

"Perhaps, but that is not why we all remember you." She returned to her chair. "So I am to be killed by the Widowmaker."

"I told you, I just want to talk."

She closed her eyes and nodded her head. "Of course you do. Poor little clone, with all the Widowmaker's skills and none of his experiences. He *chose* to become a killer, was probably driven to it, doubtless reveled in it. But you were *created* to become one, ordered to be one. No one ever asked you if you wanted to kill, did they? No one ever thought you might have other goals and desires."

Nighthawk exhaled deeply. "You understand."

"Certainly I do. Even among the outcasts and misfits who inhabit the Frontier, you are different, as I am. You were given certain physical attributes that you did not ask for, as was I. You find yourself an outsider in a galaxy of outsiders, as do I. How could I *not* understand?"

"What do you mean?" asked Nighthawk. "You look normal to me."

"Never trust the eye, which sees only the facade and never the truth," she replied. "You appear perfectly normal to me, too—and yet you are the Widowmaker, and how many men did he kill? Two hundred? Three hundred?"

"A lot."

"But less than me," she said proudly.

He frowned. "You've killed three hundred men?"

"More. And before this day is over, I will add to that total."

"We have nothing to fight about," said Nighthawk. "As you pointed out, we're two of a kind."

"What I didn't point out is that I'm as territorial as the Marquis, and you have invaded my home."

"I'll tell him I couldn't find you."

"Poor clone," she said with mock sympathy. "*You* may need a friend and confidant, but *I* do not. My life was not forced upon me; I have *chosen* to be an outlaw and a killer. You will not leave here alive."

"This is stupid," he protested. "I'm offering you your life! I could kill you in two seconds if I wanted to."

"Try," she said, amused.

"Don't push me!"

"*Push* you?" she repeated with a laugh. "I *challenge* you, Widowmaker!"

"I don't want to kill you."

"But *I* want to kill *you*."

"You're not carrying any weapons. This is murder."

"Do you really think the Marquis would want me dead if I were harmless?" responded Spanish Lace. "I don't *carry* my weapons like you lesser beings. I *am* a weapon."

Nighthawk faced her and reached for his laser pistol, but it leaped out of his holster before he could touch it and hovered, tantalizingly, about four feet away from him.

"What the hell?" he exclaimed.

"What is the loss of one weapon to a man like you?" she said, still amused. "Try another."

He reached for his sonic pistol. He closed his fingers on the handle and pulled. Nothing happened. He tightened his grip and yanked. And found that he couldn't budge it so much as a millimeter.

"*Now* do you know what happened to your powersled?" she asked.

"You're telekinetic?"

She nodded. "I have always had the ability to move material objects with the power of my mind alone. In fact, I think I was seven or eight years old before I realized that no one else could do it." She held out her hands to grab his weapons as each in turn left him and flew across the room into her grasp. "How do you feel *now* about killing a poor, helpless woman?"

"A lot better," he said, reaching into a boot, removing a knife, and hurling it at her all in one fluid motion. It flew straight and true toward her heart, and then froze in space about six inches from its target.

"Fool!" she said, allowing a contemptuous sneer to replace the look of amusement on her angular face. "Don't you realize that you are completely helpless?"

Nighthawk heard a sound above him and dove to one side just before a section of the ceiling crashed down where he had been standing. "Can you fight the Ice Palace itself?"

He began approaching her cautiously. Just as he was tensing his muscles for the final charge, a small chair flew into his back, sending him sprawling on the glittering floor.

He was on his feet in an instant, and managed to duck another chair that came at him out of nowhere.

"Very good, Widowmaker," she said. "You inherited good instincts—if 'inherit' is the proper word, and I suspect it isn't. I shall almost be sorry to dispose of you."

He stared at her, reluctant to approach, unwilling to retreat.

"Now, how shall I kill you?" she continued. "It might be amusing to use your own weapons."

Suddenly his three pistols—laser, sonic, and projectile—formed a line just to her left, five feet above the ground, and spun until they were aimed directly at him.

He dove behind the couch to get out of the line of fire. An instant later the couch moved rapidly to his left, and he scrambled on hands and knees to remain behind it as her laughter reverberated through the large chamber. He saw a doorway some fifteen feet away and dove for it. Weaponfire followed him, but he made it intact and raced through another doorway.

He moved quickly from room to room, aware of the danger behind him, unwilling to plunge blindly into potentially greater dangers ahead of him. Once he was too slow, and a beam of solid light singed his ear.

And then he came to a room from which there was no exit. It contained a huge circular bed that spun slowly a few inches above the floor, a pair of glittering silver chests, a large mirror, and a holograph of Spanish Lace herself. A small circular computer hovered near the bed. Dominating the room were some fifty clocks of all types and makes, from an ancient grandfather clock to a complex mechanism giving digital readouts in thirty-six different languages to a rotating holographic representation of Yukon divided into time zones. Nighthawk pulled his tiny circular camera out and tossed it onto the bed; if he was going to die, Malloy might as well see how it happened so the next man the Marquis sent would be better prepared.

"Ah, here you are!" said a voice from the doorway. He spun around and found himself facing Spanish Lace, with his weapons still floating in the air just next to her. "You led me quite a chase, Jefferson Nighthawk, but now it's over."

Nighthawk's gaze darted around the room, trying to find something, anything, he could use to his advantage.

He *survived a hundred or more battles. Some of them had to be against aliens or mutants with even greater powers than she possesses. Think! What would* he *have done?*

"These are my prizes," she said, gesturing to the clocks. "My booty. All else I sell or trade, but the clocks I keep, to tick off the minutes and hours of my life until I am no longer in bondage to this unwanted body." Her face suddenly became a mask of fury. "And you dare to stand among them and insult me?"

A shot rang out and a bullet ripped into the wall behind him, spraying his face with dust. He dove behind the nearest chest for cover. Two small alien statues stood atop it. He grabbed one of them, hurled it at her, picked up the second as the first bounced off an invisible barrier a foot from her head, and hurled it more carefully. She grinned as it whizzed harmlessly by her, but it hit what Nighthawk was aiming at, shattering the sonic pistol and careening off the projectile gun.

"You think I need weapons?" she said harshly, as a portion of the ceiling came loose and fell on top of him. He was up again in an instant, positioning himself directly in front of the mirror. When he sensed that the laser pistol was about to fire, he fell to the floor, and the beam bounced off the mirror. The angle brought it within inches of Spanish Lace. She ducked instinctively, then grabbed the laser pistol and hurled it through the doorway into a corridor.

You ducked! You weren't expecting the beam to bounce back at you, and you had to duck. That means it takes you a fraction of a second to erect those invisible walls and shields. Now, if I can just find a way to use that . . .

"On your feet, Jefferson Nighthawk."

He saw no reason to keep hiding, so he stood up and faced her. "What now?"

"Now we end it," she said.

And suddenly the furniture, the walls, the ceiling, *everything* began closing in on him. Vases flew at his head, lamps at his chest, the floor began swaying beneath his feet. He struggled futilely to keep his balance, fell heavily to the floor, got up again, and backed away from her until he was pressed up against the ancient grandfather clock, clinging to it desperately.

Another section of the ceiling came away, burying him. He moaned once, then lay absolutely motionless in the rubble.

Spanish Lace approached him cautiously, poking

his spine to see if there was a reaction. There wasn't. She knelt down next to him, still half expecting him to jump at her, but he was motionless.

"All right, clone," she murmured, turning him onto his back and feeling for his identity disk. "Let's see if you're who you said you were."

She deftly removed the disk, and as she was studying it his hand suddenly rose and came down on the back of her neck—burying the grandfather clock's minute hand into the base of her brain. She fell across him without a sound, dead.

Nighthawk shoved her body off his and stood up. He reached out a foot and turned her over. Her face was serene in death, as if an overwhelming burden had somehow been lifted.

You were as much of a freak as me. You could have been my friend. Why did you make me kill you?

He shook his head, as if to physically rid it of that train of thought. It didn't help.

The Widowmaker must have had brothers. Maybe cousins. Maybe even a son or two no one knows about. There could be twenty or thirty men carrying his blood. None of them are doomed to spend their lives killing everyone they meet. Why me?

But of course, they were carrying *some* of the Widowmaker's blood. He was carrying *all* of it, because he *was* the Widowmaker. Not a brother. Not a son. Not Version 2.0. But the Widowmaker. And what the Widowmaker did was kill people. Even people who might have been his friends.

Suddenly he found that he was shivering, and he realized that what had kept the interior of the Ice Palace warm was not a furnace or any heating plant but Spanish Lace, who had used a tiny portion of her abilities to keep the molecules of air in constant motion, spinning them fast enough to make the temperature habitable.

He began searching the room. The chests contained only clothes, but behind the mirror he found a small safe embedded in a quartz wall. He couldn't open it, so he cut it out with his laser pistol, tucked it under his arm, and was about to return to his ship when something caught his eye.

He walked over to it, and found it was a small holograph of a group of girls, perhaps ten or eleven years of age, their arms interlinked, all smiling at the camera. He studied it for a long moment, trying to pick out the girl who would someday become Spanish Lace, and found that he couldn't.

Interesting. One of you might have grown up to be an artist. One an accountant. One a mother of six. One a bitter, barren old woman. One a spaceship mechanic. One a professor of ancient languages. And one a notorious thief and assassin.

And suddenly he understood why she should keep that, of all holographs, of all mementos.

It was the last time you could be mistaken for normal, the last time you fit *anywhere.*

He stared at the holograph again, at all the smiling girlish faces.

I envy you. At least you had ten years.

He located his laser pistol on the way out, then hunted up her powersled and was about to take it back to his ship when he decided that she deserved to be buried. He walked back into the Ice Palace, attached his laser pistol to his power pack, rigged the charge to overload, and left both the gun and the pack right next to her corpse. Then he returned to the powersled and began racing over the frozen plains. When he was five miles away he stopped and looked back, shading his eyes against the sun and its blinding reflections. He could just barely see the Ice Palace. He waited five seconds, ten, fifteen—and suddenly he could hear the explosion. Another moment and the towers and turrets began collapsing inward upon themselves. He thought it would be appropriate to whisper a prayer, and was surprised to discover that he didn't know any.

He rejoined Lizard Malloy at the ship. The leather-skinned little man had witnessed the entire fight on his receiving device and wanted nothing more than to talk about it, while Nighthawk wanted only to put it out of his mind.

"What's the matter with you?" complained Malloy as their ship took off for Tundra. "You kill the most dangerous woman on the Inner Frontier, and suddenly you're acting like you just lost a friend."

"Maybe I did."

"Are you crazy?" said Malloy. "She did her damnedest to kill you."

"We had a lot in common, she and I," answered Nighthawk thoughtfully.

"You think so, do you?"

Nighthawk nodded his head. "She was just a friend I hadn't made yet."

"You're crazy, you know that?" said Malloy.

Nighthawk shrugged. "You're entitled to your opinion."

Malloy pulled a small cube out of his pocket. "If I show this to the Marquis, if he sees you offering that bitch her life, you're history. He'll throw you out on your ass so fast you won't know what happened."

"I can live with that."

Malloy tossed the cube into the ship's atomizer. "*I* probably can't," he said wryly. "You're still the only thing standing between me and a very slow, very painful, death."

"Then you're still under obligation to me."

"I suppose, if you put it that way," acknowledged Malloy uncomfortably.

"I do."

"I have a funny feeling you're bringing that up for a purpose."

"When we land, I want you to take a message to the Pearl of Maracaibo for me."

"I thought the Marquis told you she was off-limits," said Malloy.

"He did."

Malloy stared at him. "You're crazy, you know that?"

"I've decided that life is too short to worry about what you or the Marquis or anyone else wants," said Nighthawk. "I'm going to start thinking about *me* while there's still time, because every other person I've met, without exception, has either tried to use me or kill me."

"Not me!" said Malloy devoutly.

"You, too—or don't you want me to protect you from the Marquis?"

"That's a trade," said Malloy. "I do favors for you, you do them for me."

"Right," answered Nighthawk. "And it's about time you started fulfilling your end of the bargain."

"What the hell happened to you in the Ice Palace?" demanded Malloy. "You're different somehow."

"I realized that life is short, and that everybody goes through it alone," said Nighthawk. "Today is the first day of the rest of my life, and from now on I'm living it for *me*."

"All that from killing one woman?"

"All that, and more," said Nighthawk, wondering idly why he didn't *feel* more free for having declared his freedom.

Chapter 9

• • • • • • •

"Well, *Widowmaker*, you're as good as you're supposed to be," said the Marquis of Queensbury as he looked across his desk at Nighthawk.

"I'm not the Widowmaker. And you didn't warn me what I was going to be up against."

"You're who I say you are," replied the Marquis. "And as for the rest of it, I want my second-in-command to be resourceful. View it as a test."

"I thought my test was fighting you in the casino."

"It was."

"Well, then?" said Nighthawk.

The Marquis looked amused. "Did you think life involves only one test?"

"You're supposed to be a good businessman," said Nighthawk, trying to hide his anger. "It was bad business to send me up against someone with Spanish Lace's powers without letting me know what she could do. Why risk getting me killed by not telling me everything I needed to know before I went up against her?"

"It'd be worse business to keep you in your current high position if you couldn't improvise well enough to kill her," answered the Marquis. "Just out of curiosity, how did you finally do it?"

"By deceit and trickery. If she could be killed in any other way, it still hasn't occurred to me."

"You're young yet."

"How would *you* have killed her?" asked Nighthawk.

"Me?" The Marquis laughed aloud. "I'd have someone else do it for me. That's what being the boss is all about."

"I suppose so," acknowledged Nighthawk. "The thing is, talk like that makes me want to be a boss too."

"That's good. I admire ambition in a man." The Marquis' smile vanished as quickly as it had appeared. "But you would do well to remember that this organization only has room for one boss—and I'm him."

Nighthawk stared at him, but made no reply.

"You know," continued the Marquis, "in most employees that kind of sullen look would constitute insubordination. In your case, I think I'll write it off to the arrogance of youth. *This* time. But don't press your luck. You'll need it all just to kill our enemies."

"*Your* enemies."

"You work for me. That makes them your enemies too."

"If you say so."

The Marquis stared at him through narrowed eyes. "You know, I can't decide if you're *trying* to annoy me, or if you're so socially maladroit that you can't help it. I have to keep reminding myself that you're only a couple of months out of the lab."

"And now *you're* trying to annoy *me*," responded Nighthawk.

The Marquis shook his head. "Not at all. I'm just stating facts."

"Let's say, then, that you choose very unpleasant facts to state."

"You've got a lot to learn," answered the Marquis. "Facts are true or false. Pleasant or unpleasant is just the spin you put on them."

"That sounds reasonable, but it's bullshit and you know it."

"You're in a lousy mood. They tell me this happens in three-month-olds, so I'll forgive it this time, but if I were you I wouldn't make a regular habit of it—at least, not when you talk to me. Are we clear?"

Silence.

"Are we clear?" repeated the Marquis.

Nighthawk nodded. "We're clear."

"I think I know what's got you depressed," said the Marquis. "I'll tell you what: Let me catch up on business here and maybe I'll go to Deluros in a week or two and kill the real Nighthawk for you."

"I *am* the real Nighthawk."

"Let's not get into semantics. Once I kill him, you'll be the *only* Nighthawk."

"That's no good."

"Why not?"

"Because *I* have to kill him."

"You know, you could become a real pain in the ass without half working at it," said the Marquis irritably. "Get the hell out of here before we really *do* come to blows."

Nighthawk left the office without another word and, still annoyed with the Marquis, returned to the casino. The place was more crowded than usual. Most of the gaming tables were operating at capacity, and whores of both sexes were cadging drinks and trying to make their business arrangements for the night. The *jabob* table was surrounded by humans who found the alien game fascinating, while the craps table was populated by Lodinites, Canphorites, and a six-limbed golden-shelled Lambidarian.

Malloy was busy playing poker with a couple of flashily dressed miners and a green-hued creature of a species Nighthawk hadn't seen before. He watched as the little man bet up a flush and lost to a full house. Finally he wandered over to the bar, ordered a Dust Whore, and idly watched the various dancers until the Pearl of Maracaibo appeared on the floating platform.

He was sipping his drink and staring at her intently when she suddenly winked at him, then laughed at his reaction. He waited until her dance was through, then made his way to her dressing room, a glass in each hand. The red eye of the security system scanned him and reported his presence to the room's occupant.

"Come in," she said, and the door dilated long enough for him to step into the room.

She sat on an elegant gilt chair, naked from the waist up. A small mirror hovered in the air perhaps thirty inches from her face. She had been staring into it, meticulously removing her stage makeup, but she turned to face Nighthawk as soon as he entered.

"How nice to see you again," she said. "The Marquis tells me you're a hero."

"The Marquis exaggerates," said Nighthawk.

"A *modest* hero," she said. "Now that *is* a rarity around here."

"I brought you a drink," he said, placing it down next to her.

"I didn't ask for one."

"Try it," he said. "You'll like it."

"In a moment, perhaps." She paused and stared at him. "Do you know what the Marquis would do to you if he knew you were here?"

"I know what he'd *try* to do," answered Nighthawk, his anger returning at the mention of the Marquis.

"And you have no fear of him?"

"None." He paused. "Besides, you invited me here."

"I did?"

"You winked at me," he said. "I consider that an invitation. And you haven't told me to leave."

"Leave, then."

"Not just yet."

She smiled but chose to make no reply, and an uncomfortable silence ensued. She stared at her mirror and he looked at her. "You're a very good dancer," he said at last.

Still no reply.

"I noticed that the first time I saw you."

Silence.

"You don't have to be afraid to talk to me," he said. "I'll settle for just being friends."

She uttered a disbelieving laugh. "Just friends?"

"Yes."

"Why?"

"Because I'm lonely."

"There are many women here. Why me?"

He stared at her for a moment before answering. "Because we're both freaks," he said. "I'm sure the Marquis has told you what I am, and with that blue skin you're some kind of sport or mutant. We're each the only one of our kind here. I thought you might be lonely too."

"You were mistaken."

"I'm not so sure of that. Except when you're with the Marquis, you keep entirely to yourself."

"Did it ever occur to you that I might enjoy my own company?"

"No, it never did."

"Why? Just because you don't enjoy yours?"

He stared into her clear, almost colorless eyes for a long moment. "We're getting off on the wrong foot here," he said at last.

"Yes, I know," she said in amused tones. "You just want to be my friend."

"That's right."

"Funny," she said, making no attempt to shield her naked breasts from his gaze. "I thought you wanted to look at my body."

"That too."

"Does your notion of friendship include sharing my bed?"

"If you ask me to."

"And if I don't?"

"Sooner or later you will," he replied. "In the meantime, two lost souls can take some comfort in each other's company."

"'You do not look at me like a lost soul," she said, arching her back and stretching sensuously, "but rather like a lustful man."

"You're a very beautiful woman. How would you prefer that I look at you?"

"Perhaps, given your situation, you shouldn't look at me at all."

"The Marquis just told me that he wants his

employees to display initiative," said Nighthawk with a smile. "Besides, if no one looked at you, you'd be out of a job."

"Very clever," she said. "Now, if you're all through looking, I think you'd better leave."

"I'm still looking," he replied. "Why not have the drink?"

"I could call the Marquis."

"Yes, but you won't," said Nighthawk confidently.

"Why not?"

"Because you don't want me to kill him."

She laughed "*You*? Kill *him*?"

"That's right," he answered seriously.

"So instead of merely a lustful underling, I find myself confronted by a lustful egomaniac," she said. "I suppose I shall have to accept your drink or you will kill *me*, too."

"Now you're making fun of me."

She shrugged and turned back to her mirror.

"I've had very little experience with women," said Nighthawk awkwardly. "Believe me, the very last thing I want to do is seem comical to you."

"Not comical. Just suicidal," she replied. "And the Marquis tells me that you have had very little experience with *anything*." She stared at him with open curiosity. "Is it true that you are only three months old?"

"In a manner of speaking."

"What is it like, to remember no childhood?"

"I have vague memories of a childhood," he replied. "It's not my own, though, and the memories fade daily."

"How wonderful not to remember one's childhood," she said. "I wish I could not remember mine."

"You didn't enjoy it?"

"Would you enjoy being—how did you call it—a

sport?" she asked. "Children can be very intolerant." She paused, frowning at the memories. "That is why I came to the Inner Frontier. Here they care no more that I have blue skin than that you are three months old. They care only about what we can do—who we *are* rather than who we *aren't*."

"Interestingly put," said Nighthawk. "But I thought the Oligarchy was based on that same principle."

"They may give lip service to it, but it is valid only out here."

"Perhaps when I'm a year old I'll be less trusting," he said in self-deprecating tones.

She laughed. "You can be very amusing."

A satisfied smile spread across his face.

"You look happy," she said.

"It's nice to be appreciated for something other than my ability to kill people."

"Who was the original Jefferson Nighthawk?" she asked.

"He was the best bounty hunter who ever lived," answered Nighthawk. "He spent most of his life on the Frontier. They called him the Widowmaker."

"The Widowmaker? I've heard of him."

"I think just about everyone has."

"How did he die?"

"He didn't."

She frowned. "But I thought he lived more than a century ago."

"He did. He came down with a disease, and went into the deep freeze before it could kill him."

"It must be very strange for you to know he still exists."

"It makes me feel like a ghost."

"A ghost?"

"Insubstantial," said Nighthawk. "Like he's the real thing, and I'm just an ephemeral shadow, here to do his bidding and then vanish."

"I would hate that feeling!" she said passionately.

"I'm not especially pleased with it myself," he replied. "But it's probably no worse than dancing half-naked so all the men in the audience can lust for your body."

"Nonsense," she said heatedly. "For men to admire my body is perfectly natural. What you have described is sick!" She reached out, grabbed the drink he had brought her, and downed it in a single swallow.

"Tell me—how did you come to be known as the Pearl of Maracaibo?"

"I think we are through talking."

"We are kindred souls," said Nighthawk. "We have many things in common, many things to share. I told you how I came to be the Widowmaker; now you tell me how you came by *your* name."

"I have agreed to no trades or bargains," she said. "If you have a kindred soul here, it is more likely Lizard Malloy than me. Each of you wants things you cannot have. In his case, it is money."

"And in my case?"

"Don't play the buffoon," she said. "You are here right now because of what you want." She stood up and removed the single garment that had been wrapped around her waist. "Take a good look, Jefferson Nighthawk, for this is as close as you're going to get to it."

"I don't give up easily," he said, staring at her nude body.

"Even if I felt attracted to you, I have a strong sense of self-preservation," she said. "I belong to the

Marquis as surely as you do. He would kill one or both of us."

"I'll protect you," said Nighthawk.

"Don't be a fool. This is *his* world."

"Just promise to give it some thought."

"All right, I promise," she said. "Now go. I have to get ready to dance again."

"Your last dance of the night is coming up, right?" asked Nighthawk.

"Yes."

"I want to see you after it's over."

"You are a fool."

"I know. But you didn't answer me. Can I stop by here afterward?"

"You are a notorious killer. How can I stop you?"

Nighthawk grinned, then got up and left her in order to secure a spot at the bar where he could watch her dance again.

Chapter 10

◆ ◆ ◆ ◆ ◆ ◆ ◆

Nighthawk lay on his back, head propped on a pillow.
The bed floated a few inches above the floor, and constantly changed shape to mold itself to the forms of its
occupants.

"That was great!" he said. Suddenly he grinned.
"I'm glad I didn't have to wait twenty-three years for
it."

"From now on, whenever you go to bed with a
woman, you'll have me to compare her to," said
Melisande, the Pearl of Maracaibo.

"What makes you think I want anyone else?"

"You're a man. If you don't now, you soon will."

"No," he said. "You're the woman for me."

She turned on her side and looked into his eyes.
"But you're not the man for me."

He frowned. "I don't understand."

"I belong to the Marquis. You know that."

"But I thought . . ."

"You thought that just because I went to bed with you once, I was prepared to leave him forever?" she asked with a smile. "You really *are* very young, you know."

"Then why *did* you go to bed with me?"

"Because you looked at me like a hungry puppy dog," she said. "And because I was curious to see what it felt like to have sex with a clone."

"And?"

She shrugged. "You've got a lot to learn."

"You can teach me."

"Teaching awkward young men is not part of my job," she said with a chuckle.

"I'm sorry the experience was so unpleasant," said Nighthawk bitterly.

"I didn't say it was unpleasant," she replied.

"Not in so many words."

"It was all right."

"But nothing more."

"That's right."

"Nowhere near as good as with the Marquis."

"Don't feel badly," she replied. "Most men do a lot worse their first time."

"I don't find that especially comforting."

"Would you rather I lied to you?"

"Much," said Nighthawk.

"But then you'd insist on doing it again."

"Why not?"

She shook her head. "Once was curiosity. Twice would be infidelity."

"You've got a funny notion of morality," said Nighthawk.

"I've developed mine over a period of thirty

Standard years," she replied. "How long have you been honing *yours*?"

He made no reply, but swung his feet over the edge of the bed, stood up, and walked to the window that overlooked the frozen streets of Klondike.

"Notorious killers aren't supposed to sulk like spoiled children," she said.

"Look," he snapped, turning to her, "this is the first time I've been with a woman, and also the first time I've been rejected by one. Now, maybe the Widowmaker would know how to handle it, but I'm having a little trouble."

"You *are* the Widowmaker."

"I'm Jefferson Nighthawk."

"Is there a difference?"

"More than you can imagine."

"Well, whoever you are, do you know how silly you look, standing there without any clothes on?"

He walked over to the bed, ripped the covers off, and threw them on the floor.

"Now we're even."

"Do you feel better?" she said.

"Not much."

She stood up, examined her image in the mirror with a critical eye, brushed a few strands of hair into place with her fingers, and started searching for her clothes.

"What are you doing?" he demanded.

"I'm getting dressed and leaving," she replied. "You stopped being fun a long time ago. Now you're not even interesting."

"You're going to the Marquis."

"That's right."

He walked over and grabbed her arm. "And what if I decide not to let you?"

She winced and pulled her arm loose. "That *hurt*! Keep your goddamned hands to yourself!"

"I didn't squeeze that hard," he said. "What's the matter?"

"Nothing," she said, turning away and picking up some clothing from the floor.

"Let me see your arm," he demanded, grabbing her by the shoulders and turning her around.

"Leave me alone!"

He took her arm in his hand and studied it carefully. "That's a hell of a bruise. I can't imagine how I missed it when you were dancing."

"I cover it with makeup."

"How did you get it?"

"None of your business," she said, trying to pull her arm free.

"The Marquis gave it to you, didn't he?"

"I fell and bumped it."

"Not there you didn't, unless you fell with your arms splayed out. The Marquis did it."

"What if he did?" she said defiantly. "It has nothing to do with you."

"How often does he beat you?" demanded Nighthawk.

"I deserved it."

"For what?"

"For something a lot more serious than sleeping with a three-month-old," she said.

"He won't beat you for sleeping with me?"

"Who's going to tell him? You?"

"What kind of man beats a helpless woman?"

"What kind of man *kills* a woman?" she shot back. "Isn't that what you just came back from doing?"

"I'm not going to let him hit you ever again," said Nighthawk.

"I have no further interest in you," she said. "I want you to display none in me."

"I can't."

"Why not?"

He stared at her for a long moment. "I might be in love with you."

" 'Might'?" she repeated.

"I don't know. I've never been in love before."

"You're not now. You had a good time in bed; let it go at that."

"I don't like to think of you going back to him."

"Fine. Think of something else."

She finished dressing and walked to the door. "I have every intention of forgetting tonight. I'd strongly advise you to do the same."

"Not a chance."

"That's *your* problem," she said, walking out as the door sensed her presence and dilated.

Nighthawk walked back to the window and stared out at the frozen landscape for a long moment. Then he slowly climbed into his clothes, no longer interested in sleeping. Finally he walked over to a mirror to comb his hair, but as he looked into the glass, it seemed to him that the reflection he saw was that of a horribly disfigured old man, his eyes sunken, his cheeks hollow, the bones of his face sticking out through his rotting flesh.

The Widowmaker.

"What would *you* have done?" demanded Nighthawk bitterly.

I'd never have gotten into such a situation. I never let my libido rule my mind.

"How can you say that? I've been to bed with a woman exactly once."

You haven't been able to think of anything else since you saw her.

"You wouldn't have, either."

Never tell me what I would or wouldn't have done. You are the student here, not me.

"All right, then. What would you do now?"

Forget her.

"I can't."

She's just a woman. You're just a man. The only difference is she's had enough experience to know she can forget you. Sleep with a few more women, and you'll find her face harder to remember each time.

"Is *that* what made you such a killer? The fact that no one ever meant anything to you?"

I never said that no one meant anything to me. I said that you can't let your gonads rule your mind.

"I'm tired of hearing that. Say something else."

Don't give me orders, son. I'm the Widowmaker. You're just my shadow, my surrogate.

"Then help me, damn it! I'm out here on the Frontier trying to help *you*!"

Why do you think you're seeing me? You'd better start taking the help you can get. Don't hold out for the advice you want.

"What are you talking about?"

You want me to tell you how to win the blue-skinned girl. I'm not going to. Forget her.

"Maybe *you* could. *I* can't."

Then be prepared to kill the Marquis.

"I'm ready to do it tonight."

I know. And once you do, who's going to finger President Trelaine's assassin? Or have you forgotten why you were given life in the first place?

"The Marquis has got to be worth over five

million credits. Why don't I just kill him, confiscate what's his, and send it back to Deluros?"

Because all you really want to confiscate is the girl. And because the Widowmaker has a code of honor. If he said he'd accept an assignment, he always kept his word.

"But I'm not the Widowmaker."

You will be, one day.

"No! I'm Jefferson Nighthawk!"

So am I—and I was Jefferson Nighthawk first.

"I'm my own man! I'm not you, and I don't take orders from you!"

You are more me than you can imagine.

"No!" shouted Nighthawk furiously.

Oh, yes, flesh of my flesh and blood of my blood. You don't really think I'm here in the mirror, do you? This is just your mind's way of rationalizing my presence. I'm your conscience. More than that, I'm your essence. We are intertwined mentally, physically, in every possible way. You fall and I hurt, you laugh and I rejoice, you reach for your weapon and I aim the gun and pull the trigger. There's no getting away from yourself, son, and that's what I am: your true self. I'm the man you are striving to become. I'm the ideal you strive to achieve, and I'm always out of reach. No matter how hard you try, you'll always know in a secret chamber of your mind that I am the better man with a weapon or a woman.

"The hell you are!"

The hell I'm not. I'm thirty percent man and seventy percent disease, and I'm frozen away like a piece of leftover meat, but you're still afraid of me, still jealous. I haunt your dreams, young Jefferson; you don't haunt mine.

"I don't have to listen to this!" yelled Nighthawk. He pulled out his sonic pistol and pulled the trigger.

The beam of sound shattered the mirror into a thousand pieces.

He calmed down as suddenly as he had become enraged, and realized that he still hadn't settled on a course of action. He walked into the bathroom and stood, contritely, before the mirror.

"I'm sorry," he said. "I lost my temper. Probably you went forty years without losing yours."

A handsome young man stared out at him.

"I said I'm sorry," he repeated. "And I still don't know what to do next."

It seemed to him that the face in the mirror turned rotten with disease just long enough to say, *Of course you do*, before reverting to the handsome young man whose uncertainty and indecision showed in his every expression and gesture.

Chapter 11

◆ ◆ ◆ ◆ ◆ ◆ ◆

Nighthawk rode the ramp down to the subbasement level beneath the casino. He walked past the swimming pool and the sauna, and finally came to the shooting gallery where the Marquis of Queenbury was taking aim at a tiny target fifty meters away. The target spun, rose, and fell, remaining in constant motion— and unlike any other target Nighthawk had ever seen, this one fired back.

It was a holograph of a Navy officer, kneeling, with his pistol clasped in both hands. Tiny laser beams eminated for it—not enough to do serious damage, but more than ample to cause a painful jolt.

Nighthawk stopped and watched, silent and motionless, as the Marquis swayed back and forth, bobbing and weaving like a boxer as he evaded the laser beams and finally squeezed the trigger of his pistol. An instant later, the Electric Monitor signaled a bull's-eye.

"Nice shot," said Nighthawk, finally stepping forward.

"Thanks," said the Marquis. "You haven't been down here before, have you?"

Nighthawk shook his head. "It's impressive."

"It's more than impressive. It's essential."

Nighthawk stared at him curiously.

"There are a thousand men carrying weapons up on ground level. If I'm to be their undisputed leader, it's because they know they can't kill me and take over the operation. The reason they know it is because every month or so I'm called upon to prove it." He paused. "Most of them never pull a weapon out of a holster except to kill someone—or to try to. Their reflexes get rusty. The sights on their weapons fall out of synch. The power levels on their pistols get low. Me, I work with targets at least an hour a day, and my weapons are always in prime condition. It's the difference between the amateur and the professional."

"Very impressive," said Nighthawk.

"How are *your* weapons?" asked the Marquis.

Nighthawk, who was facing the Marquis, spun and drew his weapons and fired them, all on one fluid motion. The gun in his right hand put a bullet through the left eye of a holographic Navy man who was peeking up over a protective barrier, and an instant later the pistol in his left hand burned a hole in the Navy man's chest with a beam of light.

"They seem okay," he said, replacing each weapon in its holster.

"Even more impressive," said the Marquis. "Though somehow I knew that, of all the men on

Klondike, you were the one most likely to keep his weaponry in perfect working order. And of course, the Widowmaker could probably hit his targets at fifty meters even if he were blindfolded."

"You didn't ask me down here to watch me shoot," said Nighthawk. "And I didn't come to watch *you* shoot. So what's up?"

"They didn't teach you any small talk back on Deluros, did they?" asked the Marquis with a smile.

"No."

"All right. I sent for you because we have some business to discuss."

Here it comes. He's going to mention the Pearl of Maracaibo, and demand that I never touch her again, and I'm going to have to kill him.

"Ever hear of Father Christmas?"

"You mean like in the kid's nursery story?" asked Nighthawk.

"You should be so lucky," replied the Marquis with a laugh. "No, this Father Christmas works the Frontier. Or, rather, he used to until he got ambitious. He just pulled off a job in the Oligarchy, and now he's headed back here with maybe a dozen police ships on his tail."

"Why is he called Father Christmas?" asked Nighthawk.

"Out here you choose your name," replied the Marquis. "Or sometimes it chooses you. At any rate, he only steals from churches."

"Is there a living in it?"

"Well, if he only went after priests and poor boxes, no. But there's a lot of gold and artwork in some of the churches. Not too many of them are out here on the Frontier, which is why he went into the Oligarchy looking for a big score."

"Sounds like he got it."

The Marquis nodded. "Yeah. I gather he stole about five hundred pounds of gold from a church on Darbar II, as well as a couple of religious paintings by Morita."

"Morita? I never heard of him."

"I suppose there was a limit to what they could teach you in two months," said the Marquis. "Morita was the finest artist of the late Democracy period. His paintings go for millions, and last time I looked, gold was going for seventeen hundred credits an ounce. Which means Father Christmas has what used to be called a king's ransom in his ship's cargo hold. His problem, as I mentioned, is that he's also got a bunch of police ships on his tail."

"What sort of lead does he have?"

"Oh, maybe seven hours, maybe eight."

"He'll lose them. Seven hours is forever at light speeds."

"He's riding a Model Three-forty-one Golden Streak."

Nighthawk looked blank.

"High speed, limited range," continued the Marquis. "He's good for maybe six more hours, but then he's going to have to stop to refuel."

"I assume all this has something to do with me?"

"Of course it does," said the Marquis. "My computer has projected the possible worlds where he can freshen his atomic pile. There are only four. Two of them are military outposts, and he's too smart to stop there. The third is at war with a neighboring system, and no matter what assurances they give him, there's a fair to middling chance that he'll get blown out of the sky by one side or the other."

"Let me guess. Tundra is the fourth."

"No—but I run the fourth world. It's a little planet called Aladdin. I want you there immediately."

"And once I'm there?"

"My guess is that's where Father Christmas will put down. I want you to meet with him."

"Okay, I meet with him. What do I say?"

"You transmit my personal greetings and felicitations to him, and tell him, gently but firmly, that the price of fuel and safe passage has gone up."

"How high?"

"*Very* high," said the Marquis. "I want fifty percent of his haul."

"And if he says no?"

"Do whatever you have to do," said the Marquis with a shrug. "Just make sure that when he leaves, half of what he stole remains behind."

"How many men has he got?"

"A Three-forty-one Streak can only hold a crew of four, so the most he'll have with him will be three."

Nighthawk nodded. "Is there anything else I should know about Father Christmas?"

"You already know it: He's carrying cargo we want."

"You know what I mean," continued Nighthawk. "Has he any special talents or powers?"

"Not unless you believe that he and Jesus are in cahoots," answered the Marquis. "There are some people who believe exactly that, you know."

"Any reason why?"

"He blundered into a trap where all his men were killed and he got out unscathed. And another time the police found his hideout, back on Roosevelt III, and blew it to smithereens. He was down the block at a bar at the time. Heard the noise, stole a ship, and never looked back."

"You want me to take anyone with me?"

"You're the Widowmaker," replied the Marquis. "If I thought you needed anyone before, your last assignment proved just what you can do on your own."

"What do you have all these gunmen for if you won't use them?" asked Nighthawk.

"Oh, I use them when I need them. But you don't really hope to convince me at this late date that you need any help against four men?"

"You're a real sweet guy to work for," said Nighthawk caustically.

"Melisande thinks so."

Nighthawk took one look at the Marquis' smirking grin and knew that she had told him about the night they'd spent together.

"Every once in a while she has to go slumming, just to remind herself why she hooked up with me in the first place," continued the Marquis. "I don't blame her, since it reminds her why she stays with me. The problem," he added, "is that sometimes the man involved doesn't understand what's going on. He gets it into his head that she actually cares for him, and then he makes a nuisance of himself, and then, unhappily, I have to dispose of him." He pulled his gun out of his holster, flipped it in the air, caught it in his other hand, and pulled the trigger. There was a deafening *BANG!* and the Electric Monitor scored another bull's-eye.

"You're very good," acknowledged Nighthawk.

"We both are," replied the Marquis. "I hope we never have cause to find out who's better."

"No reason why we should," said Nighthawk.

But in his mind's eye he could see the Marquis running his hands and mouth all over Melisande's nude body. He felt a wave of jealousy sweeping over him, and he knew that they had more than ample reason.

Chapter 12

Aladdin had once held the promise of great riches—hence its name. But, like Yukon and Tundra, its mines were exhausted in less than two decades, the miners went farther toward the Galactic Core, and not much remained except a handful of prospectors who kept hoping to find another mother lode and the usual gamblers and outcasts and adventurers who were endemic to the Inner Frontier.

As with many of the Frontier worlds that no longer held major populations—or, indeed, never had—Aladdin was dotted with a number of deserted Tradertowns: quickly erected structures that had catered to the needs of a transient population. There were some worlds with forty or fifty functioning Tradertowns, but Man was an efficient animal, and usually within two or three decades of his arrival most of the Tradertowns had become ghost towns as the plunder of the planet was completed and the plunderers moved on. Such a planet was Aladdin, with seventeen ghost towns and one working Tradertown.

It was the first planet within his admittedly limited experience that allowed Nighthawk to land his ship without first requesting permission. The spaceport had fallen into disrepair and the landing pads were cracked and broken; most of the ships landed on a flat, open savannah about a mile from the Tradertown.

Nighthawk made sure that the fueling station was inoperative. Then, satisfied that his prey would have to go into town to obtain fuel, he set his ship down on the plain, activated the alarm system, and began walking across the hot, arid plain toward the Tradertown. Suddenly he became aware of the fact that he was not alone. A spherical ball—bright, yellow and fluffy, totally round, with no visible sensory organs—was rolling alongside him, purring gently to itself.

Nighthawk stopped; the ball of fluff stopped too. He started walking again, altering his direction every few strides; it matched him move for move. He stopped again, and it rolled over to him and rubbed against his boot, purring more loudly. Nighthawk kept his fingers poised above his weapon, just in case it bit, but after rubbing against him for a few more seconds it backed away, as if waiting for him to start walking again. He stared at it for a long moment, then shrugged and continued on his way.

He soon reached the town, still accompanied by the *thing*. He couldn't spot any place that was likely to sell fuel, so he tried to imagine what Father Christmas would do when confronted with the same situation.

He'd seek out some locals, of course, men who could tell him where to obtain his fuel. He'd probably keep clear of the bar and the drug den; there was always a chance that one of the patrons might consider playing bounty hunter and try to kill him for the reward. The assay office was closed; so was the postal station. That left the whorehouse, the restaurant, and the hotel. He arbitrarily chose the hotel and walked down the street until he stood opposite it. He took one more look up and down the street, just to make sure that he hadn't missed an even more likely spot, then turned and entered the hotel.

It was nondescript, much like Aladdin itself. It had changed hands so many times, and so many owners had tried to shape it to their tastes, that it seemed a catchall of influences—nonrepresentational holographic art sharing wall space with alien carvings and the stuffed heads of Aladdin's now-extinct carnivores.

The furniture was the same: angular chrome chairs floated above the floor, sandwiched between oddly shaped chairs for strangely jointed aliens and leather lounge chairs that recalled the gentleman's clubs of Earth's 19th Century.

Nighthawk approached the front desk, still accompanied by the little yellow ball of fluff. An alien, mildly humanoid, with green skin, protruding golden fangs, a bulbous forehead, and huge, luminous purple eyes, stood behind the desk. As Nighthawk approached, it spoke into a translating device that it wore attached to the shoulder of its shining silver tunic.

"Good morning upon you, sir," said its inflectionless translated voice. "How may I help you?"

"I ran short on fuel," answered Nighthawk. "I was forced to divert and land here. Where can I purchase some?"

"What type of ship do you have?" asked the alien.

"A Three-forty-one Golden Streak."

"Ah! You need your nuclear pile enhanced."

"I know what I need. Where do I go for it?"

"It is not necessary to go anywhere. I will send an experienced mechanic to your ship."

"Has he got an office?"

"No, sir. No more than one ship per Standard week needs work done on its pile. I will contact him immediately."

"Not right now."

"But you just stated that you had almost no fuel."

Nighthawk leaned halfway across the counter and lowered his voice confidently. "I have a young lady aboard the ship. Her social position is such that she must not be seen or identified. She's waiting until dark, and will then join me in the suite I intend to rent here." He paused. "Do you understand what I am saying to you?"

"Absolutely, sir," the alien assured him. "You may count upon my discretion."

"Good. What's available?"

"We have an exquisite corner suite on the third floor."

"That'll be fine."

"Will you be taking your Holy Roller with you?"

"I beg your pardon?" said Nighthawk.

"Your Holy Roller," repeated the alien. "I must know if you intend for it to stay with you."

"I don't know what you're talking about."

The alien pointed to the yellow fluffball that was about eighteen inches from Nighthawk's boot. "That is your Holy Roller, sir."

"Interesting name," said Nighthawk. "However, it's not exactly *mine*. It followed me here."

"I can see that, sir, but it's yours nonetheless," said the alien clerk. "They spend years by themselves, manifesting their presence to no one. Then, for reasons no one can fathom, one of them will suddenly appear and befriend a human. Though I have heard of such instances, I have never actually seen it prior to today—but legend has it that once it happens, they never willingly leave the human's presence again."

Nighthawk looked down at the Holy Roller, which purred and rubbed up against his boot. He frowned.

"Let me get this straight: You're telling me that I'm stuck with it?"

"Yes, sir."

"For how long?"

"They are said to be truly faithful companions," answered the alien, leaning over the counter to stare at the Roller. "It is almost always a lifetime relationship."

Nighthawk stared at the yellow fluffball. "Whose lifetime—ours or theirs?"

"They are virtually immortal."

"I don't *need* a lifetime companion."

"I'm not at all sure that your needs are meaningful to it, sir."

"Wonderful," muttered Nighthawk. "Who named them Holy Rollers?"

"They have been called that since I immigrated to Aladdin," said the alien. "I have always assumed that the name was given to them by Men." The alien paused awkwardly. "I really must know, sir: Will it be staying with you?"

"What's it to you?"

"I must program your room's security system, sir.

It is quite sensitive: if I don't inform it that you are accompanied by a Holy Roller, the alarm will go off in-
cessantly."

"I see."

"Would you like to see your suite now?"

"Not just yet." He tossed a disk on the desk. "Bill
it to that account."

"Of course, sir."

Nighthawk leaned down and picked up the
Roller. It made no attempt to elude him, and in fact
began purring louder than before as he stroked it absently with his hand.

*You'd have blown it away, wouldn't you,
Widowmaker?*

"Well, it's nice to find *something* that likes me,"
he said softly. "Maybe I'll let it stick around for a
while."

He placed it back on the floor and walked
through the lobby into the small restaurant. He found
a small table, sat down, pressed his thumb against the
scanner until it identified him and verified his credit,
and read through the menu, touching his thumb to
those items he wanted. He ordered coffee and a roll
for himself, and a small bowl of milk for the Roller.
When the robot trolley arrived, he took his food from
it and placed the bowl on the floor.

The Roller approached it, circled it warily, and finally backed away, rubbing against Nighthawk's boot
and purring loudly. Nighthawk reached down and
gently pushed it toward the bowl. It emitted a piercing
high-pitched whistle, bounced over the bowl, made a
semicircular return to Nighthawk, and was soon rubbing up against his boot again.

"All right, have it your way," said Nighthawk,
picking up the bowl and placing it on the table.

Suddenly the Roller started bouncing, gently at first, then higher and higher until it reached table height. One more bounce, and it landed gently atop the table and rolled to a spot just opposite the milk. It had no visible sensory organs, but Nighthawk would have sworn it was staring suspiciously at the bowl.

He finished his coffee and offered to show the empty cup to the Roller, which raced to the far side of the restaurant, then shyly returned to the table and lay up against his boot. He ordered another coffee, remained where he was for perhaps ten minutes, then walked out into the lobby.

"You left before I could tell you the number of your suite," announced the alien clerk. "It is three-zero-two-B, and it has been adjusted to recognize your voiceprint, thumbprint, or retinagram."

"Thank you, but I think I'll stay down here."

"Why? Nothing ever happens down here. In your room there are video entertainments, a liquor cabinet, an Imaginarium, and . . ."

"It'll give me something to look forward to."

The alien simply stared at him, as if it realized it was never going to comprehend this species into whose company Fate had thrust it.

Nighthawk walked over to a comfortable-looking chair that floated a few inches above the floor and sat down. He crossed his legs, and the Roller hopped onto the toe of his boot and remained there.

"Slow spin," he commanded, and the chair began spinning very gently in a circle. It didn't move fast enough to make him dizzy, and it allowed him to see the entire lobby in a matter of seconds without having to move or draw attention to himself.

A pair of women entered the hotel a few minutes later and went straight through to the airlift. A miner emerged from the restaurant, wearing his spotless smock, ready to direct his robots in the day's search for Aladdin's remaining riches.

Then, perhaps two hours later, a short, burly man entered the hotel, sweating profusely. He looked around briefly, then walked directly to the desk.

"How may I help you, sir?" asked the alien.

"Got a hungry Three-forty-one Golden Streak," replied the man. "I need someone to tickle its pile."

"I assume you landed to the west of town, out on the savannah?"

"That's right."

"If you will give me your ship's registration number, I can have a skilled mechanic there in fifteen minutes."

"R-three-two-zero-one-TY-four-J" was the man's answer. He slapped a wad of credits on the desk. "And get him there in *ten* minutes."

"Yes, sir!" said the alien, pocketing the money. He cast a map of the Tradertown on his computer's holoscreen, highlighted the most likely places the mechanic might be, and directed the computer to begin establishing vidphone connections to each location.

Nighthawk got out of his chair and approached the man. "Buy you a drink while you're waiting?"

"Sounds good to me," said the man. "Mighty neighborly of you."

Nighthawk turned to the clerk. "The bar's closed," he said.

"Oh, no, sir," replied the alien. "The bar is open. It just doesn't have any customers."

Nighthawk handed a few bills to the alien. "The bar is closed," he said again.

"Yes, sir. The bar is closed."

Nighthawk accompanied the man to the bar,

which was situated across the lobby from the restaurant. Like the rest of the hotel, it showed the influence of too many owners. Holographs of human and alien athletes mingled with paintings of nudes, a huge tank of alien fish, and a pair of Imaginarium games.

"What'll it be?" asked Nighthawk.

"Hot, dry day out. Anything that'll kill my thirst."

"You ought to be a little more careful how you say that," answered Nighthawk. "Someone could make the case that a bullet'll kill your thirst about as well as anything."

"A point well taken," said the man. "I'll have a beer."

"Let's make it two," said Nighthawk, punching the order into the computer. "By the way," he added, extending his hand, "my name's Jefferson Nighthawk."

"A proud name, that," said the man, accepting his hand.

"You've heard it before?"

"I think everyone's heard it before. Are you a relation, or just a pretender to the throne?"

"A little of each. And you are . . . ?"

"You know damned well who I am, Jefferson Nighthawk," said Father Christmas. "You weren't sitting in that lobby, carrying a small arsenal, just for the hell of it, and I didn't stop on Aladdin just to satisfy my thirst. You were waiting for me. Eventually you'll get around to telling me why. In the meantime, I propose to enjoy my beer."

"This world is under the protection of the Marquis of Queensbury," said Nighthawk. "He has no desire to hinder you in your flight from the police."

"That's right thoughtful of him."

"He asks only that you acknowledge that Aladdin belongs to him . . ."

"Gladly done."

". . . and that you pay him a small tribute for allowing you to refuel here."

"*How* small a tribute?"

"Half," said Nighthawk.

Father Christmas threw back his head and laughed. "Do you know what I have in my hold?"

"Yes, I do."

"And the Marquis thinks I'm going to give him the equivalent of twenty million credits just for letting me replenish my atomic pile?"

"He *hopes* you will," said Nighthawk.

"Well, he can hope. I take it you're the alternative?"

"That's right."

The two beers arrived, and each man took one.

"Well, if you're half as good as your namesake, you're twice as good as me. I freely admit it. So why don't we put off the shooting and talk a little business first?"

"That's what I thought we were doing."

"No," answered Father Christmas. "We were talking threats and extortion and the Marquis. Let's just you and me talk some business. Okay by you?"

Nighthawk sipped his beer and considered the older man's offer. Finally he nodded his agreement. "It doesn't cost anything to listen."

"By the way, what's that . . . uh . . . *thing* on your knee?"

"You should approve," said Nighthawk. "It's called a Holy Roller."

"What does it do?"

"Not much that I've been able to tell."

"That makes it holy, all right."

"I take it you're not enamored of religion," said Nighthawk.

"Yeah, that's a pretty fair assessment of the situation."

"Have you always hated churches?"

"Fact of the matter is that I used to be a minister," said Father Christmas with a grin. "Spent sixteen years saving souls, worshiping God, and avoiding the temptations of the flesh. You'd have been proud of me; I was what every mother wants her boy to grow up to be."

"So what happened?"

"There was a young man in our church. Looked a lot like you, though he was no killer. Still, he got arrested for raping and killing a pair of sisters in the congregation. A lot of the evidence pointed to him, but he swore to me on his Bible that he was innocent, and I believed him. So I did a little digging, and I found out that a surgeon, one of our wealthiest and most respected members, had actually committed the crime. Problem is, I didn't have any proof that would hold up in a court of law."

Father Christmas paused long enough to drain his beer glass. "So I figured, well, maybe I couldn't prove he was guilty to a court's satisfaction, but if I turned over all the facts to a good lawyer, he could at least give a jury a reasonable doubt that the young man had killed the girls."

"Did it work?"

"Never got a chance to. Next day my superiors contacted me and told me to tend to the spiritual and leave the temporal to those whose domain it was. The bishop explained to me that if we dragged the surgeon's name through the muck, he'd stop making generous donations to the church. Others pointed out that the young man had been arrested for robbery a few years earlier, and his loss wouldn't mean much. Then, when they couldn't scare me off, the surgeon hired the most expensive lawyer on the planet, and within two days they'd filed fifteen motions against *me*. I couldn't talk about this, I couldn't do that, I couldn't appear here, I couldn't offer an opinion on such and so. They really tied me up, let me tell you."

"Sounds like it," Nighthawk agreed.

"I went to the head of my church, back on Earth itself, and explained the situation. He promised to help me, and I went home—but when my ship landed, I found that his notion of helping was to transfer me to the Rim. And through a friend I had in his office, I learned that the surgeon had made a handsome donation to the church less than an hour before my transfer orders were written."

"So what did you do?" asked Nighthawk.

"I bought a laser pistol and burnt a hole in the middle of the surgeon's chest. Then I killed my superior, broke into jail and let the young man loose, took every credit from every bank account the church possessed, plundered half a dozen churches on Earth, and declared war on all churches from that day forward. It's my experience that they're all a bunch of money-grubbing hypocrites who deserve any misfortune I visit upon them."

"Why the name?"

"Father Christmas?" He smiled. "I declared my war on December twenty-fifty on Earth's calendar."

"So what?"

"Once upon a time, before we went to the Galactic Standard calendar, that was the date on which they celebrated Christmas." He paused. "I've been Father Christmas for fourteen years now. Never killed anyone who wasn't associated with a church, never robbed anything that wasn't owned by a church. You've got no argument with me, Nighthawk."

"Nobody's arguing."

"You're trying to exact tribute," said Father Christmas. "That's got a religious feel to it."

"I have a feeling anything you don't like has a religious feel to it."

"You put your finger on it, all right," said Father Christmas with a smile. "The Marquis wants half of what I have in my hold, right?"

"Right."

"So how much of that will he give to you?"

Nighthawk shrugged. "I don't know. Probably nothing."

"Probably, my ass," retorted Father Christmas. "You *know* you'll never see a credit of it."

"Okay, I'll never see a credit of it."

"Let me leave in peace and I'll give you ten percent. You won't even have to report it to him. Just tell him I never set down on Aladdin."

"He'll know you did."

"Tell him any damned thing you please," said Father Christmas irritably. "Do you know how much ten percent of what I'm carrying comes to?"

"A lot."

"You bet your ass!" he said emphatically. "So do we have a deal?"

"He'd know."

"All right, then. Come to work for me, and it'll be a down payment."

"Robbing churches and killing ministers?"

"And priests," added Father Christmas. "I wouldn't want it said that I was bigoted."

"God's not my enemy."

"He's everyone's enemy!" snapped Father Christmas, his eyes glowing with a private passion. "It's just that most people live their lives without knowing it."

Nighthawk shook his head. "Your god is a biblical deity with a long flowing white beard. I've *met* mine. He wears a lab coat and has a neatly trimmed brown beard . . . and I don't have any desire to kill him. I'm after the devil."

"How will you spot your devil?" asked Father Christmas. "If he doesn't have horns and a tail, what does he look like?"

"Just like me," said Nighthawk. He paused thoughtfully. "Have you got any help on that ship of yours?"

"No."

"You sure?"

"I never plan to work alone," admitted Father Christmas, "but that's the way it usually ends up."

"They desert you?"

"Or I desert them. It depends on the circumstances."

"Then why should I even consider working for you?" asked Nighthawk.

"I'm offering to pay you so much I'd *have* to keep you around. Couldn't let that kind of money loose in the galaxy; some of it might end up in a church."

The Holy Roller somehow bounced and rolled up to Nighthawk's shoulder and perched there, purring gently. He reached up and rubbed it gently. "I'm not going to come to work for you," he said after a moment's consideration, "but I'll tell you what I *am* going to do: I'm giving you a pass."

"You mean I'm free to get my fuel and leave?"

"That's right."

"Why?"

"Maybe I like meeting a dedicated man, and I don't much care what he's dedicated to."

"Maybe, but I doubt it," said Father Christmas. "As you yourself pointed out, the Marquis will know we've met. If you let me leave with my cargo intact, he'll probably kill you."

"He'll try, anyway," agreed Nighthawk.

"You *want* him to?"

She'll never come away with me if I call him out and murder him. But if I kill him in self-defense . . .

"I have my reasons."

"Pity you won't come with me," said Father Christmas, extending his hand. "I could use a man like you."

As Nighthawk reached out and clasped the outlaw's hand in his own, the alien desk clerk approached them, a pistol in one hand and a miniaturized receiver in the other.

"I regret to inform you that the Marquis foresaw this possible turn of events and commissioned me to spy upon you and take the appropriate action if it became apparent that Mr. Nighthawk was going to ignore his duty."

Slowly, leisurely, it aimed the pistol between Nighthawk's eyes. It was only a fraction of a second from squeezing the trigger when the Holy Roller went berserk.

Chapter 13

♦ ♦ ♦ ♦ ♦ ♦ ♦

At first Nighthawk thought it was simply a shrill whistle.
But it continued, and got louder, and higher, and
louder still, and suddenly he couldn't think clearly. He
doubled over and clasped his hands to his ears. Father
Christmas fell out of his chair and rolled on the floor,
also holding his ears. The alien fired its pistol, but it
was in such sense-destroying agony that the laser
beams burned two holes in the ceiling before the gun
fell to the floor. The alien began shrieking. Droplets of
blood appeared in its ears and nostrils, and soon became gushing streams. Still the Holy Roller's whistle
continued.

Nighthawk realized through a haze of pain that
the Roller was actually able to direct the force of its
whistling—that as painful as it was, he and Father
Christmas were not bearing the brunt of it. Glasses

near the alien began shattering, bottles burst; the alien kept screaming and bleeding, and finally collapsed in a heap on the floor. Instantly the Holy Roller went back to purring and rubbing up against Nighthawk.

"That's some pet you've got there," said Father Christmas groggily, rising to one knee and staring at the Roller. "It sure packs a wallop."

"It does, doesn't it?" said Nighthawk, still trying to focus his eyes.

He waited until all his senses were working properly again, then got up, walked over, and examined the alien. It was dead.

"That gonna get you in a mess of trouble with the authorities?" asked Father Christmas.

"It was probably the closest thing to an authority this world had," said Nighthawk, gesturing toward the dead alien.

Suddenly two servomechs entered the room.

"Clean up the broken glass," ordered Nighthawk. "Leave the body alone until I tell you what to do with it."

They immediately went to work straightening up the room, with special attention to the shards of glass.

"Well," said Father Christmas, "it's obvious that the Marquis doesn't put a lot of trust in you, and when his stooge doesn't report back, he's going to figure out that you killed it."

"I didn't; the Holy Roller did."

"Same difference. Who do you think he's going to blame—you or an alien animal that looks like a kid's doll and purrs all the time?" Father Christmas smiled. "If it was me, I'd pack my belongings right quick and start considering finding employment elsewhere. *I'll* still take you on, of course, but I have a feeling not too many other people in this section of the Frontier will once word gets out that the Marquis is looking for you."

"He won't have far to look," answered Night-hawk. "I'm going back to Tundra."

"Without any part of my cargo?"

"I told you—you're free to go."

"But the situation has changed," noted Father Christmas. "Now you've got a dead spy on your hands."

"I'll say you killed it."

"And you just stood by while I walked away?" asked Father Christmas.

The Holy Roller began bouncing again, while still purring, and finally bounced high enough to settle on Nighthawk's shoulder. He reached over and petted it without thinking, and the fluffball began purring so loudly that it sounded like an engine.

"You have a point," admitted Nighthawk. "I suppose I'll just have to tell him the truth."

"Thereby guaranteeing that he kills you."

"Guaranteeing that he'll *try*, anyway. It's a little sooner than I'd anticipated, but it was bound to happen. It might as well be now." The servomechs had finished sucking up the glass shards and now approached him for more orders. "Take the body to its office, lock the doors, and wait there for further orders," said Nighthawk. The machines left the bar, returned a moment later with a cart, placed the alien onto it, and took it away.

"None of this is necessary," said Father Christmas. "Just come away with me and forget about the Marquis."

"It's not the Marquis I can't forget," replied Nighthawk wryly. "He's just an obstacle."

"So it's a woman!" said Father Christmas with a grin. "But then, it always is at your age."

"It's a woman," admitted Nighthawk.

"She belongs to him?"

"People shouldn't belong to anybody."

"Absolutely," agreed Father Christmas. "It's against all the laws of God and man." He looked sharply at Nighthawk. "And you'd like her to belong to you."

Nighthawk nodded. "In a manner of speaking."

"So you need an excuse to kill the Marquis."

"Right. But . . ."

"But?"

"But he's been decent to me. He made me his second-in-command, he's trusted me . . ."

"He didn't trust you to kill me, did he?" noted Father Christmas. "If he had, we wouldn't have a dead alien on our hands."

"That's true," said Nighthawk, frowning. "But he knows what I am, and it doesn't bother him. He treats me like anyone else."

"You look like anyone else to me," said Father Christmas. "What are you?"

"I'm a clone."

"Ah! You are the Widowmaker reborn, risen from the ashes."

"He's not dead."

"He must be. He'd be a hundred and fifty years old."

"He's been in the deep freeze for the past century."

"Let me think about this," said Father Christmas. "He's alive, but he's frozen. They spent a lot of money and took a lot of risks to make a clone. Why would he freeze himself? Probably a lot of reasons. Disease. An enemy he couldn't handle. He invested a bundle of money at a good return, and hopes to be worth billions when he wakes up." He paused, considering all the possibilities. "But if it wasn't an enemy, he could wake up now. He wouldn't need a clone. If it was money, he definitely wouldn't want the potential legal hassle of sharing it with a clone. But if it was a disease . . ." He frowned. "But why a clone?"

"Costs have gone up."

"Of course," said Father Christmas. "He's been paying for the deep freeze with interest from his investments. As expenses increased, they had to dip into capital, and suddenly they're facing a situation where he won't have enough money to *stay* frozen. So they created you. . . ." He frowned again. "But what are you doing, working for the Marquis? If it's money they need, you should be here on an assignment. Gun down some killer, collect the reward, and return to wherever they're keeping the original Widowmaker."

"I'm working on it. Kind of. Things have become very complicated."

"Will killing the Marquis make it easier for you? Is *he* the one you're after?"

"No. He knows who I'm after, but so far he hasn't been willing to tell me."

"I imagine he won't be very willing, and even less able, after you've killed him."

"I've thought about it," said Nighthawk. "I'll claim he was the man I was after, take the reward, and . . ." He paused, momentarily lost in thought.

"And send it back to the Widowmaker?" suggested Father Christmas.

"No. I'll take it back to Deluros myself."

"Deluros? That's halfway across the galaxy. Why not send it?"

"I've got to deliver it in person."

"Why?"

"Because I'm probably the only man alive who can kill him," answered Nighthawk.

"I thought you said he was sick."

"I don't know if I can handle him once he's healthy. He's a killer by choice; I'm one by necessity."

"Comes to the same thing in the end," said Father Christmas.

A middle-aged man, his luggage hanging from his shoulder by a strap, entered the lobby of the hotel. When no one came to greet him, he wandered over to the bar and froze when he saw the still-wet bloodstains on the floor. Nighthawk and Father Christmas stared coldly at him, and after a moment he retreated without a word, backing up until he careered off the front desk. Then he raced out the front door.

"Well, son," said Father Christmas, "I think we'd better take our leave of this place."

Nighthawk began walking toward the door. The Holy Roller chirped in surprise, then bounced down to the floor and positioned itself about eighteen inches away from Nighthawk's left boot.

"I have no reason to stay," Nighthawk said, walking around the bloodstains and out into the lobby. He turned to Father Christmas. "Where are you heading?"

Father Christmas shrugged. "I don't know. Might be interesting to see if there are any religious goods worth stealing from Tundra."

Nighthawk looked at him, surprised.

"I've taken a liking to you," continued Father Christmas. "And I never did have much use for the Marquis. We thieves are supposed to stick together, not extort each other when we stop for a little fuel."

"You have half a dozen police ships on your tail,"

noted Nighthawk. "They're only a few hours behind you."

"I'll transfer all my goods to *your* ship," said Father Christmas. "With our alien friend dead, I'm not likely to find someone to enrich my ship's pile in the next hour anyway. Let 'em do whatever they want to my ship."

"I don't want to be responsible for your loot," said Nighthawk.

"Nobody's asking you to," said Father Christmas. "In fact, I'd deeply resent it." He paused. "Time's running short. Can I use your ship or not?"

Nighthawk considered it for a moment, then nodded his head. "I'm taking the Roller, too."

"Can't say that I blame you. Damned thing's more effective than most weapons I could name."

"I wish I knew what it ate," said Nighthawk as he walked out the front door of the hotel. "I'd like to take some along."

"It doesn't seem to have a mouth," observed Father Christmas. "Why not assume that it ingests through osmosis? Give it nice things to rub against and it'll do just fine."

"What constitutes nice things?"

"You," suggested Father Christmas with a smile.

"I beg your pardon?"

"I've seen animals with no ingestion orifices on other worlds, a couple of 'em. They feed by osmosis. Figure this critter probably kills small animals by draining the life force from them. You're too big for it to hurt, so it feeds off your energy when it gets hungry, and keeps you alive for future meals by killing off your enemies."

"You might be right," said Nighthawk. He stared

down at the Roller. "But I liked it better when I thought it was protecting me because it cared for me."

"Maybe it does. I'm just guessing."

"I wonder if it'll even go into my ship," said Nighthawk. "Maybe it'll decide it would rather stay here."

"Not a chance," said Father Christmas.

"Why not?"

"If we were back in my preacher days, I'd say that the Holy Roller—especially with a name like that—is a sign from God."

"A sign?"

"That you're protected. If God hadn't supplied you with an alien entity that can't think and can't talk but nonetheless decided to attach itself to you, you'd be dead back there in the hotel. It means God had other plans for you."

"Like killing the Marquis?"

"Who knows?"

Or spending my life with the Pearl of Maracaibo?

"You're the preacher," said Nighthawk. "How will I know when I've accomplished what God had in mind for me?"

"Easy," answered Father Christmas. "Once you've done what you're supposed to do, your little fluffball here will stop protecting you."

As if to emphasize that it wasn't ready to part company yet, the Roller began purring loudly and bounced up to Nighthawk's shoulder again.

Chapter 14

♦ ♦ ♦ ♦ ♦ ♦ ♦

Lizard Malloy looked up from his game of solitaire and saw Nighthawk and Father Christmas approaching him.

"Welcome back," said the leather-skinned little man. "Who's your friend?"

"Call me Kris," said Father Christmas.

Malloy suddenly stared at the Holy Roller. "You know you're being followed by something round and yellow?"

"Yeah."

"I assume it's alive, but I can't see any eyes or ears or anything like that."

"It's alive," said Nighthawk. "Where's the Marquis?"

"It's pretty late," replied Malloy. "I think he and the Pearl have gone off to bed."

Nighthawk tensed, but made no reply.

"Well, I'd like a drink," said Father Christmas. "You mind if we join you?"

"Ask *him*," said Malloy, indicating Nighthawk. "He's the boss."

"Sit," said Nighthawk, pulling out a chair and seating himself. The Holy Roller chirped happily and bounced up to his shoulder, where it settled down to do some serious purring.

"What the hell *is* it?" asked Malloy.

"Just a pet."

"Looks harmless," offered Father Christmas, suppressing a smile.

"Absolutely," said Nighthawk.

Malloy looked at it suspiciously for a long moment, then shrugged.

"When can we figure on meeting the Marquis?" asked Father Christmas.

"You know him, Kris?" asked Malloy.

"I know *of* him," replied Father Christmas. "I'd like to meet him. And I have a feeling that it's reciprocal."

"Well, once his lady is bedded down for the night, he usually comes back here for a nightcap," offered Malloy. "Stick around awhile and you'll probably run into him, or vice versa."

"Sounds good to me," said Father Christmas.

"And he'll probably want a report from *you*," added Malloy to Nighthawk. "Did everything go smoothly?"

"In a manner of speaking."

"Did you get the money, or did you have to kill him?"

"I've got his entire haul in my cargo hold."

"Then you killed him?"

◆   ◆   ◆

"No."

Malloy looked puzzled. "I thought this Father Christmas was a big-time Bad Guy. What kind of crook gives you everything he's got without a fight?"

"One who wants to live to see the next morning," suggested Nighthawk.

"I happen to know Father Christmas intimately," added Father Christmas, "and I guarantee that he would do almost anything to avoid a physical conflict with young Nighthawk here. Or with the Marquis, for that matter."

"Too bad," said Malloy. "The name was so interesting, I kind of hoped a really interesting crook went with it."

"Oh, he's fascinating beyond belief," said Father Christmas. "I never tire of talking about him."

"Well, you'll have to fill me in on him, Kris," said Malloy. "Only later."

"I'm happy to do it right now."

"I don't think so," said Malloy, looking across the huge casino toward the large man who was approaching him. "Here comes our lord and master. It'll have to wait."

"That's the Marquis?"

"Big, ain't he?"

The Marquis of Queensbury strode up to the table. "Welcome, Widowmaker," he said. "I hear you had a little problem."

"No problem at all," answered Nighthawk.

"You shot the wrong man, you asshole!" bellowed the Marquis.

"I didn't shoot anyone—and it wasn't a man, it was an alien."

"All I know is that I told it to keep an eye on you, and suddenly it's dead and Father Christmas's ship is empty and you're sitting here with a stranger and some kind of idiot animal and telling me that everything is okay. So you'll have to excuse me if I seem a little out of sorts, but *I* don't think everything is okay."

"I've got Father Christmas's entire haul in my ship," said Nighthawk.

"Oh?" said the Marquis, genuinely surprised. "You killed him?"

"As a matter of fact, I didn't."

"You mean he just *let* you empty his ship and move all his cargo to yours?" asked the Marquis sardonically.

"No," said Nighthawk.

"I knew it."

"He helped me," continued Nighthawk.

The Marquis looked from Nighthawk to Father Christmas. Finally he turned to face the latter. "Father Christmas, I presume."

"You certainly do. Imagine trying to extort fifty percent for the privilege of refueling."

"What are you doing here?" demanded the Marquis.

"I wanted to see what kind of thief robs his fellow thieves," answered Father Christmas.

"You're looking at him," said the Marquis with no display of embarrassment. "And I'm looking at a man who robs the deeply religious. Which of us do you suppose has more demerits in the Book of Fate?"

"It'd be a close call," said Father Christmas.

"You'd win in a walk," said the Marquis firmly.

"I would, if it was written by the same hypocrites who wrote the Bible and the church services," agreed Father Christmas. "Fortunately, they don't speak for God."

"And you do?"

"God doesn't need *my* help. I'm just a stopgap, until He Himself razes the temples to the ground."

"Temples? I thought you robbed churches."

"A poetic flourish," replied Father Christmas. "Actually, I rob any religious institution I come across."

"I know. And now you've presented me with a serious ethical problem," said the Marquis.

"I have?"

The Marquis nodded. "I've never stopped you from practicing your profession. You've robbed churches on *my* world, and I've never lifted a finger against you. But now you've taken advantage of my hospitality on Aladdin without paying for it, and one of my most trusted employees is dead. Hell, for all I know, you've corrupted the Widowmaker here." He uttered a mock-theatrical sigh. "What am I to do with you, Father Christmas?"

"Well, the way I see it, you have three choices," answered Father Christmas. "First, you can kill me. That would unquestionably make you feel better—but I suppose it's only fair to tell you that I rigged the cargo hold on Nighthawk's ship, and if you try to remove any of my treasure without knowing the proper codes, you'll blow up the ship and everything in it. Second, you can let me go, but I don't *want* to go, and I probably wouldn't avail myself of the opportunity."

The Marquis stared thoughtfully at him, more amused than outraged.

"And third?"

"Third, you can use your brain and offer to become my partner. There are thousands of churches on the Frontier, millions back in the Oligarchy. We could die of old age before we've plundered two percent of them."

"Why should I want to rob churches?" asked the Marquis.

"Because you're a thoroughly corrupt man, and there's a fortune to be made," answered Father Christmas.

"I rule eleven worlds already, and I influence twenty more," said the Marquis. "That's thirty-one worlds under my control. Why should I need a partner?"

"Because you want what every corrupt man wants."

"And what is that?" asked the Marquis.

"More," said Father Christmas.

"True," admitted the Marquis. "But if robbing churches won't make me any less corrupt, then I'll *always* want more."

"You always will," agreed Father Christmas. "That's why men like us never retire."

"And you only rob churches, right?"

"Who else forgives you for your misdeeds and prays for your soul?"

"Do I detect a note of cynicism?" asked the Marquis with a grin.

"Absolutely not," said Father Christmas earnestly. "Back on Earth—and I have plundered some of its finest churches, including Notre Dame and the Vatican—there is an insect called the ant. It lives in colonies, and is very industrious. It builds small mounds and creates incredibly complex passageways and food chambers and nurseries just beneath the surface. It takes days, sometimes weeks, to create these anthills . . . and yet you can destroy them in seconds, with the toe of your boot. And do you know what the ants do then?"

"Attack you?"

"No," answered Father Christmas. "They go right back to work rebuilding the mound."

"And you're saying churches are like anthills?"

"Only in this respect: They don't seek revenge once you've plundered them. They rebuild with all the industry of ants. It is counter to their philosophy to blame the thief. They prefer to consider me an agent of God, Who for reasons unknown to them is punishing them. It would make much more sense to think of me as the devil incarnate, but they don't really want to believe in a devil. It's easier to blame God, and hence their own sinful lives, for what I do without conscience or ethical consideration. And when disaster—meaning myself—strikes, they go about their business like the ants, rebuilding so that I can plunder them again."

Suddenly a huge smile spread across the Marquis' face. "I like you!" he exclaimed.

"Why shouldn't you?" asked Father Christmas. "I'm very likable."

"I think we can reach an agreement," continued the Marquis.

"Give me safe passage and asylum and I'll give you twenty percent," said Father Christmas.

The Marquis shoved Malloy out of his chair and sat down on it. "Take a walk," he said. "We're about to talk business."

Malloy, obviously feeling insulted, got up from the floor and left.

The Marquis turned back to Father Christmas. "Twenty percent isn't even worth talking about," he said. "Now, here's *my* proposal, my friend. You tell me what worlds you plan to hit. I'll supply you with all the firepower you need, and I'll give you safe haven on any world within my sphere of influence, for, shall we say, half?"

"I thought half was your criminal extortion rate, not your very best offer to possible partners," said Father Christmas. "I'll agree to it for, shall we say, a quarter?"

The Marquis turned to Nighthawk. "You brought back a good man, Jefferson Nighthawk. I *really* like him." He stared at Father Christmas. "In fact, I like you so much I'll do it for a third."

"Like me a little less and take thirty percent," said Father Christmas with a grin.

"What the hell, why not?" said the Marquis, sticking out his huge hand and shaking Father Christmas's much smaller one. "You've got a deal."

"Well, it's nice to be in business with you," said Father Christmas. "I think this calls for a little celebration. I'll treat for a bottle of your finest Cygnian cognac."

"I'll go get some from the bar," said the Marquis, getting up.

The Marquis of Queensbury returned a moment later with the bottle and some oddly shaped glasses on a glowing tray. He opened the bottle with a flourish, and carelessly filled each of their glasses, splashing some of the expensive cognac onto the tray and table.

"To friendship, partnership, and success," he said in a loud voice.

"To friendship, partnership, and success," echoed Father Christmas.

"And to death," added Nighthawk.

"Death?" repeated the Marquis curiously.

"In our business, how else will you know you've succeeded?" asked Nighthawk.

"True," agreed the Marquis after a moment's thought. "To death."

"May it visit our enemies first, and ourselves not at all," intoned Father Christmas.

If I work it right, thought Nighthawk, *that toast may just come true.*

Chapter 15

• • • • • • •

❖

Nighthawk sat at the bar, next to Lizard Malloy, staring at the Pearl of Maracaibo in rapt fascination. His drink was untouched, and his thin cigar had gone out. The Holy Roller sat motionless on the bar, an inch from his left hand.

Father Christmas walked into the casino, spotted him, and walked over. He looked up at the undulating, nearly nude blue-skinned girl with a bored expression, ordered a drink, and turned to Nighthawk.

"Close your mouth," he said. "You never know what might fly into it."

"Shut up," said Nighthawk, never taking his eyes off the dancing girl.

"Just trying to be helpful," said Father Christmas with a shrug. He nodded a greeting to Malloy, waited for his drink to arrive, took a sip, and reached out to pet the Roller. It allowed him to touch it, but displayed neither interest nor pleasure, refusing to purr or move closer.

Finally the performance was over and Melisande vanished backstage.

"Never interrupt me when I'm watching her," said Nighthawk, finally turning to Father Christmas.

"She won't vanish if you take the time to say hello to a friend," replied Father Christmas. He got to his feet. "Come on over to a booth. It's more comfortable, and I'm an old man with all kinds of aches and pains."

Nighthawk and Malloy picked up their drinks and followed him. The Roller chirped twice, then bounced to the floor and soon caught up with them. When they reached a booth and sat down, it came to rest on the toe of Nighthawk's boot.

"You spend a lot of time watching her," noted Father Christmas.

"What's it to you?"

"He's in love," said Malloy with a smirk.

"Have either of you got anything useful to say?" demanded Nighthawk irritably.

"As a matter of fact, I have," replied Father Christmas. "You know, you'd be immature even if you were as old as you look—and I happen to know you're a good deal younger than that."

"Get to the point."

"The point, my young friend, is that you're in the throes of first love. You're not going to want to hear this, but trust me: You'll get over it."

"I don't want to get over it."

Malloy grinned. "They never do."

"Now, I know you won't believe this," said Father

Christmas, "but girls like her are a credit a crate. Any Tradertown has a hundred just like her."

"There's no one like her!" snapped Nighthawk.

"She's the two T's, kid—trouble and trash."

"Be careful what you say," replied Nighthawk ominously. "You may be a friend, but there's a limit to what I'll let even a friend say about her."

"Listen to him," urged Malloy, enjoying Nighthawk's discomfort. "You don't know it yet, but there are a lot of women who look even better."

"And a handful who are even less trustworthy," added Father Christmas.

"What do you mean—less trustworthy?"

"I've seen her type," said Father Christmas. "They're drawn to power the way you're drawn to a good-looking girl."

"So I'll prove I'm more powerful than *he* is."

"You don't understand. I said *power*, not physical prowess. If it's not the Marquis, it'll be some millionaire or politician or something. Never an outsider like you or me."

"You're wrong," said Nighthawk stubbornly. "I can *make* her care for me."

"How? By killing her protector?"

"Oh, she'd love that," said Malloy sardonically.

"If it's a protector she wants, *I* can protect her better than *he* can."

"From outlaws, yes. From economic recessions, I doubt it." Father Christmas paused. "Let her go, Jefferson. All she is, all she'll ever be, is bad news. Believe me; I'm not an involved party."

"You don't understand," said Nighthawk. "I love her."

"You've been alive four months, and you've

found the only woman in the galaxy that you can love?" chuckled Malloy.

"Doesn't that seem just a little far-fetched, even to you?" added Father Christmas.

"She's what I want."

"I know. I'm just suggesting that *you* are not what *she* wants."

"What do either of you know about it?" demanded Nighthawk. "He's a repulsive little freak, and you're a wrinkled old man! When did you ever love anyone?"

"You think being old and gray-haired and wrinkled stops you from falling in love?" asked Father Christmas with a chuckle. "Just because you don't appeal to nubile twenty-year-old women anymore doesn't mean *they* don't appeal to *you*." He paused. "But if age has made you any wiser, you realize that there's a big difference between *wanting* them, which is acceptable, and *loving* them, which must be done with judgment and discretion. Especially when you have as many enemies as I do, or as you will if you live to be my age."

"Did you come all the way over here from the hotel just to give me a lecture on women?"

"No, though it's obvious you need one," said Father Christmas. He paused and stared at Malloy. "I think it's time we considered our next career move."

Nighthawk turned to Malloy. "Go to the bar. The drink's on me."

"Damn it!" snapped Malloy. "I'm sick of everyone always trying to get rid of me!"

"I've got business to discuss with Father Christmas," said Nighthawk.

"You think this place isn't wired for sight and sound?" demanded Malloy. "Or that it's not making a permanent record of everything you say so that the Marquis can watch and listen to it later?"

"Go away."

"Some fucking friend you are!" muttered Malloy.

Nighthawk stared at him coldly. "You are no longer under my protection. We owe each other nothing from this moment on."

"Big deal! He gives me back my life. Hallelujah." Malloy glared at him. "I don't *want* the goddamned thing back! As long as it belonged to you, people left me alone and I got to stay alive. If word gets out that I'm not beholden to you anymore, my life expectancy is about three hours, tops."

"Just go away," said Nighthawk. "You make my head hurt with all your convoluted reasoning."

"But am I still under your protection?" persisted Malloy, holding his ground.

"Whatever makes you happy."

"*That* does."

"Fine," said Nighthawk. "Now beat it."

"But if I belong to you, you shouldn't have any secrets from me."

Nighthawk whipped out a pistol and pointed it at the tip of Malloy's leathery nose.

"See?" said Malloy accusingly. "See? I *knew* you replaced me with the Roller!"

"The Roller always keeps its mouth shut and doesn't give me unwanted advice," said Nighthawk. "That's more than I can say for a certain half-pint gambler."

"All right, I'm going, I'm going!" said Malloy bitterly. "But someday you'll wish you'd been nicer to me."

"I saved your life," responded Nighthawk. "How much nicer do I have to be?"

"You'll see," muttered Malloy, stalking off to the bar.

"He's right, you know," said Father Christmas.

"You told me to dump *her*," said Nighthawk irritably. "Now you're going to tell me to be nice to *him*?"

"No," answered Father Christmas. "I mean that he's almost certainly right about the place being wired."

"Do you want to go outside and talk?"

Father Christmas considered it for a moment, then shook his head. "No. I think anything we have to say can be said in front of the Marquis."

"Okay," said Nighthawk. "Shoot."

"We have to have a serious discussion about the future, Jefferson," said the older man.

"I thought we had one on the way back from Aladdin."

"That was then, this is now."

"What's changed?" asked Nighthawk.

"I've got a bed feeling," replied Father Christmas. "The Marquis was too willing to forgive you for not doing what he sent you to do."

"I brought you back," said Nighthawk. "That was even better."

"I know you have your whole life ahead of you, but trust me: Outlaws live for the moment. He might ultimately be willing to deal with me, but it doesn't make sense that he wouldn't try to grab the gold and the Moritas first. That's hardly the mark of a criminal kingpin. It makes sense for me to deal with him; it makes less for *him* to deal with *me*."

"But you had the hatch rigged."

"That's another thing," continued Father Christmas. "He can't stay in power long if he lets people challenge his authority like that. Hell, it practically invites his henchmen to protect what they've stolen by booby-trapping the loot and then renegotiating terms with him. *I* would never allow it; neither should *he.*"

"But he did."

"That's what makes me very uneasy."

"What do you think his motive is?"

"I can't spot it. Except I know that it has nothing to do with me."

"Why not?" asked Nighthawk.

"Because my plans were fixed before I met him, and I haven't changed them one iota."

"If it has nothing to do with you, then who—?"

"You, of course," said Father Christmas. "You disobeyed his orders, and if you didn't kill his spy, you at least didn't go out of your way to save it. So I have to ask myself: Why are you still alive? He's not afraid of you; a man like the Marquis can snuff you out in an instant. He's not being altruistic, because altruism is totally alien to a man like that. He hasn't forgiven your infraction; he's chosen to ignore it. Why? Why is a four-month-old clone suddenly his second-in-command?"

Nighthawk considered what the older man had said. "I don't know," he admitted at last.

"Neither do I," said Father Christmas. "But there *must* be a reason." He paused. "Why are you here?"

"I told you."

"All right, it's part of a mission. Who sent you here?"

"Marcus Dinnisen—the Widowmaker's lawyer, back on Deluros VIII," answered Nighthawk.

"He sent you to Tundra?"

"No. He sent me to the Inner Frontier. A man named Hernandez, the chief of security on Solio II, sent me here."

"What's his connection to you?"

"He's the one who arranged for me to be created."

"Interesting."

"Is it?"

"And frustrating," said Father Christmas. "We don't know enough. Or if we do, I can't see it yet."

"You're the guy with the bad feeling," answered Nighthawk. "I still don't know what's got you so bothered."

"There's something going on here, something that reaches at least to Solio II, and maybe all the way back to Deluros," said Father Christmas. "I think we'd be well advised to get the hell out while the getting's good. There are too many things going on here that I don't like."

Nighthawk looked around, his gaze coming to rest on Malloy, who sat at the bar, and he remembered what the leathery little man had said. "Are you sure you want to be saying all this where the Marquis can probably overhear you?"

"What difference does it make?" shot back Father Christmas. "If you agree to come with me, we'll be out of here before he can stop us. If you stay here, he'll know that my best arguments couldn't make you leave him."

"What if *I* stay and *you* leave?" asked Nighthawk. "Won't that bother him?"

"Probably. That's why it won't happen."

"I don't follow you."

"Malloy is no fool," said Father Christmas. "The only thing keeping him alive is you. I plan to put myself under your protection as well."

"That's the silliest thing I ever heard," said Nighthawk. "Why would you do something like that?"

"It's a fair trade," said Father Christmas. "You're the one person on this world who can protect me and my treasure from the Marquis. And I'm the only person on this world who's been honest with you, who's tried to talk you out of doing stupid things, and who's stuck with you even when you did them. You are friendless and alone in the galaxy. I aim to be your friend, and I'll be everything a friend should be—but my price is high: my life. You're in charge of safeguarding it." He extended his hand. "Have we got a deal?"

"You ask a lot for your friendship," said Nighthawk, staring at his hand.

"If you get a better offer, take it."

Nighthawk stared for another moment, then reached out and took Father Christmas's hand.

"Good!" said the older man. "Now we stay together or leave together."

"I'm not going anywhere," said Nighthawk. "Not until *she* goes."

"Then maybe we'll take her."

"Kidnap her? The Marquis will have two hundred men after us before we're out of the system."

"You overestimate the depth of his feelings for anyone besides himself," replied Father Christmas. "He didn't get to be who he is by developing a deep and lasting commitment to every nightclub dancer who comes along." He paused thoughtfully. "Still, it would be such a public humiliation that he'd have to do something." He paused. "No, it'd probably be better to talk everyone into it."

"Everyone?"

"Even the Marquis."

"What kind of prize could get both him and her to come along?" asked Nighthawk.

"The biggest."

◆ ◆ ◆

"Deluros VIII?"

Father Christmas nodded. "The capital world of the race of Man."

"But it's half a galaxy away."

"It's got a lot of churches—and it's got the Widowmaker."

"So how do we convince them to come along?"

"We find something he wants," said Father Christmas. "Something he can't say no to."

"Like what?"

"I've got an idea," said Father Christmas. "But I need to work on it for a while."

"He knows you're trying to come up with a reason," noted Nighthawk. "Or he soon will."

"If it's a good enough reason, he'll come anyway," answered Father Christmas.

"And if it's not?"

"Then," said the old man grimly, "you'd better be prepared to prove your friendship."

Chapter 16

• • • • • • •

❖

Father Christmas entered the casino, spotted Nighthawk sitting alone at a table, walked over, and told him to don his spacesuit.

"What's the problem?"

"You look like you need some exercise," said the older man. "A walk'll do you good."

"I'm comfortable here."

"Do it anyway."

Nighthawk stared at him curiously for a moment, then shrugged, went to the airlock, and climbed into his suit. Then he and Father Christmas walked out into the frozen streets. A few robots were out clearing the snow from the streets. Here and there men would rush swiftly and silently from one building to another; other than that, the city might have been deserted.

What frequency? Nighthawk mouthed the words.

Father Christmas signaled "4748" with his fingers.

"All right," said Nighthawk, making the adjustment. "Can you hear me?"

"Yes. And nobody else can."

"Let me check that out," said Nighthawk. "I've got a pretty sophisticated radio unit. Talk, and don't say anything important."

"Lovely morning," said Father Christmas. "Reminds me of the winters back home when I was a boy."

"That's enough," said Nighthawk, scanning a panel on his radio pack. "No one's monitoring us."

"Actually," continued Father Christmas, "I grew up on a beautiful agricultural world, with waving rows of mutated wheat as far as the eye can see. I *hate* snow."

"If you brought me out there to talk about your childhood, I'm going back in," said Nighthawk.

"Actually, I brought you here to talk about Colonel James Hernandez."

"Hernandez?" repeated Nighthawk. "What's all the secrecy about? You didn't mind being overheard three days ago."

"That was then, this is now."

"Okay," said Nighthawk. "What's Hernandez got to do with anything?"

"More than you imagine," answered Father Christmas. "Why do you think he sent you here?"

"To find out who killed Governor Trelaine and to bring him to justice one way or another."

"Bullshit."

"Yeah? What makes you think so?"

"He knows who killed Trelaine," said Father Christmas as they walked slowly across the frozen surface of Klondike.

"All right," said Nighthawk. "Who killed Trelaine?"

"The Marquis, of course."

"You're guessing."

"I don't guess, kid. I'm telling you, the Marquis is the man you're here to kill."

Nighthawk stared at him. "Before we go any further, suppose you tell me how you figured all this out?"

"I did just what you'd have done if you had a little more experience," answered Father Christmas. "Two days ago I paid a substantial fee to tie my personal computer into the Master Computer on Deluros VIII."

"And?"

"And I asked it to find out everything it could about the Marquis of Queensbury. It took this long because I couldn't supply it with a holograph or a retina ID, and we were only dealing in possibilities until last night. Then I managed to swipe a beer glass that still had his fingerprints on it."

"So what did the Master Computer say?" asked Nighthawk.

"His given name is Alberto da Silva. He had a couple of other names before he became the Marquis."

"Okay, he's had other names. so what?"

"He's also had other jobs," said Father Christmas. "The last one was working as a independent subcontractor for Colonel James Hernandez."

"An independent subcontractor?"

"He killed Hernandez's enemies, and in exchange Hernandez looked the other way when he plundered Solio II."

Nighthawk frowned. "That doesn't make any

sense," he said. "If Hernandez hired him to kill Trelaine, why does he want him dead now?"

"Now we come to theory instead of fact," said Father Christmas. "But bear with me. I think it makes sense."

"Go ahead," said Nighthawk.

Father Christmas looked intently into Nighthawk's eyes and began. "What if someone saw the Marquis pull the trigger? Whoever it was would be one of the leading citizens of Solio II—remember, though Trelaine was killed at the opera, he was there to make peace between opposing factions of his party—and of course this citizen immediately took steps to protect himself. He probably hired bodyguards, and instructed his computer to release the truth about the assassination to every news organization in the sector if anything happened to him."

"Okay," said Nighthawk. "I'll buy that. What else?"

"Now that our citizen feels safe, he approaches Hernandez and says, in essence, This was *your* guy who killed Trelaine. I think you're preparing to seize power on Solio II. Hernandez denies it, of course; what the hell else can he do?"

"So far so good," said Nighthawk. "Keep talking."

"Okay. The citizen says to Hernandez, *Prove* your innocence to me. Bring in the Marquis and I'll believe you were telling the truth; otherwise, you're on the hook as much as he is. And maybe he gives him a deadline: six Standard months, a year, whatever. Now, Hernandez can't just call the Marquis in and shoot him. The Marquis has got a reputation; if he brings him in too easily, he's still a suspect. So instead he hires a bounty hunter. And not just *any* bounty hunter, but the best who ever lived."

"There are a lot of good bounty hunters out here on the Frontier," said Nighthawk. "Why me?"

"Because he could count on you not to bring the Marquis in, but to *kill* him."

"But—"

"Think back to your meeting with Hernandez," said Father Christmas. "I'll bet he told you not to take any chances, to blow the Marquis away the first time you saw him."

"Something like that," admitted Nighthawk grudgingly.

"Don't you see?" said the older man. "He expressly asked for *you* because, unlike your namesake, you've had no experience. You don't understand nuances. Subtleties are lost on you. You could never have figured this scam out by yourself. The one thing you can do is kill, and that's exactly what Hernandez was counting on."

"But sooner or later I'd have figured it out," answered Nighthawk, "and then I'd be just as dangerous to Hernandez as the Marquis is."

"He probably figures the Marquis' men will kill you before you leave the planet, once you do what you were hired to do. And I'm sure he's turned his office into a death trap, just in case you manage to make it back there." Father Christmas paused for a long moment, then shrugged. "He doubtless intends for you to die here or on Solio. And if not . . ."

He let the sentence hang, unfinished, in the air.

"If not, he figures that they'll 'decommission' me back at Deluros?"

"You're the consummate killing machine, kid," said Father Christmas, "and once this job is done, you're beholden to no one. That makes you too dangerous to live."

Nighthawk stood, silent and motionless, for a long moment while he considered what the older man had said.

"Yeah, it makes sense," he replied in a cold, passionless voice.

"It's conjecture," said Father Christmas. "Maybe Deluros will strew your path with flowers and send you out on more assignments. Maybe the Marquis didn't pull the trigger. Maybe I'm wrong about everything"—he rubbed his stomach—"but down here in my gut, it *feels* right."

Nighthawk fought back his anger at the notion that he had been *used*. His face was totally expressionless, a mask that was the very last thing 300 young men had seen more than a century ago. "It *is* right," he said at last.

"So that leads to the question: What do we do next?"

"You're the deep thinker," answered Nighthawk. "What do you have in mind?"

"Same as before: We all go to Deluros VIII. I rob some churches, you kill the original Widowmaker, and the Marquis . . . well, I'm still working on that."

"I have an idea."

"Let's hear it," said the older man.

"What if there is one man in the Oligarchy's Intelligence arm who knows he was the assassin, one person Hernandez confided in. Wouldn't it make sense for the Marquis to want to dispose of anyone who could finger him?"

"He'd have to believe the man hadn't told anyone else yet," responded Father Christmas. "Even the Marquis wouldn't try to wipe out the entire Intelligence Department." He paused. "Still, why should he believe that?"

"Because a sweet-talking old bastard like you ought to be able to convince him of almost anything," said Nighthawk. He stared at the older man, trying to martial his arguments. "For example, I fought him to a draw the day I arrived; one of these days I'll be able to beat him, and he knows it. All you have to do is convince him that once I kill the Widowmaker, I'm a free agent and I don't give a damn what happens to him or Hernandez. At the same time, come up with a name from Deluros VIII—real or phony, it makes no difference—and convince him that if he kills that name, there's no longer any connection between him and Hernandez anywhere in the Oligarchy's files."

Father Christmas lowered his head in thought for a moment, then looked up.

"You know, that's not bad at all," he replied. "You're going to be damned frightening if they let you live another twenty years or so." He paused. "No wonder they still talk about the Widowmaker."

"I don't want to hear about him," said Nighthawk irritably. "He's just a frozen old man who's never going to wake up."

"He's you and you're him, whether you like it or not," said Father Christmas.

"I don't," said Nighthawk. "And if you say it again, you'll wish you hadn't."

"You got a lot of hang-ups for a four-month-old," muttered Father Christmas.

"Just remember what I said."

"I'll remember," said the older man. "But sometimes you make it very hard to be your friend."

"It's a lot harder to be my enemy."

"Let's hope so." Father Christmas turned back toward the casino. "Shall we go back, or have you got anything else to say that we don't want the Marquis to overhear?"

"No, I think that's pretty much everything." Suddenly Nighthawk stopped in his tracks. "Well, there *is* one more thing to consider."

"Yeah?"

Nighthawk nodded. "I see how we're going to get the Marquis' permission to leave, and how we're going to convince him to come with us. But . . ."

"But what?"

"After you rob your churches and I kill the Widowmaker, what do we *do* with him?"

"Well, that's pretty much up to you, isn't it?" said Father Christmas.

"Yeah," said Nighthawk thoughtfully. "Yeah, I suppose it is. And of course, if he doesn't come back, if he's killed while he's away on a job . . ."

"Don't even think about *her*," said Father Christmas. "You kill him, she'll be on her way so fast it'll make your head spin."

"I'll be in charge here. I'll have the power, *and* the ability to protect her. She'll stay."

"Not a chance."

"You'll see," said Nighthawk. "I'm young. If she sticks with me, I can get her anything she wants."

"Others can get it faster," replied Father Christmas. "Some of them already have it. She's the type who can sniff them out from two thousand light-years away."

"Have you even spoken to her?" demanded Nighthawk heatedly. "What makes you think you know anything about her?"

"Experience."

"You don't have any experience with her, because there's never *been* anyone like her."

"Blue skin doesn't make her any different."

"It's not the skin," said Nighthawk. His voice lowered. "She's perfect."

"Son, take it from a minister," said Father Christmas. "Even God isn't perfect."

"What do you know about God *or* women?" demanded Nighthawk. "All you do is rob God's churches, and you're so old and wrinkled no woman would look at you."

"Kid, if I wasn't sure you'd blow me away, I'd show you just how fast I could get that dancing girl to go to bed with me." He sighed. "Let's skip it. We're agreed on what we have to do, right?"

"Right."

"Then let's get the show on the road."

He turned and began walking back to the casino.

Chapter 17

◆ ◆ ◆ ◆ ◆ ◆ ◆

◈

"So where is he?" demanded Nighthawk, *stalking angrily* through the control cabin of his ship. Father Christmas sat in a passenger seat, while the Holy Roller perched atop the navigational computer, purring softly to itself.

"He'll be here," said Father Christmas reassuringly.

"Are you *sure* he bought your story?"

"I'm sure."

"Then why isn't he here?"

"He's the Marquis of Queensbury, and he rules eleven worlds," answered Father Christmas easily. "He's allowed to be twenty minutes late. He knows you won't leave without him."

Nighthawk came to a stop and looked at Father Christmas. "What if he doesn't show? We're already committed to leaving. We'll look damned silly changing our minds just because he didn't come along."

"I don't know why old people, who have so much less time remaining to them, develop patience, while young men like you, with a century ahead of them, go a little crazy when they have to wait for anything."

"He believes someone in Intelligence can finger him, right?" said Nighthawk, ignoring Father Christmas's statement.

"Yes, he believes it."

"If *I* thought someone could put me out of business, or bring the authorities down on me, I'd be early, not late."

"Maybe that's why *he* runs the show, instead of someone like you," suggested Father Christmas. "Do you mind if I change the subject?"

"Talk about anything you damned well please," said Nighthawk irritably, as he recommenced his pacing.

"Fine. I will. Because you're worrying about the wrong thing. The Marquis will be here, never fear. What *you* should be thinking about is how you're going to kill the Widowmaker."

"Gun, knife, hands, what difference does it make?"

Father Christmas shook his head. "You don't follow me. If you can make it to the chamber where he's frozen, I'll grant you can kill him by any means you choose. But only the very, very wealthy can afford to be frozen. The Widowmaker was only a millionaire when he went in there, but he's lying side by side with billionaires, with people who created financial empires and have every intention of waking up and ruling them again at some time in the future. How do you plan to get past the kind of security they've paid for with those enormous annual fees?"

"I'll find a way."

"Have you considered that you might not even be able to get through Customs on Deluros VIII? All they really have to do is report the Widowmaker's passport missing. You'll give them an ID disk, it'll set off twenty alarms, they'll incarcerate you until someone who can identify Jefferson Nighthawk shows up—and you can bet your ass he'll show up with a gun."

"Why?" asked Nighthawk. "They don't know I'm coming to kill the Widowmaker."

"They don't have to know why you're coming," answered Father Christmas. "All they have to know is that they've created the deadliest killer in the galaxy and told him to go out to the Frontier. Suddenly he's disobeying their orders and coming to Deluros without giving them any prior notice. Losing control of their creation will scare 'em more than knowing you want to kill the Widowmaker."

"All right," said Nighthawk. "I'll start thinking about it." He paused. "*You're* wanted on dozens of planets. How do you get around it?"

Father Christmas smiled. "I never go back, so it's a moot point."

"But even when you go to a new planet, they must know who you are, and that you're wanted."

"I mostly stay on the Frontier, and most Frontier worlds don't have extradition treaties with the Oligarchy. Hell, most of 'em don't have any laws at all."

"Okay," said Nighthawk. "But now we're going to the capital world of the Oligarchy. So how will *you* get past Customs?"

"How many passports do you possess?" countered Father Christmas.

"One."

"Well, I've got fifteen," replied the older man with a triumphant smile, "each and every one able to pass a close inspection by a Customs computer. I use the one that fits the situation."

"Tools of the trade?" asked Nighthawk.

"Even the original Widowmaker must have had a handful of them," answered Father Christmas. "No sense announcing your presence when you're trying to sneak up on someone who doesn't know you're on his trail."

"I may need some myself," said Nighthawk thoughtfully. "Where do you get them?"

"There are forgers all over the galaxy," said Father Christmas. "After we're through with our business on Deluros, I'll introduce you to some of them."

"Some of whom?" said a familiar voice from the direction of the airlock, and they turned to see the Marquis of Queensbury, his arm around the Pearl of Maracaibo.

"What's *she* doing here?" asked Father Christmas.

"I never go anywhere without the necessities of life." He ran his fingers through her hair and down her neck to her breast, then leaned over and kissed her on the ear while she grinned at Nighthawk. "Hi, Jefferson," he said when he looked up again. "How's it going?"

Nighthawk realized that he'd been staring at the blue-skinned girl. He had no idea what his expression had become when the Marquis fondled and kissed her, but he realized there was enough tension in the air that the Roller had stopped purring. Suddenly he snapped to life.

"You're late," he said. "I wanted to leave half an hour ago."

"Your victim can wait," replied the Marquis easily. "He's past knowing what time it is."

"You should have said you'd be late," repeated Nighthawk. "It's only common courtesy."

"This is *my* world," answered the Marquis. "It obeys *my* laws." He looked into Nighthawk's eyes and smiled. "That means you were leaving half an hour too early."

Melisande laughed, her eyes never leaving Nighthawk's.

"All right," said Nighthawk. "Let's get going now, if it's all right with you."

"Just fine."

"It'll be a little cramped. I didn't know we were going to have another passenger."

"No problem," said the Marquis easily. "We only need three beds."

"I was referring to oxygen and meals."

"Then we'll put down on some world or other and get more when we need it."

"There's only room for three people on the bridge," said Nighthawk.

"That's not a problem," said the Marquis. "She and I will share the captain's cabin. You can bunk with the old man." Before Nighthawk could protest, he added, "Take her down there and show her around."

Nighthawk could smell her perfume as she passed him. There wasn't much room, and she had to turn sideways to enter the corridor that led to the sleeping cabins. She took a deep breath, and he couldn't help looking down her neckline. She grinned at him and undulated her way past him, then slowed her pace so he had trouble avoiding bumping up against her.

"You've gone too far," said Nighthawk a moment later, stopping by the door to his cabin. She turned back and managed to lean against his arm and shoulder while the door slid into the wall. "This is it," he said, taking a step into it while she followed.

"This is your cabin?"

"It *was* my cabin."

"It's more like a prison," she said, looking around. "Like the kind of place where you spend long, lonely nights." She turned to him. "Do you?"

"This is the closet," he continued, ordering a door to slide open.

"What's that?" she asked.

"What's what?"

"*That*," she repeated, pointing to the Holy Roller, which had followed them and now bounced up to Nighthawk's shoulder. "I've seen it near you when I was dancing. At first I thought it was some kind of toy, and then I realized it was actually alive. Is it a pet?"

"Kind of."

"It doesn't *do* much," she said. "Why do you keep it?"

"It loves me and it's loyal to me," answered Nighthawk. "That's more than I can say for any person I know."

"Let me see it," she said, approaching him and reaching out for the Roller.

The Roller tensed and stopped purring.

"That's not a very good idea," said Nighthawk, stroking the Roller as he felt it stiffening. It calmed instantly beneath his touch.

She pulled her hand back and glared at the Roller. "Who wants to touch such an ugly thing anyway?"

There was an awkward pause, and then Night-hawk spoke again. "Behind that door's the bathroom. It's got a dryshower and a chemical toilet."

"Maybe you'll come by later and scrub my back," she said, lowering herself to the bunk and stretching.

Nighthawk stalked out and returned to the control cabin.

"Welcome back," said the Marquis, who was now sitting in the captain's chair. "What kept you?"

"That's *my* chair," said Nighthawk.

"Not anymore."

"I own this ship."

"And I own *you*," said the Marquis. "Now sit down."

"I've got to lay in a course to Deluros," said Nighthawk.

"I've already done it. We'll be jumping to light speeds any second now." He turned to Father Christmas. "Well, old man, have you got your churches all picked out yet?"

"Sure do," said Father Christmas. "Just waiting to narrow 'em down to a reasonable number."

"I take it you've been studying them?"

"All my adult life," answered the older man. "There's a lot of gold in the churches of Olympus. I think I'll take some of it back with me."

"Olympus? What is that—a city?"

Father Christmas chuckled. "A continent."

"So who can know the geography of a thousand worlds?" said the Marquis with a shrug.

"Anyone who wants to get rich off 'em," replied Father Christmas, as the ship suddenly lurched and jumped to light speeds.

"Touché," laughed the Marquis. He turned to

Nighthawk. "What about you, Jefferson Nighthawk?" he asked with a certain smug amusement. "Do you plan to get rich on Deluros?"

"No," answered Nighthawk. "I plan to get free on Deluros."

"Free of what?"

"Of a lot of things."

"For instance?"

"Ghosts, mostly."

"Of men you killed?"

Nighthawk shook his head. "Of the man I was . . . or the man I was supposed to be."

"Not much profit in that," remarked the Marquis with a faint air of disapproval.

"More than you can imagine," said Nighthawk firmly.

The Marquis shrugged. "Whatever makes you happy." He glanced down the corridor toward Melisande's cabin, and added, "Within reason."

Nighthawk tensed again, and the Holy Roller reacted instantly. It stopped humming and began a very low whining sound. Nighthawk picked it up, cradled it in his arms, and stroked it gently.

"You ought to get rid of that thing," said the Marquis.

"I like it."

"As far as I can tell, it serves no useful purpose— and it wastes space."

"Not as much as Melisande."

"*She* has advantages that outweigh her disadvantages," said the Marquis.

Nighthawk forced himself to relax, muscle by muscle, and tried not to think of the blue-skinned woman stretched out on his bunk. Finally the Holy

Roller began purring again, and he realized that he had succeeded.

"You're going to have to learn to control that hot young blood," remarked the Marquis, who had been watching him closely. "And you're also going to have to learn who gives the orders around here."

"We're learning just as fast as we can," said Father Christmas, before Nighthawk could make a caustic reply.

"That's what I like to hear," replied the Marquis.

Melisande suddenly appeared in the corridor. "I'm hungry," she complained. "What have we got to eat?"

"Don't ask *me*," said Nighthawk coldly. "Ask the ship."

Nighthawk walked to the galley and ordered it to life. Suddenly it was awash with lights, and an illustrated menu appeared in midair, the three-dimensional images of the food rotating slowly before the ship's occupants.

"Is that really steak?" she asked.

"It's all soya product," answered Nighthawk. "But you won't be able to tell the difference."

"Sounds good to me," said the Marquis. "If it looks like steak and tastes like steak, who cares what it is?"

And if someone looks like the Widowmaker and thinks like him and kills like him, thought Nighthawk, *don't ever get him mad by taking over his ship and flaunting your woman in front of him.*

"What'll you have, my love?" asked the Marquis.

"Nothing," replied Melisande.

"You're sure?"

"I don't eat substitutes." She paused briefly. "Besides, what I want now isn't in the galley."

She sauntered down the corridor and gave the Marquis a sexy smile as she passed by the cabin door.

"You can wait for him in the control room," suggested Father Christmas as she reached the end of the corridor.

She walked slowly through the galley and came to a stop a few feet from Nighthawk.

"There are only three chairs," she noted.

"That's right," said Nighthawk.

She stared at his lap until he shifted uncomfortably on his chair, then turned around and returned to the galley, brushing against Nighthawk as she did so.

"By God, she looks good when she walks away!" said the Marquis enthusiastically. He got to his feet. "I think we'll retire to our room for a little while." He headed toward the captain's cabin.

Nighthawk watched them, his face expressionless, his body rigid. The Roller bounced back down to the floor and began whining softly. Suddenly he felt a heavy hand on his shoulder, and found that Father Christmas had walked over to him.

"Don't do anything foolish, son," said the older man.

"Am I supposed to let him fuck her on *my* bed and just sit by doing nothing?" demanded Nighthawk in strained tones.

"It's her choice."

"It's *not*! He'd kill her if she said no."

"I don't want to disillusion you," said Father Christmas, "but she probably hasn't said no since she was twelve."

"Shut up!" snapped Nighthawk, and the Roller, still whining ominously, jumped to his shoulder.

"I'm not the enemy," said Father Christmas, back-backing away and lowering his voice. "Try to remember that. I'm just trying to keep you alive."

"All right," said Nighthawk after a long moment. "We'll stick to the plan. He lives until you've robbed your church and I've killed the Widowmaker. But then . . ." He reached out and absently petted the Holy Roller, which twitched a couple of times then rubbed up against him.

"Just make sure you don't underestimate him," said Father Christmas.

"I can take him," said Nighthawk grimly.

"You sound awfully certain."

"I didn't ask to be the best killer in the galaxy," said Nighthawk. "But that's what they made me." Suddenly Melisande's moans of ecstasy could be heard through the closed door of the cabin. Nighthawk's face became even grimmer. "They had their reasons back on Deluros, and now I've got mine."

A mechanical voice spoke out. "Pursuer alert. Ten minutes three seconds stroke four off the port bow."

Nighthawk frowned and ordered his ship to change course. The voice was silent for a moment, then repeated its message with slightly different coordinates. "What is it?" asked Father Christmas.

"Someone's on our tail."

"Who?"

"He doesn't want to identify himself. But we've ID'd his registry number, and traced a signal he's sent elsewhere to learn his frequency. The computer will find out who he is before too long."

"Maybe we should tell the Marquis."

Another muffled moan came from Nighthawk's cabin.

"And then again, maybe not," amended Father Christmas.

Nighthawk sat absolutely motionless, forcing himself to stare at a computer screen. A moment later an amused expression flashed across his face. "The gang's all here," he announced.

"What do you mean? Who's in the other ship?"

"Lizard Malloy. He's probably been on our tail since we took off."

"So tell him to go away."

"Don't be silly. He's not going to go away just because I ask him to. He's there for a reason."

"*What* reason?" demanded Father Christmas.

One final sound of sexual frenzy rang through the ship, reaching a crescendo and culminating in a satisfied moan.

"I wish I knew," answered Nighthawk.

"Maybe if you'd spend less time concentrating on what's happening thirty feet away from here and start worrying about what's a parsec away, we might get something accomplished," said Father Christmas.

"I *am* concentrating on Malloy."

"Sure," said the older man, unimpressed.

"*And* the Marquis."

"Did the Marquis order him to track us?"

"How the hell should I know?"

"Why not ask him?" suggested Father Christmas. "It sounds like they'll be through in a minute or two. Just give him a chance to put his pants on."

"And if he doesn't know why Malloy's out there?"

"Then it might be interesting to know who *did* send Malloy after us."

Nighthawk tried to think about Malloy, or the Marquis, or the Widowmaker, but he kept coming back to the same thing again and again: *Goddamn it, she never sounded like that with me!*

He knew he wanted to kill someone, but at the moment he wasn't sure if it was the Marquis, or perhaps the Pearl of Maracaibo, or maybe even himself.

Chapter 18

◆ ◆ ◆ ◆ ◆ ◆ ◆

Nighthawk was sitting in the galley, nursing a cup of coffee a few feet away from the command chair, as the ship sped through the void on autopilot. Father Christmas was asleep in his half of the crew's cabin, and the Marquis was snoring noisily across the corridor.

Finally Melisande emerged from the captain's cabin, wearing nothing but a towel she had wrapped around her.

"May I sit down?"

Nighthawk indicated the empty chair across from him.

"And could I have some coffee, please?"

"Don't ask me," he said. "Ask the galley."

She repeated her request as an order, and a moment later a cup of black coffee was deposited on the table in front of her.

"Thank you," she said.

"If you're waiting for it to say you're welcome, you're out of luck," said Nighthawk. "Only the control deck talks back to you."

"Why?"

"Because that's the way I like it."

"Don't be so defensive," she said with a smile. "I'm not criticizing you."

"I'm not defensive."

"You sound like you are."

"I'm not!"

"Okay, have it your way," she said with a shrug. The shrug caused the towel to come loose and slip to her waist. "Excuse me," she said with a catlike smile.

"Cover yourself up!" snapped Nighthawk.

"What's the problem?" she asked innocently, as she slowly adjusted the towel. "This isn't anything you haven't seen before—or have you forgotten already?"

"I haven't forgotten."

"Come over and help me do this," she said, wrapping herself again in the towel.

"Fix it yourself."

"All right—but I can't promise that it won't slip again."

Nighthawk grimaced, got to his feet, and walked over.

"Right here," she said, pointing to the spot where she wanted it joined.

She handed Nighthawk a gaudy, ornate clasp and he put the two ends together, trying to ignore the scent of her perfume.

"You're all right now," he announced, walking back to his chair.

"You're sure?" she asked, getting to her feet. "It's very short."

"So what?"

"So what if I have to raise my arms like this?" she said, starting to do so.

"Just sit down and it won't happen again."

"I can't sit for the whole voyage."

"Then get dressed."

"I don't want to wake the Marquis." She grinned. "I think I wore him out."

Nighthawk made no reply.

"This is very good coffee," she said at last.

"How do you know?" he answered. "You haven't tasted it yet."

"But it warms my hands." She reached out and laid her hand on top of his. "See? No one wants to be touched by a cold hand."

"It doesn't bother me."

"Well, maybe it wouldn't bother your hand, but there are other places I could touch you where you'd jump." She paused. "Or you would if my hands were cold. Next time they are, I'll prove it to you."

"Not necessary."

"I don't mind," she responded. "After all, we're all friends here, aren't we?"

"Maybe you should stick with the friend that brought you," suggested Nighthawk tightly.

"But he's sound asleep," she said. "If you listen, you can hear him snore."

"So what?"

"He needs his sleep . . . but I've already had mine. It's boring in there, just watching him." Suddenly she smiled. "Of course, he *is* naked."

"I'm sure you find that wildly exciting."

"Well, it all depends," she said. "I mean, it's no fun being excited all by yourself. I *could* find it exciting if *he* did. Would you like me to tell you how I would excite him?"

"No."

"Are you sure?" she said. "It might even excite you."

"Leave me alone!" he snapped, getting to his feet and walking to the command chair.

"I thought you liked me."

"I do," he said softly.

"I even thought you wanted me," she continued.

"How come you only come on to me when both cabins are in use?"

"You think we have to have a cabin?" she said. "All a cabin has is a bed." She stood up and removed her towel. "We've got everything we need right here." Mock hurt. "You're frowning. Don't you like what you see?"

"I like it."

She approached him slowly, making sure to avoid the Roller, which was perched on a panel a few feet away. "Yes, I can see that you like it," she said, staring at his groin.

He grabbed her arm, pulled her onto his lap, and kissed her hungrily.

"Careful," she said, shifting her position. "You're going to impale me."

"That's the general idea," he said.

"What if the Marquis wakes up and walks out into the corridor right this second?" she said.

"I'll have to kill him."

"But how can you if I'm in the way?"

"Stop talking so much."

"Maybe I should check and make sure he's still asleep."

"Forget it."

"No," she said, getting up. "I really should. I don't want to be caught in the crossfire."

Before he could stop her, she walked back to the galley and wrapped her towel around her, then disappeared into the captain's cabin. She emerged a few seconds later and mouthed the words *Sound asleep.*

Then, as she was approaching Nighthawk again, Father Christmas's sleepy voice rang out. "What the hell's going on out there?" A moment later he emerged from his cabin, stopped apruptly, and sized up the situation as he stared at Melisande.

"Dressed in a bit of a hurry, didn't you?" he said sardonically.

"I just came out for some coffee," she said.

"Galley, serve up two coffees," commanded the old man. Two cups filled with black coffee appeared a moment later. The Pearl of Maracaibo turned to Nighthawk and shrugged helplessly, almost falling out of her towel.

"So how long was I asleep?" asked Father Christmas.

"Maybe four or five hours," replied Nighthawk.

"Too bad I didn't sleep another hour," he said. "You might have made a little progress with the lady here."

"Not a chance," answered Melisande. "I'm totally loyal to the Marquis."

"And I'm the reincarnation of Ramses II," said Father Christmas.

She turned to Nighthawk. "Are you going to let him talk to me like that?"

"You're totally loyal to the Marquis," said Nighthawk. "Let *him* defend your honor."

"Some hero," she snorted contemptuously.

Suddenly the Marquis stuck his head out into the corridor and stared at the galley. "What's going on?"

"Nothing," she said. "We're just talking."

"You woke me up."

"We didn't mean to," she said. "Go back to sleep."

"Come on back to bed," he said. "I don't like to sleep alone."

"Whatever you say."

"*That's* what I say," answered the Marquis.

She stood up, clutching the towel to her, and turned to Nighthawk. "Perhaps we can continue our discussion later."

"Perhaps," he said noncommittally.

"Get your ass in here," said the Marquis, withdrawing to the interior of the cabin. She joined him a few seconds later.

"You're a little young to have a death wish," said Father Christmas as the door to the cabin slid shut. "I hope what I think was going on here wasn't going on."

"I don't want to talk about it."

"I'll just bet you don't," said the older man. "I wonder how many pets she tortured to death when she was a little kid."

"Shut up!"

"Have it your way," said Father Christmas. He took a sip of his coffee. "How long until we reach the Oligarchy?"

Nighthawk looked at a screen. "We entered it about five hours ago."

"And when do we hit the Deluros system?"

"At this speed, maybe another thirty hours."

"Thirty hours more," mused Father Christmas. "That's a long time for her not to precipitate a killing."

"I don't want to discuss her," said Nighthawk ominously.

"We still got our shadow?"

"Malloy? Yeah, he's back there a couple of million miles."

"Sounds like a lot until you realize it's, what, maybe ten seconds?"

"A little less."

"You want some sleep?" asked Father Christmas. "I can keep an eye on things."

Nighthawk shook his head.

"You've been awake a long time," continued Father Christmas. "I want all your reactions to be one hundred percent when we get there. Get some sleep."

"How can I sleep when I know she's in bed with him not twenty feet away?" demanded Nighthawk irritably.

"So *that's* what it is," said Father Christmas. "You think if you stay here in the control room maybe he won't fuck her any more?"

"They're not fucking—they're sleeping," said Nighthawk. "Or, at least, *he* is."

"And you don't like that any better, do you?"

"No, I don't," said Nighthawk.

"Well, then," said Father Christmas, "I have a suggestion."

"Oh?"

"You won't like it, but it makes the most sense."

"Let's hear it."

"This girl is messing up your mind, son," said Father Christmas. "She's tying you into knots. She's all you're thinking about, and that's deadly."

"You want me to kill the Marquis?"

"You can't kill the Marquis . . . yet," said the older man. "Don't forget your original assignment: You need him to finger the assassin for you."

"Then what do you want?"

"Kill *her*."

"Are you crazy?" snapped Nighthawk.

"Not even a little bit," said Father Christmas. "Every time the Marquis takes a nap or turns his back she's teasing the hell out of you. Don't bother to deny it; I've got eyes. You let her live, eventually she'll precipitate a fight between you and the Marquis before you're ready for it."

"But the whole purpose of this trip was to kill the Marquis so I could finally have her," said Nighthawk.

"She's not worth having, son," said the older man. "Let me plunder my churches while you're killing the Widowmaker, and then let's both blow this life and go retire somewhere where neither the Good Guys *or* the Bad Guys will ever find us."

"Sounds good to me."

"It's a deal, then?"

"As soon as I kill the Marquis," said Nighthawk. "We'll take Melisande with us."

The old man sighed once, deeply, but made no reply.

Chapter 19

◆ ◆ ◆ ◆ ◆ ◆ ◆

They were thirty-eight hours out of Tundra, and life wasn't getting any easier for Nighthawk. When he wasn't busy fantasizing about Melisande, she was there in front of him, sending him secret smiles, finding reasons to accidentally brush against him, taunting him with the touch and smell of her.

Her behavior radically altered whenever the Marquis was around. She never willingly left his side at such times. No portion of her anatomy was forbidden to his hands, even in plain sight of Nighthawk and Father Christmas. But the Marquis had no interest in the workings or navigation of the ship, and he spent most of his time in his cabin. As quickly as he was out of sight she went back to teasing Nighthawk with the same single-mindedness with which she ignored him when the Marquis was around.

Nighthawk was experiencing one of his few brief moments of solitude, staring absently at one of the ship's viewscreens. He ordered it to go to high magnification, hoping to get a glimpse of Malloy's ship, but all he could see were stars and the endless blackness of space.

Finally he decided to radio Malloy yet again to find out why he was being followed—but he couldn't raise Malloy's ship. It was there, it was tracking him, but it wouldn't respond to his signal. He frowned. Neither Malloy nor his ship presented a physical threat, but he didn't like things he couldn't understand, and he didn't understand why the little grifter was following him into the Oligarchy.

"If he bothers you so much," said a voice behind him, "let's slow down, let him catch up with us, and blow him into a million pieces."

It was the Marquis, who had wandered over while Nighthawk was preoccupied with the radio.

"I didn't say he bothered me," replied Nighthawk defensively.

"You didn't have to."

"I just want to know why he's there."

"Someone sent him, obviously," responded the Marquis.

"Who—and why?"

The Marquis shrugged. "Beats the hell out of me." He paused, then smiled as a thought came to him. "If you don't want to blow him away, let him catch up with us and then threaten to lock him in a room with the Holy Roller. Five'll get you ten that he'll suddenly be overjoyed to talk to us."

"It's a pet, not a weapon," said Nighthawk, stroking the Roller as it bounced up from the floor to his shoulder.

"It's a little of each," said the Marquis. "You're not the first I've ever seen with a Holy Roller. I've known two other men that Rollers attached themselves to." He paused and looked at Nighthawk's Roller admiringly. "Get one of those things angry, it can wipe out a roomful of men in ten seconds flat. *I'd* call that a weapon."

"I'd call it a friend."

"That's because you don't think big enough," said the Marquis. "You don't understand what you could do with a thing like that."

"But you do?" said Nighthawk sardonically.

"Of course I do," answered the Marquis. "That's one of the differences between us."

"If you're that hot to get one, go to Aladdin."

"I've been to Aladdin. Never saw one."

"So go again."

"Waste of time," said the Marquis. "I've been there a dozen times." He paused. "I think I'd rather trade for yours."

"It's not for trade."

"You haven't heard my offer yet."

"You don't have anything I want," said Nighthawk.

"Oh, I think I do," said the Marquis with a grin. "Melisande!"

The blue-skinned girl emerged from the cabin and walked over to join the Marquis.

"Well?" said the Marquis.

"*Her?*"

"For the Roller."

"It's a deal," said Nighthawk.

"Don't I get some say in this?" demanded Melisande.

"I'm afraid not, my dear," said the Marquis.

"You can't trade me for some alien animal as if I was a piece of property!" she said.

"We are all property," answered the Marquis. "It is only the intelligent ones who know it." He paused. "I am sure Mr. Nighthawk will cherish you as I have, my love."

"And what if I don't want to be cherished by Mr. Nighthawk?" she said.

"That's hardly my concern." The Marquis paused. "I'm sure that he'll treat you with the same compassion that I have displayed up to now."

"Which is to say, none at all," she snapped.

"Please don't make this more difficult than it is," said the Marquis. "You have given me an inordinate amount of pleasure, and I regret losing you"—he smiled apologetically—"but the galaxy is full of women. There are very few Holy Rollers. For all practical purposes, there is really only one. Surely you would do the same thing in my position."

"I've never been in your position," she said bitterly.

"Well, there you have it." He reached out for the Roller, which suddenly became rigid and started humming softly.

"I don't think it likes the thought of you touching it," offered Nighthawk.

"Well, explain to it that we've got a deal."

"I don't know its language."

The Roller began whistling a little louder.

"Make it stop!" said the Marquis. "I've seen them do this before."

Nighthawk plucked the Roller from his shoulder and cradled it against his chest, stroking it gently.

"We made a trade," said the Marquis, backing away slowly. "It's up to you to deliver your end of it."

"Don't you think I *want* to?" shot back Nighthawk. "It doesn't like you, and there's nothing I can do about it. The alien back on Aladdin told me that it chooses one person and sticks with him for life."

"Too bad," said the Marquis. "You had your chance, and you blew it." He turned to the Pearl of Maracaibo. "It looks like we're reunited in eternal love, my sweet." She glared at him but didn't say anything. "Go back to the cabin," he continued. "I'll join you in a few moments."

She stood still and glared at him.

"Now," he said in a tone that brooked no disobedience.

She stalked off to the cabin without a backward glance.

"My offer stands for the duration of this trip," said the Marquis. "You teach the Roller to accept me, and she's yours." He paused and suddenly grinned. "Maybe I'll have to teach her to accept *you*."

Nighthawk made no reply.

"Well, she may be yours any day now," said the Marquis, starting to walk back toward his cabin. "I think I'd better enjoy her while I can."

He grinned again and disappeared into the cabin. The Holy Roller squeaked loudly, and Nighthawk realized that he was squeezing it painfully. He released it, and it rolled down his leg onto the floor.

"Mind if I join you?" asked Father Christmas, emerging from his cabin and walking down the corridor toward the galley and the control cabin.

"Why not?" said Nighthawk without enthusiasm. "You heard it all?"

"Yep. Hard to keep secrets on a ship. Especially one as small as this." He paused. "Sounded like a soap opera. Makes for an entertaining trip."

"So how do I make the Roller like him?"

"You don't," said the older man. "They choose one person, and when all is said and done they're a lot more loyal than any man or woman I've ever met."

"You're not much help, are you?" said Nighthawk bitterly.

"I would be, if you'd ever listen to me."

"You don't say anything I care to hear."

"Nobody ever really wants the truth," agreed Father Christmas.

"Let it be."

Father Christmas shrugged. "Whatever you say." He glanced at the viewscreen. "Malloy still tracking us?"

"Yeah. I tried to raise him, but he's not answering his calls today."

"Assuming the Marquis was telling the truth—always a dangerous assumption—I wonder who the hell Malloy *is* working for?"

"I don't know."

"Why don't you think about it for a minute?" said Father Christmas.

"I'm thinking," said Nighthawk. "Nothing's coming."

"You know, the guys who built you could have spent two less school days on killing people and two more on spotting subterfuges."

"What are you talking about?"

"Use your brain, son," said Father Christmas. "What is Malloy doing?"

"Tracking the ship."

"Why?"

"I don't know," said Nighthawk, feeling just like a frustrated schoolboy.

"What *do* you know?"

Nighthawk frowned. "What do you mean?"

"Let's assume for a moment that the Marquis is telling the truth, that he has nothing to do with Malloy or the ship. What does that tell you?"

Nighthawk looked blank.

"Look," said Father Christmas patiently, "if he's not here for the Marquis, and he's not here for you, and he's not here for me, who the hell else *is* there?"

Nighthawk's eyes widened. *"Melisande?"*

"Right."

"But why?"

"Beats me," admitted the older man. "But I'd say she's probably a little more than she seems to be."

Nighthawk said nothing, but sat motionless, petting the Holy Roller absently, lost in thought. Finally he looked up, cleared his throat, and spoke.

"Maybe his employer wants to know where the Marquis is and what he's doing."

"Would *you* send someone like Malloy up against the Marquis of Queensbury?" retorted Father Christmas. "If it was up to me, I'd hire someone who could handle himself when the going got rough—someone like you."

"Then why is he following us?"

"I've got a notion or two, but let's wait a little longer and see what happens."

"How much longer?"

Father Christmas shrugged. "We'll know before we get to Deluros." He pulled out a deck of alien cards. "Care for a quick game of *jabob?*"

Nighthawk shook his head. "They never taught me the rules."

"The rules are easy," said the older man with a smile. "The odds are impossible."

"Then why do so many humans play it?"

"Because the rules are simple," answered Father Christmas. "So they figure they ought to be able to beat it." He paused. "Most men don't suffer from an abundance of intelligence—or hadn't you noticed?"

"I've noticed," said Nighthawk.

The two of them sat silently for a few minutes, the older man shuffling and reshuffling his cards. Then the Marquis emerged from his cabin once again.

"Still here, I see," he said.

"See what I mean?" whispered Father Christmas. Then to the Marquis he said, "We're traveling at sixty-four times the speed of light in a three-man ship. Just where the hell did you think I'd be?"

The Marquis shrugged. "Sleeping. Eating. Pissing. How should I know?"

Father Christmas laughed aloud. "You'd better work on your muscles, son," he said to Nighthawk. "It's a cinch she's not hanging around with him because of his brainpower."

"Watch your mouth, old man," said the Marquis ominously. "I want part of your haul, but I don't *need* it. Never forget that."

"My sincere and most humble apologies," said Father Christmas, bowing low from his seated position and somehow losing his smile before he straightened up again.

The Marquis glared at him silently for a long moment, muttered "Old fool!," then ordered a drink from the galley.

"Well, Nighthawk," he said at last, "are you still looking forward to killing the Widowmaker?"

"That's why I'm here," answered Nighthawk.

"It must feel a little like killing your father."

"Not really."

"Ah, I forgot," said the Marquis. "You don't *have* a father, do you?"

"Well, if I do, he's been dead a couple of centuries," said Nighthawk.

"Then maybe it's really more like killing your brother," suggested the Marquis. "Perhaps you are Cain to the Widowmaker's Abel."

"If you say so."

"I don't say anything. I'm just trying to understand what it feels like, as one killer to another."

"I'll tell you after I've done it," said Nighthawk. He sighed deeply. "I rather suspect it'll feel like laying a bad memory to rest."

"I thought you'd never seen him," said the Marquis. "How can you remember him?"

"Maybe I expressed myself poorly," replied Nighthawk. "He's the ideal to which I have always been compared. His accomplishments created the hopes and expectations that I've been measured against." He paused thoughtfully. "Most young men simply have to forget the role models that have been chosen for them. Me, I get to eliminate mine permanently. I find that a very satisfying notion."

"If he's half of what they say he was, you might not be able to kill him."

"He's a diseased, disfigured old man who can't move or breathe without help," said Nighthawk. "Besides, I have no intention of waking him up. This is an exorcism, not a contest."

"An exorcism," repeated the Marquis with a smile. "I like that."

"I'll like it when I've finished it."

Melisande stepped through the cabin door then, sauntered into the galley, and paused to run her hands through the Marquis' tousled hair.

"I want a drink," she announced.

"Order it yourself."

"I don't like this galley," she complained. "It doesn't mix them right."

"What the hell do you want *me* to do about it?" asked the Marquis.

She nodded toward Nighthawk. "Make *him* mix me a drink."

"I don't mix drinks," said Nighthawk.

"Just a minute," said the Marquis, turning to face Nighthawk. "It's okay for *me* to tell her you don't make drinks. It's not okay for *you* to."

"Why not?" said Nighthawk. "Has she suddenly become my commanding officer?"

"No," replied the Marquis. "But *I* give the orders around here, so when I'm around you don't refuse any request until you find out what I want you to do about it."

"Some chain of command," said Father Christmas with a contemptuous snort.

"You stay out of this, old man," snapped the Marquis. He turned to Nighthawk again. "Fix her a drink."

"I don't do coolie labor," said Nighthawk. "Let her fix her own."

"I'm ordering you to."

"I kill very dangerous people for you," said Nighthawk. "That's my job, and I'm goddamned good at it. It's *not* my job to mix Melisande's drinks just so you can prove to her that you can give me orders. Everything that makes you look good in her eyes makes me look like shit. If you want a drink mixed, mix it yourself."

The Marquis got to his feet. His left arm moved out slowly, sweeping Melisande behind him.

"I'm ordering you one more time. Mix her drink."

"Go fuck yourself," said Nighthawk, still sitting comfortably on his chair.

"I'm not going to ask you again," said the Marquis ominously.

"You didn't *ask* a first time," said Nighthawk. "Besides, what are you going to do? Fire me and make me walk home?"

"That's not a bad idea."

"Of course it's not," said Nighthawk. "*You* didn't think of it."

"You guys don't want to fight in here," said Father Christmas suddenly. "A stray shot could go right through the bulkhead and kill us all."

"Then it's damned lucky for you that I never miss, isn't it?" said the Marquis.

Suddenly the Holy Roller, distressed by the tension in the room, became rigid and started humming.

"Turn that damned thing off or I'll kill it," warned the Marquis.

"I wouldn't even if I knew how," said Nighthawk, finally getting to his feet. "Which of us are you going to shoot first, and what do you think the other's going to be doing in the meantime?"

"I beat you before and I can beat you again!" snapped the Marquis.

He pulled out his laser pistol and fired it—and a beam of solid light almost split the Roller in half. It screeched once, burst into flames, and died. But as it did so, Nighthawk had his own gun in his hand and fired one shot. The bullet lodged between the Marquis' eyes, and he plunged, face forward, to the floor.

Father Christmas knelt down next to the Marquis and rolled him over, examining the wound.

"Goddamned lucky the bullet didn't ricochet off

and go through the bulkhead," he said. "Either of you idiots could have killed us all with one bad shot."

"What did you want me to do—arm-wrestle him?" said Nighthawk.

"No," said Father Christmas with a deep sigh. "But you might have mixed the lady's drink. He had information you needed, remember?"

"Fuck it," said Nighthawk. "I needed that information so I could deliver an assassin and collect enough money to keep the Widowmaker alive until they came up with a cure for what ails him." He paused. "Well, what's about to ail him is *me*, and there's no cure for what I plan to do. That makes the Marquis' information kind of meaningless, doesn't it?"

"What about *her*?" asked the older man.

"She's mine now," said Nighthawk, turning to face Melisande. But what he found himself facing was the business end of one of the Marquis' sonic pistols.

"I'll decide who I belong to," she said coldly. "If you take one single step toward me, you'll be dead on the floor right next to him." She looked him square in the eye. "I mean it."

Nighthawk gently holstered his pistol and sat back down on his chair.

"I hate to say 'I told you so,'" said Father Christmas with an ironic smile, "but . . ."

Chapter 20

◆ ◆ ◆ ◆ ◆ ◆ ◆

◈

"Well," said Father Christmas, breaking a long, tense silence, "we've got some decisions to make."

"I've made mine," said Melisande.

"You don't have the slightest idea of what I'm talking about," said Father Christmas, making no attempt to keep the contempt out of his voice. "Now put that gun away. I guarantee that Nighthawk's not about to pounce on you while I'm here and there's still a dead body on the floor."

She stared at Nighthawk for a long moment, then placed the pistol down on the galley table.

"All right," continued Father Christmas. "First thing we have to do is . . ."

"First thing we have to do," interrupted Nighthawk, "is jettison what's left of the Roller."

"Forget it," said the older man. "We've more important things to consider."

"How can you stand the smell?"

Father Christmas inhaled deeply, made a face, and nodded his consent. Nighthawk picked up the little Roller's charred corpse, carried it past the galley while Melisande and Father Christmas tried not to retch, and jettisoned it into space. On the way back he activated a small servomech that cleaned up the spot where the Roller had bled, and then had it deodorized.

"Better," agreed Father Christmas when Nighthawk returned to his chair.

"All right," said Nighthawk. "Now, what decisions do you think we have to make?"

"Well, the first one's already out of our hands," said the older man. "All we have to do is acknowledge it."

"What are you talking about?"

"We're going to have to alter course," said Father Christmas. "We can't go to Deluros."

"Why?" demanded Nighthawk.

"Because Deluros has the best security in the galaxy." Father Christmas paused. "In fact, we'd better get the hell out of Oligarchic territory while we have the chance."

"Why should you give a damn about Deluros's security now?" said Nighthawk. "It didn't bother you when we were planning this job."

"We didn't have a dead body in the ship when we were planning this job," answered Father Christmas. "There's no way you can hide that from Deluros security."

"Then we'll just jettison it, the way I did with the Roller," said Nighthawk.

Father Christmas turned to Melisande. "Do you want to tell him, or should I?"

"Tell him what?" she asked, honestly confused.

"Jesus!" muttered Father Christmas. "I wonder if either of you have enough brains to write your name in the dirt with a stick!"

"Get to the point," said Nighthawk irritably.

The older man turned to face him. "You can't jettison the Marquis' body because a slimy little bastard called Lizard Malloy is still tracking us, and the second you dump it into space he's going to pick it up and either blackmail us if we to return to Yukon or Tundra, or turn us in for the reward if we stay in the Oligarchy."

"Malloy," repeated Nighthawk. "Shit! I'd forgotten all about him."

"Well, it's a goddamned good thing that *I* don't forget the scum that's following me across the galaxy."

"All right," said Nighthawk, trying to control his temper. "We can't go to Deluros until we get rid of the body, and we can't jettison the body while Malloy's tracking us. That seems to leave us two choices: We land on a planet long enough to dump the body, or we go back to the Frontier with it."

"You've only got one choice, son," said Father Christmas. "You've got to go to the Frontier and lose the body there."

"But there are hundreds of thousands of planets right here," protested Nighthawk.

"You might park the ship in an orbiting hangar, or dock it at a space station without getting searched," said the older man, "but I guarantee that you'll be thoroughly scanned if you try to put down on a planet, and there's no way to hide the body from the kind of scanning they'll do. And if you can't jettison it with

Malloy around, I guarantee you can't jettison it at an orbiting hangar or a space station."

"But I've got business on Deluros!" insisted Nighthawk.

"That's the seat of human government," said Father Christmas. "They're more sensitive about security there than anywhere else in the Oligarchy. They'll scan you ten times between the moment you enter the system and the moment you park in orbit around Deluros VIII. And a couple of hundred police will be waiting for you to emerge from the ship once they've spotted the corpse." He paused. "Now, if you'd killed him with your hands, we could try to pretend that he tripped and fell against something hard, and if you'd killed him with your sonic pistol we might have been able to blame the Holy Roller, at least if you hadn't jettisoned it—but it's gonna be goddamned difficult to tell them that he shot himself right between the eyes while he was cleaning his pistol. Or *your* pistol, once they got done examining the bullet. You see what I mean?"

"I see what you mean," said Nighthawk. "But I still want to get to—"

"Forget it!" snapped the older man. "First things first. We've got to go back to the Frontier and lose the Marquis. Otherwise, you'll never get within five hundred miles of Deluros VIII's surface, and that's a fact."

Nighthawk fell silent, considering his options, rejecting each in turn. Finally he looked up and stared at the Pearl of Maracaibo.

"Just a minute," he said, his eyes narrowing.

"What is it?" asked Father Christmas.

"We had a problem a few hours ago. We discussed it, but never solved it—and then, because of the killings, we forgot all about it."

"I don't think I follow you."

"Neither does Malloy," said Nighthawk. "But *he* follows *her*. Maybe we should ask why."

"You're making foolish accusations," said Melisande angrily. "Malloy is *your* friend, not mine."

"What reason would he have for following me?" asked Nighthawk.

"How the hell should *I* know?" demanded Melisande.

"Nobody knows," said Father Christmas. "There isn't any reason." He paused. "Now, what reason does he have for following *you*?"

"I don't even know him!" she protested. "I've seen him in the casino. He spends most of his time with you."

"Just a minute," said Father Christmas. "Suppose you tell us who you worked for before you hooked up with the Marquis."

"I don't have to tell you shit!"

"That's what you think, lady," said Father Christmas.

"Leave her alone," said Nighthawk.

"Damn it, son," said Father Christmas, "I know you've got the hots for her, but we're in a helluva dangerous situation here. You've killed one of the most powerful men on the Frontier, we've got a potential enemy tracking us—and we might have another one right here in the ship. So stop thinking with your gonads and start using your brain. We are in serious trouble, and I can't get us out of it alone."

"We'll get out of this," said Nighthawk. "Just stop harassing her."

"Goddammit!"

"You heard me."

"All right," said the older man with a heavy sigh. "We can't stay in the Oligarchy. We can't jettison the body. I say that we don't return to the Inner Frontier. Too many people know we left with the Marquis; they'll figure out that you killed him. Lord knows *I* couldn't have done it."

"So what?" responded Nighthawk. "He was just a crook, a little more powerful than most. It's not like some government will post a reward for me."

"You don't understand," said Father Christmas. "There was a limit to what they could teach you in a couple of months."

"What don't I understand."

"The very people who are thrilled that he's dead, so they can divide the spoils and advance up the ladder, will be the ones who come after you. If you could kill the Marquis, you could kill any of them, and since they don't know for a fact that your current employer won't finger them next, you're a marked man." The older man paused and cleared his throat. "So I say we stay away from the Inner Frontier."

"Where do we go?"

"The Rim, the Outer Frontier, the Spiral Arm—at least that portion of the Arm that's not officially a part of the Oligarchy."

"That's awfully far away," said Nighthawk.

"Of course it is," replied Father Christmas. "That's the whole point of this."

"I don't want to go the Rim or the Outer Frontier," said Melisande. "I haven't killed anyone."

"Fine," said Father Christmas. "We'll drop you off at the next oxygen planet and you can make your way back home—or hitch a ride with Malloy."

"The hell we will!" snapped Nighthawk.

"Son, she doesn't want you," said the older man. "Now, that seems pretty devastating to you right now, but there are trillions of women in the galaxy. Believe me: You're young, you'll find another."

Nighthawk stared into Melisande's eyes. "You're the one I want."

"That's *your* problem," she said. "I have problems of my own. One of them is getting back to Tundra."

"I'm stronger than *he* was," continued Nighthawk. "I can take better care of you, protect you better."

"But I don't want you to."

"I'll go back to Tundra and take over," said Nighthawk. "I'll be as rich as he was. Richer. I'll be able to buy you anything you want."

"I want the Marquis," she said. "Buy me that."

"You didn't give a damn about the Marquis," said Nighthawk. "It was the money, the power he wielded."

"It was *him*."

"Bullshit."

"It was him, and the way he could please me," she said. "But that's something you couldn't possibly know about, could you?" she added with a cruel smile.

"I'm naive, but I'm not stupid," said Nighthawk. "You enjoyed it. I know you did."

"You can enjoy many meals in a restaurant," she replied. "But there might be only one that you would pay to have again."

"There's nothing he could do that I can't do," persisted Nighthawk. "I'll learn."

"Not with me, you won't."

"It'll work out. You'll see."

"Foolish, foolish clone," she said, making no attempt to hide her contempt. "Conceived in a test tube, nurtured in a chemical bath. An educated blob of protoplasm. A laboratory *thing* that walks and talks like a man." She paused. "I'll bet the original Widowmaker knew how to please a woman. Bring *him* around and maybe I'll stay."

His gun was out and aimed at her so quickly that she couldn't even reach for her own. She just sat there, stunned by the speed with which he had moved.

"Don't ever say that again!" he whispered so softly that she could barely make out the words.

Both Melisande and Father Christmas had seen Nighthawk under many conditions. They had seen him angry, and they had seen him bitter, and just a few minutes earlier they had seen him kill a man—but neither had ever been physically afraid of him until that instant.

Chapter 21

• • • • • • •

◈

Nighthawk carried the Marquis' body belowdeck, deposited it in the cargo hold, and sealed it in a quick-hardening plastic since he didn't know how long it would remain aboard ship. Then he returned to the control room, set a course that would take them to the Rim while avoiding the Oligarchy, and finally stopped by the galley. He couldn't remember the constituent parts of a Dust Whore, so he settled for ordering a beer.

"It should take us ten, maybe eleven days to get to the Rim," he announced. "I've never been there, so I don't know which worlds have been opened up, which ones might be friendly to us. Hopefully my ship's computer is up to date."

"Well, *I* don't want to go to the Rim," said

Melisande. "I haven't killed anyone, and no one wants to kill me. I want to go back to the Inner Frontier."

"I'm afraid that's out of the question, my dear," said Father Christmas.

"Am I your prisoner?" she demanded.

"Nobody's a prisoner," said Nighthawk. "You're a guest. Hopefully more than a guest."

"The hell I'm a guest," she said. "I'm here under protest. I want to go home."

"Where *is* home, now that the Marquis is dead?" asked Father Christmas.

"What makes you think it's anywhere but Tundra?" she demanded pugnaciously.

"Because nobody goes to Yukon and Tundra unless they have business there," answered Father Christmas. "What's *your* business? Surely you're not going back there just to dance with your clothes off?"

"My business is none of your concern!" she snapped.

"Then you *do* have business there?" he persisted.

"I've told you before to stop baiting her," interrupted Nighthawk.

The older man shrugged. "Okay. What would you rather talk about?"

Nighthawk glared at him and made no reply, and an uneasy silence descended on the ship for the next ten minutes. Then he ordered another beer.

"I'll have one too," said Father Christmas.

"How about you?" said Nighthawk to Melisande. She shook her head.

"Something to eat, then?"

"No."

"You must want *some*thing," said Nighthawk.

"I want to go back."

"I can't take you back just yet," he said.

"Why not?"

"I'm not ready to be a target. Once word gets out that I killed the Marquis, dozens of men, maybe hundreds, will be after my scalp. None of them live on the Rim."

"The Rim has *its* share of bounty hunters, too," she pointed out.

"Yeah, but there won't be a price on my head," noted Nighthawk. "Have you ever seen a bounty hunter kill anyone for free?"

"Just one," she said. "You."

"I'm not exactly a bounty hunter," he corrected. "And I didn't kill the Marquis for free. I killed him for you."

"I didn't ask you to."

"Not in so many words."

"Not in any way whatsoever!" she snapped. "You've killed him, and now you're taking me half a galaxy away from where I want to be. And then you wonder why I don't like you."

He stared at her. "Would you like me better if I took you back?" he asked.

"No," she answered. She smiled a slow, seductive smile. "But I might hate you less."

Nighthawk was silent, as if thinking about his options.

"You can't do it, son," said Father Christmas softly. "Not if you want to live to an old age."

"I know," said Nighthawk at last. He turned to Melisande. "You're coming to the Rim with us. It won't be so bad. You'll see."

She stared at him coldly, then stood up and stalked off to her cabin.

"You want a suggestion?" said Father Christmas.

"Not particularly."

"I'm going to make it anyway. If you join her in the cabin, frisk her before you climb into bed with her."

"I'm not joining her."

"Good decision."

"I don't want to rape her," continued Nighthawk. "I love her. I want her to love me."

"You're a little new to the game to understand what love is," said the older man. "As for her, she doesn't love anyone but herself. Never has, never will."

"Shut up."

"You're the boss."

They were silent for a few minutes. Then Nighthawk got to his feet. "I need some sleep."

He went off to the crew's cabin and fell into a deep, dreamless sleep . . .

. . . that was broken by the high-pitched wailing of the ship's alarm sirens.

He shot up, banged his head against the bulkhead, sat down heavily on the bed, tried to clear his head while the sirens kept screaming, and finally lunged out into the corridor. Father Christmas was in the control room, looking for the mechanism that would deactivate the alarms.

"Off!" shouted Nighthawk. The sirens stopped immediately. "They're keyed to my voice," he explained to the older man.

"No wonder I couldn't find a way to turn them off."

"What happened?" demanded Nighthawk, glancing around. "All the systems seem to be working."

"The airlock's been opened and closed," said Father Christmas. "So has the aft hatch. I tried to stop her—but it seems that half the ship's protective devices are keyed to your voiceprint."

"*Her?*" repeated Nighthawk. He turned to a viewscreen. "Magnify." He couldn't see anything. "Extreme magnification."

And now, suddenly, he was able to make out two tiny figures: the spacesuited Melisande, and the plastic-coated corpse of the Marquis.

"What the hell's going on?" murmured Nighthawk. "This doesn't make any sense."

"*Now* it does," said Father Christmas, as Lizard Malloy's ship suddenly came into view. It stopped and hung motionless in space, waiting for Melisande to maneuver herself and the corpse into an open hatch. A moment later they both disappeared inside the ship. It turned its nose back toward the Inner Frontier, then accelerated and vanished from the screen as it reached light speeds.

"As soon as the ship's computer can dope out its course, we'll go after it," announced Nighthawk, finally looking away from the screen.

"And do what?" asked Father Christmas. "This isn't a military ship. We don't carry any weaponry. You can't blow him apart. So what will you do? Follow him into the middle of the Marquis' territory?"

"What makes you think he's going there?"

"They've got the Marquis' body. Where do *you* think they're taking it?"

"To claim a reward."

"There isn't one," said Father Christmas. "There was never any paper on him, or someone would have killed him long before you did." He paused. "Face it, son—Malloy and your ladyfriend are partners, or at least they work for the same employer." He paused. "I

told you before that Malloy had to be following us because of her. It was the only logical conclusion. If you
decide to chase them, someone's going to get blown
out of the sky, all right—but it won't be *him*."

"All right," said Nighthawk bitterly. "You have all
the answers. Who do they work for?"

"I don't have 'em all, but I do have a logical
mind," answered Father Christmas. "You start by asking who wants the Marquis dead, and everything else
follows."

"There's no price on him," said Nighthawk,
frowning. "You said so yourself."

"There's no price on your head either, but I think
we can safely assume there are people who want *you*
dead."

Nighthawk lowered his head in thought for a
moment, then looked up. "I don't know."

"Well, I suppose not many four-month-olds could
dope it out," said Father Christmas. "But you're going
to have to grow up fast if you want to survive out
here."

"Spare me the lecture and get to the point," said
Nighthawk in annoyed tones.

"All right," replied Father Christmas. "Who sent
you after the Marquis in the first place?"

"Colonel Hernandez, back on Solio II."

"Well?"

"Well *what*?" demanded Nighthawk. "He told me
the Marquis would know who shot Trelaine."

"The Marquis knew, all right," said Father Christmas. "But then, so did Hernandez."

"What are you talking about?"

The old man lit a cigar and settled more comfortably into his chair. "Let me do a little serious
hypothesizing here," he said at last.

"Go ahead."

"All right. Let's say my name is Hernandez. I've been in charge of security on Solio II for years, which means I command the best-trained forces of armed men on the planet. Now, we call the big boss our Governor, but he's just a more accomplished tyrant than the rest. You with me so far?"

"So far," said Nighthawk.

"Let's say I decide that *I* would make a better Governor than Trelaine. What would I do?"

"Kill him."

Father Christmas shook his head. "Too many potential witnesses, too much chance of being seen. But that doesn't mean I can't carry out my plan. All I have to do is contact a criminal who operates on my world—and would like to operate even more freely— and suggest that *he* do it. Maybe I pay him money, more likely I forgive all his past crimes and promise him a free hand in the future. Now, I don't care if the Marquis pulls the trigger or hires it out; all I care is that he sees to it that Trelaine gets killed. And so he does."

"But you're not Governor."

"I know," said Father Christmas with a smile. "I guessed wrong. Remember, Trelaine went to the opera to make peace between two warring factions. What if neither of them was strong enough to take over, but both of them were strong enough to stop *me* from taking control? In fact, suddenly I have to prove that I had nothing to do with the assassination." He paused and puffed on his cigar. "Well, I can't bring the Marquis in. He'll never go quietly to the gallows; if he stands trial, he's a cinch to implicate me. So I want him dead. Now, how do I got about it so no one will know?"

◆   ◆   ◆   241

"You hire me."

"Right," said Father Christmas. "Not because you're the best killer in the galaxy, though that's a pretty good job qualification. I insist on a clone of the Widowmaker because I know he'll be all of two or three months old in real time when he gets out to the Frontier. I not only need someone who can kill the Marquis, but I need someone so naive, so innocent, that in all the time he's out here he never puts two and two together to figure out *why* I've finessed him into a situation where he almost *has* to kill the Marquis rather than bring him in."

"It's an interesting hypothesis," said Nighthawk uncomfortably. "But what does it have to do with Malloy or Melisande?"

"Melisande is Hernandez's spy," answered the older man. "She wasn't there to have you fall in love with her. She was there to sleep with the Marquis and let Hernandez know if he ever had an inclination to talk—or to blackmail Hernandez, which was much more likely.

"And Malloy?"

"I doubt that he was working for Hernandez at all. From what you told me, if you hadn't shown up exactly when you did, the Marquis would have killed him or he'd have frozen to death trying to get away. No, my guess is that once you became friendly with him, Melisande reported it and that was when Hernandez hired him." Father Christmas took another puff of his cigar and looked at Nighthawk. "Well, what do you think?"

Nighthawk considered the scenario for a long moment. Finally he looked at Father Christmas. "I think you're probably right," he admitted.

"Probably?"

Nighthawk angrily slammed a fist against the arm of his chair. "Okay, you're right. Period. Are you happy now?"

"Thank you," said Father Christmas. "I presume this means you're going to set a course to the Rim?"

"I haven't decided."

"But I told you what a double-crossing bitch your Pearl of Maracaibo is!"

"I know."

"Well, then?"

"You don't love someone because she's perfect."

"You're kidding!" exclaimed Father Christmas. "We're not talking about a woman who falls a few notches short of perfection. We're talking about someone who is, and always has been, in the employ of the enemy and wants you dead. What the hell is the matter with you?"

"You haven't been to bed with her," said Nighthawk. "You can't know what you're asking me to give up."

"A quick death!" answered Father Christmas. He stood up as if to pace off his frustration, then realized there was no room to do so and sat down tensely. "If you'd ever fucked anyone else, you'd know there's nothing unique about her. And remember: It was all an act, all in the line of duty. She'll never go to bed with you again, now that you know who and what she is."

"She doesn't know I'm aware that she works for Colonel Hernandez."

"She jumped ship with the Marquis' corpse," said the older man sardonically. "She's got to figure that even you can draw the logical conclusion about whose side she's on."

"I want her."

"I want to be King of Deluros VIII," retorted Father Christmas. "We're both doomed to be disappointed."

"Speak for yourself," said Nighthawk.

Chapter 22

◆ ◆ ◆ ◆ ◆ ◆ ◆

Father Christmas sipped his beer and tried to control his temper. "Goddammit, son—will you please, just for once, use your brain?"

"What are you talking about?" demanded Nighthawk.

"I know it's difficult, but try to think things through. You want to follow the girl, right?"

"Right."

"And you know she's with Malloy, and they're almost certainly in the employ of this Colonel Hernandez."

"Have you got a point?"

"Just this," said Father Christmas. "Where do you suppose they're going right now?"

"Probably Solio II."

"And if you follow them, that's where you'll wind up, right?" continued the older man.

"So what?"

"So how much does Hernandez owe your creators?"

"I'm not sure," said Nighthawk. "Somewhere around five million credits."

"But you haven't told your people on Deluros that you've accomplished your task and killed the Marquis," Father Christmas pointed out. "So if you land on Solio, what is Hernandez's most reasonable course of action?"

Nighthawk was silent for a moment, considering the possibilities. Finally he grimaced. "He kills me, or has me killed, and saves the money."

"Exactly!" said Father Christmas. "You've already killed the man he wanted dead. Now all he has to do is kill you, dump your body on any Frontier world except Solio II, and then report to your people on Deluros that you told him you were following a very promising lead. The next thing he knew you'd been ambushed and killed." The older man finished his beer. "Just remember that Hernandez controls security for the whole planet," he continued. "He's probably got ten times as many guns working for him as the Marquis had, and they're better disciplined. If you go there, you won't have a chance."

"All right," said Nighthawk angrily. "You've made your point."

"So we go to the Rim, right?"

"Wrong," said Nighthawk.

"But I've explained that it's suicide to go to Solio," said Father Christmas.

"You've warned me what I'll be up against."

"Then what's the problem?"

"I want her."

"There's nothing wrong with *wanting* her," said the older man. "Just don't go after her."

"I love her. I'm not leaving her."

"You're a fool!"

"Nobody says you have to come along," said Nighthawk. "I can set you down on the first inhabited world we come to."

"How do I know it'll have a church?" replied Father Christmas. "You need a keeper, son. That's me."

"Then you're coming with me?"

"When we're ready."

"I'm ready now," said Nighthawk.

"The hell you are," said Father Christmas. "The second Hernandez speaks to the Pearl of Maracaibo—and he doesn't have to wait for her to land on Solio to do that—he's going to know you killed the Marquis and that you're probably coming after the girl. First thing he'll do is put a price on your head."

"But I killed the man he wanted dead."

"Yeah—but now that the Marquis is dead, and there's no proof linking him to Trelaine's assassination, the easiest way to save however many millions of credits he owes to your people on Deluros VIII is to kill you before you can explain *why* you think the Marquis was the hit man or was at least connected to the crime. He'll have posters transmitted to every Frontier world, and if his people don't kill you, the bounty hunters will. Hell, once he tells your people on Deluros that their illegal clone is off the reservation and killing people on his own, they'll probably double the reward."

"So what do you suggest?"

"A little subtlety, a little misdirection," answered the older man. "Remember I told you about phony passports and IDs? That's what we need now. He's looking for you to sneak onto his world, to land where no one's around to challenge you and then come after him under cover of night. I think you'll do better walking boldly in the front door. You don't identify yourself until you're behind ninety-nine percent of his defenses."

"How long will that take?" asked Nighthawk, seriously considering the suggestion.

"It all depends," said Father Christmas. "How far are we from Purplecloud, Terrazane, or Antares III?"

"I have no idea," replied Nighthawk.

"Neither do I. That's what we have a navigational computer for."

A moment later the ship informed them that the closest of the three worlds, Purplecloud, could be reached in seventeen hours.

"Lay in a course for Purplecloud," said the older man, ordering another beer.

"That's where one of your forgers lives?"

"One of my equipment managers," Father Christmas corrected him with a smile.

"Equipment?"

"You'll see," Father Christmas assured him.

Chapter 23

◆ ◆ ◆ ◆ ◆ ◆ ◆

Purplecloud wasn't all that impressive a world, despite the fact that it lay firmly within the boundaries of the Oligarchy. It had been opened as an agricultural world early in Man's galactic expansion, supplying food to fifteen nearby mining worlds. But the soil wasn't very rich in nutrients, and other worlds with far better farmland were soon opened up.

So Purplecloud was deserted and forgotten for close to two millennia. Then gold was discovered in one of its mountain ranges. There wasn't all that much of it, and the veins were soon played out, but not before half a dozen Tradertowns were built. Two of them still existed, one serving the employees of the huge corporations that had taken over the abandoned farmland and were now growing hardy hybrid crops, the other acting as a refueling stop on the way to the Inner Frontier.

Nighthawk set his ship down near Tomahawk, the second of Purplecloud's Tradertowns. He and Father Christmas emerged, passed a row of advertising and Wanted holographs, and caught an airbus into town.

"I know this place," said Father Christmas, as they came to a small restaurant. "Great food."

"Good," said Nighthawk, following him inside. "I was getting sick of the ship's menu."

The older man found a table that suited him and sat down. "It was a fine menu. Problem was that everything was made with soya products. You can get real meat here—a kind of mutated buffalo they farm a few hundred miles to the west. You ought to see those suckers: blood red, and maybe six thousand pounds apiece. They make great eating."

"What are they called?" asked Nighthawk.

"Redbison," answered Father Christmas. "Get yourself a tenderloin. Fabulous piece of meat."

They ordered, and as they were waiting for their meals to arrive, Nighthawk turned to Father Christmas.

"Where's your contact?"

"Just up the street."

"You're sure he's still here?"

"I'm sure, and he's a she."

"How did you ever find her on a little backwater world like this?" asked Nighthawk.

"I ran into some associates with better-forged papers than my own and asked them where they got the work done."

"I wouldn't have thought they'd reveal a source like that."

"I had a partner at the time. Young feller, a lot like you." Father Christmas grinned. "The survivor was more than happy to share his information with me."

"Yeah, I can see where he might have been," said Nighthawk, as the food arrived at the table. He cut off a small piece of meat, chewed it thoughtfully, and nodded his approval.

"Anyway," continued Father Christmas, "I came here, introduced myself by returning the dead men's papers to her, and suggested that since I had cost her some clients, it seemed only fair that I take their place. We did a little negotiating, and that's all there was to it."

"If she's so good, why do you also have forgers on Terrazane and Antares III?"

"Great steak—as good as I remember it," said Father Christmas, cutting into his meal. Finally he got around to answering Nighthawk's question: "You never know when you'll blow a particular identity, or need a new one in a hurry—and you can't go racing halfway across the galaxy when you need new papers. There probably aren't more than a dozen topnotchers in the whole damned galaxy."

"You'd think there'd be more," commented Nighthawk.

"There were."

"What happened to them?"

"People like you happened to them," said Father Christmas. "This is, shall we say, a highly competitive business. A man of your talents could make a handsome living hiring out as an assassin to one forger after another. In fact, a lot of men of your particular talents have done just that."

"Well," said the older man when they were through with the meal, "was it as good as I said?"

"Better," answered Nighthawk, wiping his mouth on his sleeve. "I'm going to have to stop here whenever I come to this part of the Oligarchy."

"Tell you what," said Father Christmas. "Before we leave, we'll buy a couple of dozen frozen Redbison steaks and put 'em in the galley."

"Sounds good to me," agreed Nighthawk.

"Let me pay for this," said the older man, pressing his thumb against a sensor. "You don't have any accounts in the Oligarchy, and it'll take forever for a Frontier account to clear."

The computer took less than twenty seconds to verify his thumbprint and match it with his bank account on a nearby world.

"What now?" asked Nighthawk, as they stood up and walked to the door.

"Now I visit my supplier and haggle out a price for everything we need," said Father Christmas. "It's probably best if you don't come along. If she doesn't know you, she might not let either of us in."

"No problem," said Nighthawk. He looked around as they left the restaurant. "I'll be at that bar across the street."

"Fine," said Father Christmas. "I'll meet you in about twenty minutes."

Nighthawk nodded and walked slowly to the tavern. It was dimly lit inside, and housed an equal number of Men and aliens. He entered, looked around for an empty table, spotted one, and walked over to it.

He sat down, lit a small, thin cigar, and surveyed his surroundings. Though well within the Oligarchy, the place was primitive even by Frontier standards. The furniture was made of a native hardwood and didn't float, or adjust to fit his form, or indeed do anything but sit there. The lighting, though poor, was direct: the lights didn't move, raise, lower, or adjust their intensity to accommodate his pupils; all they did was cast a dim illumination throughout the place. The bar was also made of a poorly finished hardwood; it neither sparkled, glittered, nor shone. It also didn't house a complex computer. A small three-legged alien, a native of Moletoi II, walked from table to table, taking orders and dispensing drinks, while a human bartender, a bored expression plastered permanently on his face, mixed the drinks and manned the cash drawer.

The little Mole approached Nighthawk and spoke into its translating device.

"How may I help you, sir?"

"Bring me a Dust Whore."

"I would love to oblige you, sir," responded the Mole, "but this is a tavern, not a brothel. I regret that I cannot bring you any kind of prostitute."

"That's the name of a drink."

"Truly?"

"Truly."

"I have never heard of it."

"I'll bet we could fill a book with things you've never heard of," said Nighthawk. "Just tell the bartender what I want. He'll know."

"Have you a second choice, in case he too has never heard of a Dust Whore?"

"Just do what I told you to do."

The Mole bowed and waddled off to the bar, where the bartender nodded and began mixing up Nighthawk's Dust Whore. When he was through he handed it to the Mole, who dutifully carried it back to Nighthawk.

"He has heard of it, sir."

"Why am I not surprised?" said Nighthawk sardonically.

"I have no idea why you are not surprised," answered the Mole, "but if I were to hazard a guess, it would be that this drink is popular among Men."

Nighthawk stared at the Mole without responding, and finally it began to feel uncomfortable and waddled over to another table to serve some Lodinites.

Nighthawk sipped his drink, and had just decided that the bartender might have heard of a Dust Whore somewhere but had never actually made one before, when Father Christmas entered, spotted Nighthawk, and walked over to join him.

"She's still in business?" asked Nighthawk.

"I told you she was," said Father Christmas, sitting down wearily.

"Well?"

"She can supply everything we need."

"How soon?"

"Tomorrow, if we want it."

"We do."

"There's just one little problem," said Father Christmas. "Oh, nothing we can't take care of before the night's over, or certainly by tomorrow," he added hastily.

"What is it?"

"She's got a computer expert handling her financial transactions," said the older man, "and this young man says that the police have put a Watch-and-Track on all my Oligarchy bank accounts."

"What does that mean?"

"It means any time I transfer funds, an alarm will go off in some computer somewhere, and they'll follow the money to find out who I paid."

"Well, hell, they already know you're here on Purplecloud," said Nighthawk. "You charged dinner, remember?"

"I know."

"So what's the problem?"

"Well, if all they find is that I charged dinner and some uranium rods for the ship's pile, there's nothing to lead them to my friend, who definitely doesn't care to have the government looking into her business."

"All right," said Nighthawk. "You said we could get around the problem. How do we do it?"

"The answer should be obvious," said Father Christmas with a smile. "We go out and rob a couple of churches."

"I don't rob churches."

"You can make an exception this time," said Father Christmas. "We need some untraceable money. The gold from Darbar II is too easy to spot."

"We wouldn't need a thing if you hadn't let Melisande go," said Nighthawk.

"No use dwelling on the past, son."

"The past?" exploded Nighthawk. "That was yesterday, for Christ's sake!" He glared at the older man. "You couldn't have slept through all that clamor. If you couldn't stop her yourself, why didn't you wake me?"

"Good riddance to bad rubbish," said Father Christmas. "That girl was going to get you killed."

"That girl is the reason we're here, trying to get new identities."

"Well, we're not getting anything until we rob a church," said the older man sullenly.

"And what happens if I agree to rob it?" demanded Nighthawk. "Will your forger accept payment in candlesticks?"

"Certainly not. We'll have to go to a fence first."

"The woman I love is racing for Solio, and you want me to go out robbing churches and visiting fences?" said Nighthawk angrily.

"You know a faster way?" said Father Christmas pugnaciously.

"You bet your ass I do!" snapped Nighthawk.

He pulled his gun out of its holster, aimed it at a man who was huddled with three friends at the bar, and shot him in the back of the head. Before the body had hit the ground every patron had ducked for cover.

"Have you gone crazy?" yelled Father Christmas.

"There's a reward for that man, dead or alive," answered Nighthawk. "I saw his face on a poster at the spaceport."

He stood up and faced the dead man's three companions.

"There's paper on all of you," he announced. "But I'm not interested in you. Your friend will bring me all the money I need. If you want to live, drop your weapons and walk out of here."

"Who the hell *are* you?" demanded one of the men.

"I'm the man who's offering you your lives."

"Yeah? Well, here's what I think of your offer!"

The man reached for his pistol. Nighthawk put a bullet between his eyes, then crouched and whirled to face the other two. Both had gone for their weapons. Nighthawk took out the man who actually had his hand on his gun, then waited for the other to take one wild shot and blew him away.

"Stupid," muttered Nighthawk. "They should have listened to me!"

"You think *they're* stupid?" said Father Christmas disgustedly. "How about the man who killed them for nothing?"

"What do you mean, nothing?" demanded Nighthawk. "The four of them are worth close to fifty thousand credits."

"And the second you collect it, your people on Deluros will know where you are."

"Who gives a damn?" shot back Nighthawk. "We're not waiting around to meet them. The second I collect it, we visit your forger and then we're out of here."

Father Christmas looked at the four bodies on the floor. "You sure as hell didn't give that first one much of a chance," he said.

"He was a killer with a price on his head."

"He was a man."

"He was an obstacle," said Nighthawk. "He stood between me and Melisande. I plan to handle any other obstacle the very same way."

And as he looked into the young man's eyes, Father Christmas realized that he meant every word of it.

Chapter 24

◆ ◆ ◆ ◆ ◆ ◆ ◆

◈

They picked up the reward money the next morning— fifteen thousand credits for the first one Nighthawk killed, ten apiece for the other three. Father Christmas immediately converted the credits into Maria Theresa dollars and Far London pounds. He then explained to Nighthawk that once they got back to the Frontier, where people had very little faith in the Oligarchy's longevity and even less in its currency, the other currencies would be worth much more. Nighthawk, who had seen all kinds of currency on Tundra and the other Frontier worlds, had no objection.

Then, their financial transactions completed, they went down the main street until they came to the forger's place of business: an apartment above a weapons shop. There was no airlift, not even an elevator, simply a set of stairs leading up to the second floor.

The door was plain, made of wood, with no name or number in evidence. Still, as they approached it, it scanned them briefly, then opened long enough to let them through to the foyer.

A small, wiry woman, her auburn hair turning gray and in need of brushing, stood in the living room of the apartment, staring at them.

"Did you bring the money?"

"Yeah, we've got it," said Father Christmas.

"You know better than to bring credits," she said, anticipating him. "We'll use the exchange rates on Sirius V as of nine o'clock this morning, Standard time." She paused and stared at him, as if expecting an objection.

"Fine by me."

She walked over to Nighthawk and studied his face. "So this is your young friend."

"Any problem?" asked Father Christmas.

"Not if you have the money."

"Here it is," he said, pulling a wad out of his pocket.

"Just lay it on the table," she said, walking over to a desk, unlocking one of the drawers, and reaching in. She took out a large envelope, which she brought over to the two men.

"Now this," she said, withdrawing a small cube and handing it to Father Christmas, "is your passport. You are Jacob Kleinschmidt, a platinum miner from Alpha Bednares IV."

Father Christmas studied the cube for a moment. "Shouldn't this be round and flat?"

"They've changed them in the Altair sector, and that's where you're coming from." She reached into the envelope and pulled out more items, none of them more than an inch square, most made of titanium.

"Your birth certificate. Your employment record. Your most recent tax form. Your health certificate. Three blank visas, good for most of the worlds within the Oligarchy."

She turned to Nighthawk. "Have you ever been to the Deneb system?"

"No, ma'am. I come from—"

"I don't want to know where you come from," she interrupted. "And if you're using your real name, I don't want to know that either." She paused. "You know," she added, studying his face, "you don't have to be from Deneb after all. You're young enough to be on a field trip from Aristotle."

"Aristotle, ma'am?" he repeated.

"A university world. I understand that you wish to approach the chief of security of one of the Frontier worlds."

"Yeah. He's—"

"I don't want to know who or where he is. Just his job." She paused thoughtfully. "You can't study security—they don't give degrees in it—let's see, yes, I think we'll make you a student of ciphers. That at least is associated with security, and should validate any request you have to speak to your prey."

"Will you need a holograph of me, ma'am?" asked Nighthawk.

"I took it when you were waiting for the door to open," she replied. "Your passport is being processed right now."

"Fine."

"It'll just take a moment."

She left the room.

"Has she got a name?" asked Nighthawk. "I feel awkward calling her ma'am all the time."   •

"I'm sure she does," replied Father Christmas. "But she's never felt compelled to reveal it to me."

"It doesn't make sense," said Nighthawk. "If you're caught, and they want to know where you got your papers, you can give them her address as easily as her name."

"There are no addresses on this street, in case you haven't noticed. And this building is identical to the next three or four. With no name for the police to ask after, by the time they get to this apartment, she's seen them coming for at least half an hour and has managed to hide anything incriminating."

"For a whole hour, actually," said the woman, returning to the room. She walked over to Nighthawk and handed him his envelope. "Everything is here. You are Vincent Landis, a student from Aristotle, majoring in ciphers with a minor in communications. You are twenty-one years old, and you come from Silverblue, out on the Rim. Your parents are farmers."

"Got it," said Nighthawk. He turned to Father Christmas. "Are we done here?"

The older man laughed. "Not by a long shot." He turned to the woman. "Have you got what we discussed last night?"

"The pistol?" she said. "Yes. But as I told you, it will be expensive."

"Makes no difference," said Father Christmas. "He'll never get past Customs or any of the security checkpoints with what he's carrying now."

"What are you talking about?" demanded Nighthawk. "I'm happy with the weapons I have."

"I'm sure you are," answered Father Christmas. "But they've got to go."

Nighthawk was visibly upset. "But they're the ones I was trained with!" he protested.

"Son, you try to get anywhere near the colonel with them," said the older man, scrupulously avoiding mentioning Hernandez by name, "and you'll set off every alarm on the planet."

"What kind of gun have *you* got for me?" asked Nighthawk unhappily.

"May we see it, please?" asked Father Christmas.

The woman walked to the desk, unlocked another drawer, and handed him a small carrying case.

Father Christmas opened the box.

"Lovely," he said, looking at the small pistol. "Just lovely!"

"It looks like one of *my* guns," said Nighthawk. "What's so special about it?"

"It's made of molecularly altered ceramics," explained the woman. "Trust me: it can pass through any security device yet created."

"Looking like *that*?" said Nighthawk sarcastically.

"Of course not." She quickly, expertly broke the pistol down into four pieces. "This part, with the trigger, will pass for your belt buckle," she explained, demonstrating for him. "These two pieces will act as orthodic inserts in your boots. And I've tampered with the molecular structure of this final piece: just touch a match to it and it expands and loses its physical integrity. You can use it as a hatband or belt or anything else you can think of. Then, when you're ready to assemble the pistol, just touch it to a cold metal surface and it will instantly revert to this shape."

"I don't see any bullets," said Nighthawk.

She smiled. "That's the beauty of it. Even if they suspect what it is, even if they confiscate it, they'll never find the ammunition, and eventually they'll have to return it to you and let you go."

"So where is it?"

"In your pocket."

"My pocket?" he repeated.

"It shoots coins," she said. "I have this one configured to shoot gold Maria Theresa dollars."

"Well, I'll be damned!" said Nighthawk.

"Nice idea," said Father Christmas. "Could get expensive in wartime, though."

She ignored the older man's attempt at humor. "I think you'd better practice with it before you use it," she said. "It's not balanced like a normal handgun. At more than thirty yards, you'll have to adjust for a tendency to shoot low—about an inch per yard."

"I won't be that far away."

"All right. Our business is done." She escorted them to the door. "Your face is familiar," she said to Nighthawk as he stood in the doorway, "yet I'm sure we've never met before."

"You don't want me to tell you why," he said.

"No, I don't."

"I'll let you know when I've succeeded."

"I'd rather you didn't," she said. "It would only remind me of all my clients who didn't succeed."

"How do you know there are that many?" asked Nighthawk.

"An identity is an ephemeral thing," she replied. "The successful ones come back for more."

The door opened.

"Go," said the woman. "And good luck to you."

"What about me?" asked Father Christmas with a smile.

"You don't need any luck, old man," she said. "You'll never be half the man your young friend is, but you're a survivor. I *know* I'll see you again."

Then they were walking down the stairs and heading for the ship. Father Christmas was basking in the glow of being called a survivor, but Nighthawk was too busy planning his approach to Solio to wonder why he had not been considered one as well.

Chapter 25

◆ ◆ ◆ ◆ ◆ ◆ ◆

◆

They were two hours out of Purplecloud and headed for the Inner Frontier when his lawyer on Deluros VIII finally tracked him down.

"This is Marcus Dinnisen of Hubbs, Wilkinson, Raith and Jiminez, trying to contact Jefferson Nighthawk."

Nighthawk ignored the signal.

"Please come in."

"You're gonna have to talk to him sooner or later," said Father Christmas.

"Damn it, I know you're on that ship, Jefferson!" said Dinnisen angrily. "Please respond. I'm not going to break contact until you do."

"All right," said Nighthawk after another lengthy pause. "How did you find me and what do you want?"

"Finding you was easy," said Dinnisen. "You put in a claim for forty-five thousand credits."

"You learned about it awfully fast."

"We're a very powerful law firm," replied Dinnisen. "We have connections all over the Oligarchy."

"All right, so you know I did some bounty hunting," said Nighthawk. "So what?"

"So what?" repeated Dinnisen, surprised. "So what the hell are you doing on Purplecloud?"

"Killing bad guys, just like you and Kinoshita told me to do."

"Damn it, Jefferson—you were sent to Solio II to accomplish a specific mission. If it's not done, I want you to go back there immediately. If it *is* done, then we want you to come back to Deluros VIII."

"What you want doesn't matter to me," replied Nighthawk easily.

"What the hell are you talking about?" yelled Dinnisen.

"You heard me. I have business to take care of. Leave me alone."

"The only business you have is working for the team that created you!"

"You're welcome to think so," said Nighthawk.

"Look," said Dinnisen placatingly. "Let's stop before we say things we'll both regret. Why don't you come to Deluros and we'll talk it over?"

"Not a chance," said Nighthawk.

"I think it would be best, Jefferson," continued Dinnisen in persuasive tones.

"Yeah? Well, *I* think it would be suicidal."

"What are you talking about?"

"The second you get your hands on me, you'll toss me back into a vat of protoplasm."

"Don't be melodramatic, Jefferson," said Dinnisen, trying to control his temper. "We don't have vats of protoplasm, as you well know. We just want to talk."

"Anything you've got to say, you can say right now."

"We're not the enemy, Jefferson," continued Dinnisen. "We *created* you. You're like family to us."

"That's funny," said Nighthawk. "You don't feel like family to *me*."

"You're being difficult, Jefferson," said Dinnisen. "You've changed since I last saw you. What's happened, son?"

"I'm not your son, and the galaxy is what happened to me. I've been out here, and I'm not going back."

"No one wants you to stay on Deluros VIII," said Dinnisen. "I'll be perfectly frank with you: You represent an enormous investment in time, money, and technology. Since you're alive, it means you've been able to interact with the scum that live out there on the Frontier and survive. We'll have many lucrative assignments for you."

"Most of the scum I've interacted with would look down their noses at a lawyer," said Nighthawk. "Any lawyer. But especially you."

"Why are you being like this? We just want to examine you and make sure you're holding up all right. One day and out. Is that so much to ask?"

"I have work to do."

"Our work?"

"*My* work."

"You don't *have* any work!" exploded Dinnisen. "You're less than six months old, for God's sake!"

"Wrong," said Nighthawk coldly. "I'm the Widowmaker, and I was an old man when your great-grandfather was less than six months old."

He terminated the communication.

"Well?" he asked, turning to Father Christmas.

"Does it bother you when I call you son?" asked the older man.

"No. But it bothers me when *he* does." He paused and suddenly grinned. "Hell, it bothers me when he calls me Jefferson."

"Well, I hope you enjoyed your conversation with him, because it's going to cost you."

"Money?"

"Everything *but* money," responded Father Christmas. "Five'll get you ten he's already contacting Hernandez to warn him that you're off the reservation."

"Why?"

"Because he and his people have created the perfect killing machine, and suddenly you've got your own agenda. They don't know what it is, but they're going to warn the guy who commissioned you." Father Christmas smiled suddenly. "And you can bet your ass *he'll* know what your agenda is."

"I hope so," said Nighthawk. "He's responsible for it all: Trelaine, me, the Marquis, Melisande, Malloy, everything. I want to look into his eyes when I kill him."

"He's awfully well protected," noted Father Christmas. "It may be a very short look."

"That'll be enough," said Nighthawk.

Chapter 26

* * * * * * * *

◈

They sold their ship as soon as they reached the Inner
Frontier, then took their new ship and their new identities straight to Solio II.

"You know," said Nighthawk, when they were
still half an hour out from Solio, "I know why *I'm* going back, but I sure as hell can't figure out why *you're*
going."

Father Christmas shrugged. "Why not? Solio's
got churches, just like every other world."

"It's also got a top-notch security force. We may
fool them for a while with all the stuff we picked up
on Purplecloud, but eventually they'll dope it out. If
not before I kill Hernandez, then after. Either way,
anyone who was seen with me is going to be pretty
high up on their Wanted list."

"You want me to leave?" asked Father Christmas.

"I didn't say that," replied Nighthawk. "I asked why you *hadn't* left."

The older man leaned back on his seat, stared at the ceiling for a moment, then exhaled heavily. "I think it's curiosity more than anything."

"To see if you were right about Hernandez hiring the Marquis?" asked Nighthawk, puzzled.

Father Christmas shook his head. "No, I'm pretty sure about that. And if it's not that, then it's something similar. These guys feed on lies and subterfuge the way we fed on Redbison two nights ago."

"Then what are you curious about?"

"You."

"Me?"

"Yeah," said Father Christmas. "I want to see if you're as good as I think you are."

"I assume that's a compliment?"

"All depends. I don't think you can steal the girl and get off the planet, but I'm curious to see how close you come."

"You left out killing Hernandez."

"That, too."

"Getting to him will be the toughest part of the job," said Nighthawk thoughtfully. "Once I've killed him, the rest should fall into place."

"Have you given any thought as to how you're going to get to him?" asked Father Christmas.

Nighthawk lit a small, thin cigar. "Not really. Create some story that'll get me in to see him, I suppose."

"You can't be the only man who's ever wanted to kill him," suggested Father Christmas. "There probably aren't too many stories he hasn't heard—or that his subordinates haven't encountered."

"Well, if push comes to shove, I'll just shoot my

way in and shoot my way out," said Nighthawk with a shrug.

"Just like that?" asked the older man, snapping his fingers.

"Why not? I took the Marquis, didn't I?"

"And if you run into someone better?"

"Anyone who's better than the Marquis isn't working for peanuts on some security force," answered Nighthawk. "He's set up shop somewhere on the Frontier, and he probably controls a dozen or more worlds."

"Well, at least consider this: There's no silencer for the gun you're carrying. The first shot will draw everyone within five hundred yards."

"There's only going to be one shot," responded Nighthawk. "That's all I ever take."

"One, five, a dozen—it'll make noise."

"Hernandez carries a laser pistol. By the time my gun's made a bang, I'll have his weapon, and it's silent except for a little buzzing. If no one years a second shot, they'll think the first one was something else."

"You hope."

"Actually, I don't much give a damn. If they worked for Hernandez or so much as touched my Melisande, I *want* to kill 'em."

"Well, I, for one, would feel a damned sight safer if you had some means of approaching him other than to tell one ridiculous story and then shoot your way in if the story doesn't work," said Father Christmas.

"Just say the word and I'll put down on a neighboring world and let you get off."

"I don't want to get off, son," said the older man. "I just want you to take it a little slower and more carefully so that you live through this episode."

Nighthawk looked at Solio II, a green and blue world spinning in the viewscreen. "She's there right

now," he said. "The slower I go, the longer it'll be before we're together again."

"Son," said Father Christmas, "I hate to keep
bringing this up, but she doesn't *want* to be together
with you."

Nighthawk's expression hardened. "She will," he
said adamantly.

Chapter 27

◆ ◆ ◆ ◆ ◆ ◆ ◆ ◆

They touched down at Solio II's single spaceport, about ten miles outside the planet's major city, which was also called Solio. Unlike many Frontier worlds, Solio II was large enough and busy enough to have a Customs department, and their documentation was given its initial test as they were ushered into separate booths.

"Please insert your passport, sir," ordered the Customs computer.

Nighthawk did so.

"Thank you. Please sit down."

Nighthawk sat down opposite the holographic screen.

"Name?" asked the computer.

"Vince Landis."

"Your passport says Vincent Landis."

"Vince is a shortened version of Vincent."

"Checking . . . verified. Home planet?"

"Silverblue."

"Your passport says you live on Aristotle."

"I do live there now, but I am a student and that is a temporary residence. My permanent residence is with my parents on Silverblue."

"Considering . . . accepted. Age?"

"Twenty-one."

"Purpose of visit?"

"Research."

"What is your area of study?"

"As you see," answered Nighthawk, "I am majoring in ciphers. My doctoral thesis will concern the use of ciphers by security forces on the Inner Frontier. I intend to visit a number of worlds on the Frontier, questioning the security forces about the use of ciphers in their daily work."

"Where will you stay while on Solio II?"

"I have no idea," said Nighthawk. "Can you recommend a good hotel?"

"I will append a list of all hotels and room rates to your visa," said the computer. "Have you any weapons to declare?"

"I'm just a student," said Nighthawk with a smile. "What would I do with a weapon?"

"You did not answer the question."

"No, I don't have any weapons."

"Have you any existing medical conditions?"

"None."

The machine returned his passport, along with a thirty-day visa and a list of hotels.

"You have cleared Customs, Vincent Landis," it announced. "Welcome to Solio II."

"Thank you."

Nighthawk got up and walked out of the booth, and found Father Christmas waiting for him.

"How'd it go?" asked the older man.

"No trouble. And you?"

"Nothing to it."

"Then let's get out of here," said Nighthawk, heading toward an exit. They followed the departing crowd to an airbus and rode into the city. When they reached a street that seemed to have lots of hotels, they got off.

"What now?" asked Father Christmas.

Nighthawk studied the area carefully. "I'm trying to remember where the Security Division is." Finally he shrugged. "It doesn't make any difference. We'll find it later. Let's go get a couple of rooms."

They registered at one of the hotels, and met a few hours later for dinner.

"Did you locate it?" asked Father Christmas.

"The Security Division?" said Nighthawk. "Yeah, it's about half a mile away."

"And teeming with armed men?"

"It is now," said Nighthawk. "We'll walk by and see how it looks after dark."

They ate dinner in the hotel's restaurant, and Father Christmas spent most of the meal complaining that the meat seemed insipid next to a cut of Red-bison. They waited until dark, then walked outside and headed over toward the large building that housed Hernandez's office.

"I'm nervous," said Father Christmas.

"Why?" asked Nighthawk.

"I don't know. Maybe because it's been so easy to get this far. I keep thinking someone's watching us and is getting ready to pounce."

"Won't do 'em much good," said Nighthawk with

a grim smile. "I must be walking around with thirty Maria Theresa dollars in my pockets."

"You mean you've already assembled the gun?" asked Father Christmas.

"I thought I'd attract less attention assembling it in my room than in front of the Security Division," said Nighthawk wryly.

Father Christmas kept looking nervously off to his right and left. Finally Nighthawk stopped and turned to him.

"Look, if you'd be happier robbing a church, I'll point a couple out to you and—"

"I don't want to rob a church."

"Well, you sure as hell need *something* to do with your hands," said Nighthawk. "You're even making *me* nervous."

"Sorry," said Father Christmas, thrusting his hands into his pockets.

"All right," said Nighthawk, giving his companion a reassuring pat on the shoulder. "Let's keep going."

They walked another two blocks, and finally found themselves staring at a large building.

"This is it?" asked the older man.

"This is it."

"Well, how do you approach it—from the front, the rear, or the side?"

"The front," answered Nighthawk. "Isn't that why I'm a student from Aristotle? Tomorrow I'll just walk up and make an appointment."

They were about to leave when a window on the third floor opened, and a sleek figure stepped out onto a balcony. It was Melisande, dressed all in gold.

"It's *her*!" whispered Nighthawk.

"I *knew* those IDs were too good to be true," muttered Father Christmas.

"What are you talking about?"

"They know we're here, son, or at least they expect us any moment," said the older man. "Look at her, dressed in gold and glitter and leaning out over the edge of the balcony. They're using her as bait."

"For me?"

"Who else?"

"And they think I'm going to burst into the building and shoot my way up to the third floor because she's standing there?" continued Nighthawk.

"Yeah," said Father Christmas. "Pretty damned foolish, aren't they?"

"Sure are."

"So what do we do now?" asked the older man. "Go back to the hotel?"

"You can go if you want."

"What about you?"

"Me?" repeated Nighthawk. "I'm going to burst into the building and shoot my way up to the third floor."

"I thought I just explained: That's exactly what they're expecting," said Father Christmas.

"They're expecting a man," replied Nighthawk, checking his ceramic pistol and thrusting it back into a pocket. "What they're getting is the Widowmaker."

He turned and began climbing the ornate stairs to the main entrance.

Chapter 28

* * * * * * *

◈

Nighthawk entered the building, passing through the security scanner without setting off any alarms. Father Christmas, after a moment's hesitation, followed him at a safe distance.

A young man sat behind a desk in the main foyer. He looked up at Nighthawk with a bored expression on his sullen face.

"May I help you?"

"My name's Landis. Vince Landis. I'm a graduate student from Aristotle. I'd like to arrange an interview with Colonel James Hernandez."

"Are you seeking employment?"

"I told you—I want an interview."

"Concerning what subject?"

"I don't see that it's any of your business," said Nighthawk.

"Rudeness will not get you your appointment," said the young man punctiliously. "I must know the purpose of your request."

"I'm a student of ciphers and communications," said Nighthawk. "I want to speak to him about his use of them."

"I will transmit your request to him, Mr. Landis," said the man. "Have you an address where you can be reached?"

"I'll wait right here."

"It may take days or even weeks for an appointment," said the man. "And that's *if* he'll agree to see you at all."

"I haven't got days or weeks," replied Nighthawk. "I'm leaving Solio II in a couple of hours. It'll have to be right now."

"That's out of the question."

"Contact him and let *him* decide."

"Are you giving me orders?" demanded the young man, rising to his feet.

"I'm trying to save your life," said Nighthawk. "Now call him."

"I'll do no such thing!"

Nighthawk pulled out his pistol and fired at point-blank range. The man collapsed behind his desk, and Nighthawk, without another look at him, sought out the nearest airlift.

"Don't go that way," said a voice behind him, and he turned to find himself facing Father Christmas.

"Someone's got to be monitoring the lobby here," continued the older man. "They know you've killed that young feller. You get into an airlift now, you've obliged them by confining yourself, and they won't let you out until there are more guns facing you than even you can handle. If I were you, I'd find a stairway

instead. Even if they come after you, you'll have a little more room to maneuver."

"Makes sense," said Nighthawk, heading for the
ornate curving staircase that led to the upper levels of
the building. "Keep clear once the shooting starts."

"I ain't no hero, son," Father Christmas assured
him. "Once the guns come out, you're on your own."

"That suits me fine."

"Somehow I thought it would," said Father Christmas wryly.

Gun in hand, Nighthawk began climbing the
stairs, alert for any sign of movement above or below
him. He made it to the second floor without any op-
position. Then, as he was about to climb to the third
floor, a door opened behind him and two thin beams
of light burned into the railing. He whirled and got off
three quick shots, and two men, each holding a laser
pistol, fell to the floor.

"Nice job," said Father Christmas's voice from
well below him.

"Thanks," said Nighthawk.

"Be careful," urged Father Christmas. "They won't
be that dumb again."

Nighthawk surveyed the staircase. Given the way
it curved, the top of his head would be a target for
anyone on the third floor before he could see to fire
back.

"Right," he said.

He stepped back and considered his options, then
turned and walked quickly to the office in which the
two men had been hiding. There was a large window,
and he opened it and leaned out. The sides of the
building were as smooth as glass; climbing up on the
outside would be impossible.

He stepped back into the hall and picked up

the dead men's weapons. Now that his presence was known, the more firepower he had, the better.

He approached the stairs, then paused. There had to be another way to the third floor besides the stairs and the airlift. Perhaps a service lift. He was about to look for it when a door opened at the far end of the hall. A man stepped out, saw him, and started shouting. Nighthawk quickly silenced him with a burst of solid light from a laser pistol.

There was certainly a service elevator, but he didn't have time to hunt for it. Besides, if he started walking down the hallway, he'd have cut off his options since the airlift and the stairway would both be behind him and it wouldn't take much to isolate him.

So it was back to the stairs. He began climbing them in a semi-crouch, ceramic pistol in one hand, laser in the other, not so fast that he was an easy target, not so slow that Hernandez had time to send more men to meet him. When he was almost halfway up, just reaching the turn where his head would become visible, he measured the angles by eye and fired his laser once more, holding the pistol steady as the deadly beam burned through the floor above him. There were exclamations of surprise and a scream of pain, and he knew he'd gotten at least one of the men who were waiting for him. The problem was that he didn't know how many were left, or where they were positioned.

He heard a footstep below him and spun around, half expecting to see Father Christmas. But it was a uniformed guard, taking aim. He dropped down and got off a shot as he tumbled down a couple of stairs. When he regained his balance long enough to look, the guard was dead.

He fired upward, blindly, just to make whoever was on the third level keep their distance, but he knew he couldn't remain trapped on the stairs between floors for much longer. He'd just about made up his mind to go back to the second floor and look for some other means of reaching Hernandez's office when he heard Melisande's voice ring out from above.

"Jefferson!"

He paused just an instant. Then, pocketing his ceramic pistol, he took a laser in each hand, swept every part of the third floor he could see with deadly light, and raced up the stairs, which were already starting to smoke. Two men moved to stop him; both were dead by the time he reached the top step. Two more bodies lay where he had shot them through the floor.

He looked around for Melisande but couldn't see her. The corridor ran about sixty feet in each direction from the stairway, and he began walking down the hallway to his left, guns at the ready.

Suddenly a man burst out of a room behind him and hurled himself at Nighthawk's back. Nighthawk went sprawling, and both laser pistols flew from his hands. He tried to get up, only to have a large forearm come down heavily on the back of his neck. He rolled onto his side, and was able to see his attacker: a huge man some six and a half feet tall, topping three hundred pounds without any fat on him at all.

Nighthawk twisted and turned, trying to free himself, but the man wouldn't budge. Finally he snaked his hand down to his side, then moved it slowly, painfully, inch by inch, until he found what he was looking for—his attacker's testicles. He grabbed and squeezed, and the man let out a howl of pain and tried to roll away. Nighthawk held on, squeezing and twisting; the man shrieked and squirmed, and finally, with one enormous effort pulled free.

The man, red of face, breathing heavily, got to his

feet and pulled a wicked-looking knife from his belt.
Nighthawk looked for his pistols, but they were too far
away. The man hunched over, holding the knife like
someone who was experienced with the weapon, and
edged forward.

Nighthawk, his back to the railing, realized the
man would reach him momentarily. He got to one
knee, checked for escape routes, found none. Then,
suddenly, he grabbed one of the railing's smoldering
supports, pulled it loose, and swung it toward the
man's head, all in one motion. It split his opponent's
head open with a sickening thud. The man fell forward, and Nighthawk bent down, letting the huge
body somersault over him and past the railing. By the
time it hit the floor two levels below, Nighthawk had
picked up his laser pistols and was once again stalking
down the corridor.

He heard a sudden sound behind him and saw
Melisande, well past the landing, almost at the end of
the opposite corridor, struggling to free herself from
two uniformed men. They overpowered her and
pulled her back into the room from which she had
come.

He raced down the corridor, past the landing, toward the room she was in. A shot rang out, and he felt
a bullet bury itself in his shoulder from behind. The
force of the bullet spun him around, and he got a
quick glimpse of a man ducking back into a room,
almost at the spot he had reached before seeing
Melisande. He fired his laser, but it was too late; the
corridor was empty. As he turned back, ready to race
to Melisande's room, a sonic pistol hummed, and suddenly he staggered as a field of solid sound over-
whelmed him. He fell to one knee, his ears and nose
bleeding, and fired back. The man with the sonic

pistol fell into the hallway, dead—but even as he did so, another bullet dug deep into the back of Nighthawk's left thigh. He turned and fired at where he knew the shot had come from, and this time he burned off the sniper's hand. There was a scream, then silence.

And now, suddenly, every room seemed to hold a sniper. Dozens of doors up and down the corridors slid open and shut, just long enough for the occupant to take a shot at Nighthawk. A laser put a smoking hole in his left foot, and another burned off part of his ear. He fired back, and two more men were dead. A bullet smashed his right knee. He fell to the floor, but he melted the man who'd shot him. Another bullet hit him in the back, then two more, and as he tried to regain his feet he found that he couldn't get up—either because of the knee or the bullet in his lower spine, he didn't know which. He dragged himself to a doorway, trained a laser on it, and tried to burn a hole through to the interior where he would momentarily be out of the line of fire. But the door, made of a tightly bonded titanium alloy, only glowed red and didn't melt. A bullet burst through his hand, and he felt the bones splinter as the laser dropped to the floor.

He inadvertently grabbed his broken hand with his left hand, dropping his other laser in the process. A molecular imploder disabled both lasers, and suddenly he was lying on the floor of the corridor, bleeding from more than a dozen wounds, unable to move.

A door at the end of the corridor opened, and James Hernandez stepped out. He walked over to Nighthawk and stared down at him.

"You should have stayed away," he said.

"Couldn't," rasped Nighthawk, choking on his own blood.

"Why? You killed the Marquis, you saved your
. . . ah . . . progenitor—or at least bought him a few
more years. You must have known that I'd kill you if
you came back here."

Nighthawk couldn't force any words out. He
settled for nodding his head weakly.

"Then why?" asked Hernandez, genuinely puzzled. "There's no price on *my* head. Why did you come
back?"

He tried to mouth the word "Melisande" and
found that he couldn't. "For *her*," he grated.

"Ah." Hernandez smiled. "I didn't think anyone
was that young or that foolish." He turned and spoke
to someone who was out of Nighthawk's line of vision.
"Come say good-bye to the bold young hero who was
going to rescue you from my nefarious clutches."

And then, suddenly, she was standing next to
Nighthawk.

"You're a fool," she said.

He convulsed with pain. "I know."

"And now you're going to die."

"Everyone dies," he replied, coughing blood.

"You could have just stayed in the Oligarchy,"
said Melisande angrily.

"Probably," he grated, as a wave of pain and dizziness overcame him.

"Then why didn't you?"

His lips moved, but no words come out.

"Well, this is all very touching," said Hernandez,
"but I'm afraid the time has come to deliver the coup
de grace. Have you any last statement to make?"

Again the lips moved silently.

"Kneel down and tell me what he's saying," ordered Hernandez.

"Why me?" demanded Melisande.

"You slept with him. Who better to hear his final words?"

She glared at Hernandez for a moment, then knelt down next to Nighthawk and leaned over until her ear was next to Nighthawk's lips.

Suddenly there was the sound of a gunshot, and the blue-skinned girl jerked spasmodically just once, then rolled over with a coin-sized hole in her chest.

"I saved you the trouble," whispered Nighthawk as Hernandez kicked the ceramic pistol out of his hand and aimed his gun at the young man's head.

Epilogue

◆ ◆ ◆ ◆ ◆ ◆ ◆ ◆

They buried Nighthawk the next morning, in an un-
marked grave beside the Pearl of Maracaibo.

Father Christmas walked across the large cemetery, looking neither right nor left, ignoring the dozens
of armed, uniformed men who watched his every
move. When he reached the grave he stopped, crossed
his hands sedately in front of him, and lowered his
head.

"I rather thought I'd see you at the ceremony,"
said Hernandez, joining him.

"I hate services."

"But you like churches."

"This was a little one," said Father Christmas.
"Hardly anything worth stealing, except for the cross
behind the altar."

"How did you know about that?" asked Hernandez. "No one saw you check it out."

The older man smiled. "If people could spot me when I'm casing a job, how long do you think I'd stay in business?"

"You have a point," conceded Hernandez. "But a moot one. I'm putting you out of business this morning."

"Be quiet and show some respect for the dead," said Father Christmas.

"When you're through praying for *him*, you might say a brief one for yourself," continued Hernandez. "You're going to be joining him, wherever he's at."

"Don't be foolish," said Father Christmas easily. "You don't really think I'd show up here without protection, do you?"

Hernandez looked around the cemetery. "I don't see any protection."

Father Christmas chuckled. "And you won't— unless I turn up dead."

"What do you think you've got?"

"This is hardly the place to discuss crass worldly matters," said Father Christmas.

"What *is* the proper place?"

"You got any drinkin' stuff in your office?"

"Yes," replied Hernandez.

"That'll do."

The two of them turned and walked across the cemetery together, then entered the impressive Security headquarters, and took an airlift to the third floor.

"It's a lot easier to get here today," noted Father Christmas. "How many of your people did he take out before you killed him?"

"Enough," said Hernandez grimly.

They stepped out of the airlift and onto the third level.

"You cleaned up the mess pretty quickly," said Father Christmas.

"It looks better than it is," replied Hernandez. "There was some structural damage to the staircase. Everyone above the second floor is required to take the airlift.

"Well, when all is said and done, lots of things look better than they are," said Father Christmas. "I hate to think of how many industries would go broke if that weren't so."

"Spare me your quaint homilies."

They reached the door to Hernandez's office, where the colonel waited for the standard retina and palmprint scan, after which the door slid into the wall.

"What's your preference?" asked Hernandez.

"Anything that's wet."

Hernandez poured them two drinks, handed one to Father Christmas who seated himself on a leather chair, then went behind his desk and sat down himself.

"All right, old man," he said, "what do you think you have on me?"

"You hired the Marquis of Queensbury to kill Governor Trelaine," replied Father Christmas. "And then you got them to create young Nighthawk to kill the Marquis so you could cover it up."

"Why would I do that?" asked the colonel, lighting up a thin Antarean cigar.

"Oh, lots of reasons," answered the older man, sipping his drink. "The way I see it, you wanted to be Governor. You hired the Marquis to kill Trelaine . . . but then he began blackmailing you. He probably got a little too greedy, and eventually it was a matter of kill him or be exposed."

"You couldn't be more mistaken."

Father Christmas shrugged. "The reason doesn't make much difference. What matters is that you hired the Marquis to pull the trigger, and he confessed to it before Nighthawk killed him."

"Rubbish. Why would he tell you?"

"Maybe he was trying to buy his life."

"Nonsense," said the colonel. He noticed that his cigar had gone out and relit it. "The Marquis was as brashly fearless as young Nighthawk."

"Maybe he was bragging," said Father Christmas. "Who cares what the reason was? I've got recordings of it stashed on three different worlds in the Oligarchy. If I don't report in to each of them every month, those recordings go—"

"To the Oligarchy?" interrupted Hernandez. "Somehow, I'm not trembling in my boots."

"To the press on Solio II, and to half a dozen select politicians just down the street."

Hernandez stared at him. "I think you're bluffing."

"Ah, but would you stake your life on it?" said Father Christmas. "All I want is to go out to the Rim and plunder God's churches at my leisure. If you let me go, you'll never hear from me again. If you kill me, you'll be joining me within, not to be too pessimistic about it, a year."

Hernandez downed his drink in a single swallow, then carefully placed the empty glass on a corner of his polished desk. "Do you want to know the truth of it?"

"I'd like to," said the older man, glancing out the window at the cemetery. "But I can live without it. It's up to you."

"Trelaine was a tyrant, but he was a *weak* tyrant. He allowed the Marquis to rob the Solio system because he didn't have the guts to stand up to him." He paused. "The Marquis had once worked for me on, shall we say, a freelance basis. We'd had a cordial relationship. I finally managed to convince him that if he killed Trelaine, I would put in a puppet who would allow him even greater freedom in plundering Solio II."

"Yourself?"

"If I could have rounded up the support, yes. If not, then a man who was amenable to my suggestions. The Marquis' muscle would help keep us in power, and we'd show our gratitude by looking the other way. At least, that was the plan I laid out to him." He paused. "Of course, the moment we took power we'd have driven the Marquis and his henchmen out of the system"

"The Marquis might have considered that a bit of a double cross," observed Father Christmas.

"By then it wouldn't have mattered," answered the colonel. "I'd have had the power to make it stick, and he could have been just as rich and happy preying on other worlds."

"So he killed Trelaine. . . ."

Hernandez nodded. "But he was smarter than I had anticipated. He had his own puppet, and he took me by surprise. The new Governor kowtowed to him even more than Trelaine did. *That's* why I contacted Deluros about the Widowmaker. I'm a *patriot*, damn it!"

"Patriot, murderer, we'll leave it to posterity to judge," said Father Christmas. There was a meaningful pause. "Or we can leave it to your peers. It's your choice."

Hernandez stared at him for a long moment. "All right," he said at last. "You've got a deal."

"Good," said the older man. "It's a pity you had to waste a promising young man."

"Nighthawk? There was no place for him in our plans," said Hernandez. "And this way we justify our decision not to pay millions more to his people back on Deluros. The official line is that he died before accomplishing his mission."

"It just means they're going to make another one, you know," said Father Christmas. "Who knows? Maybe next time they'll do it right."

"What was wrong with this one?" asked Hernandez curiously. "He was good enough to kill the Marquis, and wipe out half of my staff."

"Oh, he had all the physical skills," said Father Christmas. "They made sure of that. Trained him to kill from the instant he was born, if 'born' is the right word." He finished his drink. "But when all is said and done, they couldn't give him the heart of the Widowmaker. He was too soft."

"Soft?" repeated Hernandez, surprised. "Look at the people he killed!"

"Makes no difference," said the older man. "He had a fatal flaw, one that's maybe even worse than a bad aim or a shaky hand: the poor son of a bitch *cared*. The one thing you can never do in his business is get emotionally involved." He paused. "The Widowmaker *chose* to become a killer. Jefferson Nighthawk's tragedy is that he was never allowed to choose *not* to become one."

"I think perhaps he was toughening up there toward the end," offered Hernandez.

"Oh?"

The colonel nodded. "His last words. He knew that I'd have killed her if he hadn't. She'd outlived her usefulness, and she knew too much."

"Well," said Father Christmas, "I think I'll have one more drink, and then I'll take my leave of you."

Hernandez got up and poured them each a refill.

The older man held up his glass. "To lost innocence."

"Whose?" asked Hernandez.

"Everybody's," answered Father Christmas.

ABOUT THE AUTHOR

◆ ◆ ◆

MIKE RESNICK is one of the major names in science fiction, both as a writer and an editor. He is the author of almost 40 novels, 8 collections, and more than 100 stories, and has edited 23 anthologies. He has been nominated for 13 Hugos and 8 Nebulas since 1989, and has won 3 Hugos and a Nebula, as well as scores of lesser awards. Among his best-known works are *Santiago, Ivory, Soothsayer, Paradise,* and the Kirinyaga stories, which have become the most honored story cycle in science fiction history. He lives with his wife, Carol, in Cincinnati, Ohio, where he is currently at work on the second book in the *Widowmaker* trilogy.

Two unique voices
come together to create one gripping vision in

PALACE
a novel of the Pinch

Katharine Kerr & Mark Kreighbaum

Bestselling author Katharine Kerr teams with newcomer Mark Kreighbaum to create the lush world of Palace, a futuristic city located in a region of space known as the Pinch. In this riveting tale of espionage and cybervengeance, Vida L'var is thrust into the world of the ruling classes, threatened with a loveless political marriage. Because she attempts to make a difference in a world that grows more corrupt with time, Vida's very life is in jeopardy. Now she is being stalked by a vicious assassin, and should he succeed in his mission all of Palace may pay the price. Politics, intrigue, and a chilling vision of the future are seamlessly assembled in the tradition of classic space opera.

____57373-X PALACE: A Novel of the Pinch $5.99/$7.99 Canada